# JUNGLE FIRE

# JUNGLE FIRE

Dana Mentink

MOODY PUBLISHERS
CHICAGO

The author is represented by MacGregor Literary, Inc.

Edited by Sandra Bricker
Interior Design: Ragont Design
Cover Design: Dog Eared Design, LLC
Cover Image: iStock 1034176 / 5314048, Shutterstock 59420941
Author Photo: Snap Pea Photography

Library of Congress Cataloging-in-Publication Data

Mentink, Dana.
Jungle fire / Dana Mentink.
pages cm
ISBN 978-0-8024-0594-4
1. Missionaries—Guatemala—Fiction. 2. Drug traffic—Guatemala—Fiction. I. Title.
PS3613.E496J86 2013
813'.6—dc23

2013004867

This is a work of fiction. Names, characters, places, and incidents either are the product of the author's imagination or are used fictitiously, and any resemblance to actual persons, living or dead, businesses, companies, events, or locales is entirely coincidental.

We hope you enjoy this book from River North Fiction by Moody Publishers. Our goal is to provide high-quality, thought-provoking books and products that connect truth to your real needs and challenges. For more information on other books and products written and produced from a biblical perspective, go to www.moodypublishers.com or write to:

River North Fiction
Imprint of Moody Publishers
820 N. LaSalle Boulevard
Chicago, IL 60610

1 3 5 7 9 10 8 6 4 2

*Printed in the United States of America*

The most powerful weapon on earth
is the human soul on fire.

—FERDINAND FOCH

# CHAPTER 1

Nina never imagined her life would end on a bus.

Not a dilapidated bus filled to groaning, departing the soggy Guatemalan town of Solitar, three hours from the Mexican border. Not sitting next to a dark woman with a haggard face and oddly green eyes who gazed at her with peculiar intensity from under lowered lids, peppering her with questions about her destination.

*Especially not,* she thought as the uniformed soldier raised his automatic weapon, *one short day after her missionary furlough began.*

Maybe she should have anticipated just such a thing. Violence was part of life in Central America, deeply rooted like the thorned kapok tree. Victims had been carried through the doors of their small clinic suffering a range of injuries from snake bites to stabbings. Some would walk out healed, and some would not walk out at all.

Still, perhaps the malice she saw in the gunman's demeanor was a product of her exaggerated imagination or the attitude she'd picked up from virtually every Mayan she'd encountered. Soldiers were to be regarded warily. After thirty-plus years of brutal civil war that staggered to a bloody end in the mid 1990s, the suspicions were not easily shed. The soldier, standing atop a grassy knoll on the side of the road with his dripping cap pulled low over his face, might just be looking to collect valuables from unwary passengers, especially Americans. It had happened before when they arrived at the clinic some four autumns prior.

"It's just money," her father had whispered to her, her fingers squeezed between his as the men pushed through the vehicle collecting valuables with eager smiles on their faces. "More will come when we need it."

Bruce William Monte, a veteran of two tours of duty in Vietnam, had tasted fear but never bowed to it—at least as far as Nina knew. He'd certainly never lost his cool for a moment when the bandits held up the passengers.

The terror she'd felt then had taunted her with shame. Fear was against the rules; not just the written ones recorded in the Bible, but also within the precepts upon which her father lived.

I will trust and not be afraid. Isaiah 12:2.

Still, she'd been ice-cold terrified and sick with fear.

Now, however, as the small collection of passengers stared at the gun-wielding soldier through the mud-spattered windows and the bus rolled to a stop, a surreal sense of detachment embraced Nina. Not courage, really, but disbelief. She felt as though an old movie unfolded before her eyes.

The man with the gun did not smile. He stood with slouched shoulders, braced against the wind that whipped the clouds into long roiling columns so common to *el invierno*, the Central American winter. He appeared to reconsider his situation, turning slightly, as if to walk away.

Juan Carlton, a fellow missionary who had served with her, shoulder to shoulder for the past six months, gave her a relieved, good-natured smile.

The soldier outside paused again. After a moment more of consideration, he lazily switched off the safety and opened fire. Nina noted the smile frozen on Juan Carlton's face in spite of the horror that blazed in his eyes.

In a deafening display, bullets punched through the windows like a stream of angry hornets, sending glass rocketing in all directions. Shards sliced into worn seat covers around Nina and skimmed her long brown hair.

"*¡Dios mío, perdóname!*" wailed the woman.

God forgive me.

Nina saw the driver's head snap forward. As he slumped over the steering wheel, the bus began to drift toward the side of the graveled road as if the driver's foot had lost contact with the brake. They drew nearer to the road's edge, where a sharp drop preceded a rugged boulder-strewn slope and bushes clung to the rocky soil with long roots like clawed fingers.

"Hold on," Nina yelled in English, her Spanish forgotten as the tires skidded sideways on shuddering axles.

"No, no, no," the woman cried, fingers pressed to her mouth.

Nina tried to grab her in vain as she flew from the seat. Bodies, bags, and glass eddied around her in a violent storm.

Something cut into her cheek, then her shoulder. Her body collided with the leg of Juan Carlton. The breath hammered out of her as she hurtled against a seat.

Still, Nina did not feel the surge of fear that should have accompanied the scene. It was odd that she felt no pain, even as blood washed across her field of vision. Odd too, that the screams from the handful of passengers stopped as the bus toppled one final time on its way to the bottom of the ravine. Strangest of all was that the green-eyed woman had, a split second before the soldier began to fire, given him a smile, the gentle smile of . . . *a woman in love*.

* * *

The clouds rolled across the sky above the cluster of ramshackle buildings optimistically regarded as a town. As Shaw Wilder exited the crooked shed that served as the town garage, he looked again along the graveled road crowded with tangled vegetation.

Axel whined, and Shaw calmed the big German shepherd.

The dog paced in a restless ebb and flow in the sticky ground around Shaw's feet as Shaw's own muscles tensed. He knew enough to trust the dog who had proven infinitely more perceptive than any human he'd met.

Axel generally sensed much more than the presence of the land mines he sniffed out, and this was no exception. His nose quivered as he looked out across the hills turned phosphorescent by the continual rains. Shaw had arranged a meeting with his friend and employer, but he saw no sign of the man.

"Señor Wilder," Tito said, gasping for breath as he approached at a rapid clip. "*¡Tenemos un problema!*"

Trouble in any other language still sounded the same. "*¿Qué pasó?*"

Tito rattled off the information. The basic facts Shaw already knew. Otto Solis—the larger-than-life character with the lush black mustache and heavy silver pocket watch who had brought him to Solitar, hired him and Axel to rid his newly purchased land from explosives left over from the torturous civil war—was missing.

Overlooking an appointment in San Francisco or Paris was one thing; missed appointments in middle-of-nowhere Guatemala had more than a whiff of disaster about them. Death waited around every hill here and lurked in the quiet caves, nestled in clumps of trees on solitary roads. He'd come to expect it from the country that had destroyed his sister, her life drained away like the chicle sap that oozed from raw gashes in the sopadilla trees.

Perhaps Otto had gone to his plantation, a wild sprawl of oil palms nearer the mountains. He opened his mouth to ask Tito, and then thought better of it. Otto would have told him. The man was as reliable as the sunrise when it came to business. He'd gone to town with the promise of meeting Shaw upon his return at ten o'clock. It was now ten-thirty. Not surprising for the relaxed Central American attitude toward time, but Otto had never shared that philosophy.

"I'm a Guatemalan, born on New York time. Who can figure it?" He'd often said it with a characteristic chuckle. Otto was indeed a puzzle.

Shaw sent Tito to start the phone calls to Otto's regular business contacts and headed for his truck, Axel trotting along at his heels. He called Otto's satellite phone from his own once more. No answer. He gunned the motor and headed straight for the neat brick house Otto called home. The gravel pinged against the wheel wells as they progressed. For a moment, he thought he heard a rattle of gunfire. Stomping on the brakes, he waited, ears straining.

Nothing. His imagination. He continued on.

Mud sucked at the tires, splatting at the undercarriage where the gravel on the road had worn thin. Rolling down the windows did not allow for any refreshing breeze. Humidity reached in and squeezed the breath out of him.

Four years and counting, and Shaw hadn't yet gotten used to the weather. Winters brought daily drenchings and the threat of hurricanes while the long summers sank into stifling heat, stinging insects, and adventure-seeking tourists eager to visit the ancient Mayan ruins of Tikal. The topography still confounded him, too. The massive jungle region of Petén flowed into cloud forests and dumped into coastal areas along two oceans, a continent as diverse as the people who lived there. Guatemalans were by nature a somewhat wary people, but the *ladinos* of Spanish European heritage were so different from the indigenous Mayan, that they might as well be from two different worlds. And Shaw supposed they were.

*It's not the location, Shaw. It's you.*

True enough. He felt at home precisely nowhere since his sister had died trying to be some sort of missionary zealot like her friend Nina Truman. As far as he could tell, being a missionary was like shoveling sand uphill; useless. Beth never should have stayed in Guatemala, never should have married a man so much older than her that he could have been her father. She never should have died there.

He pictured Beth, with his sandy blond hair and eyes caught somewhere between gray and blue, and the ball in the pit of his stomach tightened. He should go home, return to the States where he didn't have to look over his shoulder for pit vipers and drug smugglers, but Beth was buried deep in the heart of this wild place, a fact that stuck him in the gut with the sharp force of an ice pick. He'd desperately wanted to take her body home, but her husband, a wealthy and powerful man with his fingers in every money pot in Guatemala, would not hear of it. She was trapped there and, in some ways, he wondered if he was too.

Axel seemed to sense Shaw's mood and pulled his head inside the window to give Shaw a wet nose poke to the thigh.

"I know. It doesn't pay to live in the past. Maybe we'll go back to the States soon, get ourselves a boat and a couple of corn-fed T-bone steaks."

Axel ignored the comment and shoved his head back through the open window, shaking off the rain droplets that fell with a gentle whoosh. Shaw rounded the twisting road, mercifully graveled, the engine grinding in complaint as he took the steep grade.

The smell got him first. A mixture of fuel and something much more frightening. The tang of a newly fired weapon.

The hair on the scruff of Axel's body stood on end, as if charged by an electric current. Shaw was more electrified by the sight of Otto's Jeep pulled off to the side of the road.

He hurtled out of the truck and ran to it. Empty. The feeling of foreboding hiked up a notch.

Axel didn't bother with the Jeep. He took off running up the slope, lanky shepherd legs quickly outpacing his master and carrying him out of view in a moment.

"Come, Axel," Shaw shouted to no effect.

Shaw hastened back to the truck and retrieved a sheathed knife from under the seat. He jammed it into his waistband before he took off upslope after the dog.

Quickly covered in sweat despite the rain, a noise came to him over the sound of the pattering droplets. He stopped to listen. Again, he heard nothing but rain hitting leaves and his own harsh breathing. The quiet didn't soothe him. The silence rang with an unnatural alarm, stripped of everything, even the squawking of ever-present jungle birds.

Pulse pounding, he sprinted up the road. Cresting the top, he didn't see anything unusual at first glance . . . until his eyes traveled to the path. Deep ruts in the mud filled in the picture and he ran to the edge of the road. Looking down, he spotted the battered remains of a chicken bus, one of the many decrepit old school buses that carried everything from people to poultry. The metal body stretched like a dying animal halfway down the ravine, wedged against an outcropping of rock. Bullet holes showed in the few windows that remained intact. He scanned the tree line, the rock above and the tangle of shrubs below. The shooter was long since gone.

Disgust rose thick in his throat. Shaw didn't consider himself a man of great imagination, but the scenario played out in his mind's eye, and he winced at the broken bodies, moans of the dying, or worse, the all-encompassing silence that might greet him inside the ruined bus.

He started down the slope but stopped after a few steps. The police would be there within minutes, he could hear their approach. Best to stay away from anything involving the authorities. The lengthy explanations that would be required, the money that would likely need to change hands to end the questioning. Otto would have made the same decision. He was well-to-do by Guatemalan standards, but he could pinch a penny until it yodeled. And he had no love for the police.

"Axel!" he hollered. An answering bark came from somewhere in the deep screen of trees. He wondered what the dog had gone after. Mud stuck to his boots as he took a step toward the bus again. For the second time, he stopped.

Leave it to the police, he told himself, or the almighty missionaries who came to this nowhere jungle to shine their light in the darkness, or whatever it was they did.

"It would take a massive inferno to change the smallest thing about this place," he grumbled.

His attention lassoed by a delicate bloom of orange from inside the bus, Shaw squinted at the light playing crazily behind the broken shards of glass still clinging to the frame as the flames sprang suddenly to life.

* * *

Nina's face pressed against something rough. Her mind fought the return to consciousness as flickers of pain shot up her arms and legs. A crackling noise buzzed in her ears like some enormous jungle insect. She opened her eyes and blinked against the blurriness. She pushed against the stuff that scraped her cheek.

Cloth. Strange.

Realization jerked her upright with such force that she nearly passed out. The cloth on her face materialized into someone's sleeve; her missionary friend, Juan Carlos. He was dead. Even without her nursing background, she would have known from the odd angle of his broken neck, the lifeless pallor of his dark skin.

She thought it odd that she didn't feel grief. Nor anger. Nor anything. All she could manage was to stare at the man who had been alive only moments before, clutching a guidebook and a cheap ballpoint pen in his hands and reading snippets about the Mayan ruins they intended to visit before she returned to the States. She'd only planned to remain in Guatemala for two more days, tops. Just long enough to welcome the incoming team of missionaries. Oddly, she'd had to fight her father on that point. He'd wanted—demanded, really—that she fly out with him, leaving their precious clinic untended. But Nina had prevailed in her objections, and Juan Carlos had cheerfully agreed to stay and assist where needed.

*Juan Carlos.* The affable, easy going, humble man who did the dirtiest jobs without complaint and never lost his wide grin.

Now he was dead, and the world had turned upside down.

*Pray, Nina. That's what you should do.*

But she couldn't.

She could do nothing but stare at him as the rain washed over his face, coursing down the laugh lines around his mouth, and dripping off his chin.

Someone pulled at her arm.

"*Vamanos, por favor*."

The green-eyed woman. A trickle of blood snaked down her forehead, glistening black against her skin.

Nina allowed herself to be pulled to her feet, fighting a wave of dizziness. She understood now that she'd been thrown clear of the bus which was turned over, stuck on a clump of rock halfway down the slope, wheels still turning lazily. Nearby, two men laid curled on their sides, mercifully still breathing. An old woman cradled a whimpering child in her arms, stroking his hair and shielding his face from the rain with her body.

*Someone caused this. Purposefully.* Her mind whirled, following the rhythm of the spinning tires. *Bullets. Ruined people. Ruined bus.*

She stared into the windows through the jagged teeth of glass. A shadowed head appeared, a small hand thrusting through the wreckage. A child. At the same moment, she watched smoke rise up around the tiny figure, wreathing him in a black shroud.

A child. A child. A child!

Her mind screamed, but her body refused to move in the right direction as the green-eyed woman pulled her away toward the trees.

"We must run," she said in accented English. "He will come back."

Nina finally found the strength to resist the woman's strong grip. "There's a child," she managed, stabbing a finger toward the bus. "There. In there."

"There is no time," the woman continued, her grasp surprisingly strong on Nina's arm.

A dog barked from somewhere deep in the trees. One pane of

glass from the rear window of the bus suddenly exploded into hundreds of glittering missiles. When the green-eyed woman flinched, Nina used the moment to wrench her arm away, and she took off running toward the small hand that had begun to slide slowly down the window.

# CHAPTER 2

Nina felt the heat on her face as she approached. Smoke from burning metal and melting plastic scalded her nostrils and throat. The rear door stood partially open, and she squeezed through, disoriented by the black curtain of smoke and the upside-down position of the bus. A piece of plywood torn free from who-knew-what shifted under her feet.

"*¿Dónde estás?*" she yelled into the interior. Glass crunched under her feet as she crept forward. "Where are you? Answer me!" she shouted again, interrupted by a fit of coughing.

Hearing nothing, she eased toward the middle of the bus where she'd estimated she'd seen the child. A crack made her dive to the floor, a pane of glass shattering to her right. More shots? She stayed low, crawling gingerly across the floor, planting her palms on spots clearest of debris. The air around her pressed in, hot and growing hotter.

"*Estoy aquí,*" she called in Spanish, hoping he would understand she was there to help.

She thought she heard an answer, or perhaps it was the blood pounding in her own ears. Smoke curled along the dirty floor, now an ersatz ceiling, and the seat cushions began to smolder. She headed toward what she calculated as the front of the bus. The child must have thought he could escape through the main door.

Suddenly, he was there, his face nearly obscured by the smoke, but a wild thatch of black hair clearly visible, the same color as the soot that stained his cheeks. His broad face and generous features identified him as Maya, in spite of the fear written there as he turned to run back into the smoke.

Nina shot to her feet.

She knew of at least thirty-five different languages spoken by the indigenous people, and she could manage a few words at best from any of them. Her brain seized on a bit of information from her first days in country.

*"Ch'qapjp'kin pewi . . .* clinic." *I'm from clinic. A nurse.* She'd fractured the phrase completely. Kekchí was a widely spoken language she prayed he'd understand in spite of her rough attempt.

It was enough. The boy started as if he'd received a shock. He nodded, the tiniest of gestures, and turned again toward the driver's compartment.

"Wait," she called.

The burgeoning fire crackled louder as Nina crept after him. The bus rocked as a tire exploded, nearly bringing her to her knees.

*What am I doing?*

She couldn't hear the voice of reason or the calm reassurance of the Lord. The chaos around her seemed to press inside, filling her with a terrible confusion. One foot in front of the other, shoulders hunched to avoid the scraps of ruined seat that hung inches from her head, she made her way to the driver's compartment. The heat rose with every passing minute until she thought her lungs would burn by breathing in the scorched air.

A man lay crumpled on the ceiling which was now their floor. He lay on his back, blood oozing from an angry channel on his neck. Same broad face, same generous features. The boy's father. The child stared at her, hands balled into fists with a look of utter desperation. She turned away, keeping herself between the stricken man and his son, and she pressed her fingers under his chin, feeling the precious throb of life there. She shot the boy a smile and a nod.

He returned the smile, his teeth white in the gloom, and his face transformed into something beautiful within that soot-filled horror. How would they get him out? The top and bottom of the driver's compartment were smashed together, collapsing the front windows and leaving only a narrow margin filled with glass shards in the gap. The side window offered a wider space, but Nina couldn't be sure it was large enough for an adult, even one of small stature like the bus driver appeared to be. She feared too that moving him without some sort of stabilization might result in spinal cord damage. The answer to that question came in a flash. The plywood she'd seen in the rear of the bus. Not quite long enough, but it would do.

She gestured to the boy to wait there and crept back into the belly of the bus. The smoke stung her eyes and tears ran down her face. She collapsed to her hands and knees and pushed along until a sudden deafening roar shook the floor and the surface beneath her tilted. The bus had begun to slide farther down the slope. She froze, her heart jackhammering against her ribs.

After a terrible groan of distressed metal, the sliding sensation tapered off and the bus stopped, jammed again against the rock. Nina scrambled gingerly to her feet, a difficult task since the pseudo floor was now even more steeply pitched. She didn't dare move any closer to the rear of the bus for fear that her weight might provide the final push sending the bus careening the rest of the way down the gorge.

She returned to the boy and his fallen father. They would have to move the injured man without stabilizing him and pray it wouldn't cause further damage to his spine. At this point, paralysis took a backseat to incineration.

"We'll have to get him out the side window," she said, more to herself than the child. Using the bottom of her shoe to push out the remaining shards of glass, she took his small hand. "You need to get out first," she said, pantomiming.

The boy looked from her to the window and slowly shook his head. He pointed to his father.

Nina took a breath and kept her voice low. "You have to go first, to help pull him out." It might have been the second roar of breaking glass or the oven-like temperature that finally convinced the boy, but Nina sighed in relief as he shimmied through the hole. At least he was safe. She glanced at the thickening blanket of smoke and the narrow sliver of opening and felt the despair start to take root, the hopelessness of their predicament pressing down on her. This was where it would end, her strange journey. She imagined consumption by fire, ignoring the fact that death would come first from the choking smoke. Her knees weakened and she dropped to the floor, head spinning and face wet with acid tears.

The boy's face appeared again, and his hands thrust through the opening. They were such tiny hands, so delicate and finely boned. How could those hands reach through such overwhelming heat? Those yearning fingers reached out for the father.

Something flickered deep inside Nina and she forced herself to her feet. Maybe if she could turn the man on his side. Grabbing hold of his thick shoulder, she heaved him into position, hoping not to hear the crackle of broken bones as she did so. Sweat ran down her face, stinging the multiple cuts as she tried to shove him toward the window.

He didn't budge.

Nerves firing frantically, she took off the light jacket she wore to keep off the perpetual winter rain. Rolling him forward and back, she got the material underneath his torso and tried again. Pushing with all her strength, she cried out as her efforts yielded slow movement. When her vision blurred and the heat grew intolerable, his foot touched the frame of the window.

The boy took hold of his father's ankle and began to pull, crying out in words she did not recognize, but understood anyway. She tried to push, but the scene swam before her eyes, a kaleidoscope of black smoke and glittering needles of glass.

* * *

Shaw saw the bus shudder and slide a few feet farther, metal screeching over the rock. It remained wedged, but precariously so.

"Axel," he shouted again, and this time the dog answered, barking furiously. Shaw scrambled back up the slope in time to see the shepherd burst from the trees with something clasped in his mouth, followed by a short man with a lush mustache.

*Otto.* Shaw sighed in relief.

Wiping his forehead with the back of his hand, Otto walked in his customary brisk gait. Shaw clapped him on the shoulder, noting a gash on his cheek and a torn pant leg.

"I was starting to worry."

Otto flashed him a grin. "Worry? About me?" He squinted toward the accident. "I am on my way to town and what do I see? A crazy *soldado* shooting up the bus." He shook his head. "The bus is nearly empty fortunately, and the passengers begin to jump out the windows before it goes over the side, but still I wonder why this soldier shoots up a bus."

Shaw sighed. "So you decided to find out?"

Otto's face grew mournful. "I begin to run after him, but he is faster." He sighed. "Somewhere in my fiftieth year, the speed has left." He shook his head. "Anyway, I am walking back to help when your dog meets me." Otto cocked his head, catching the sound of male voices. "*La policía.*"

"Yeah."

"Then that is my cue to depart."

"They'll want to know about the shooter."

Otto waved a hand. "I will send Tito to the station to tell them what I have seen."

"And if they want more?"

He smoothed his mustache. "Then they can make an appointment. *Adiós,* Shaw." He took his hat from Axel who still held it patiently grasped between his teeth. "*Gracias*, Axel, but next time perhaps without the holes bitten through, eh?"

Otto squeezed his wide frame into his Jeep and pulled the

vehicle into a tight turn, pausing to poke his head out. "It will be the best thing for you to leave now, too. Speaking to those buffoons causes you to lose your temper and I am not wishing to come and bail you out of jail." Tipping his hat, he sped away.

Axel began to creep in the direction of the ravine until Shaw ordered him to sit. The dog obeyed, staring at his master with an unmistakable expression of disapproval.

"We're going, Ax."

Each triangular ear swiveled on the dog's head. Shaw pulled back into the shadow of the trees as a police car appeared, climbing to the top of the slope.

"Police will take care of it. We'll be in the way."

Axel's whiskers twitched, his eyes locked on Shaw's.

Shaw knelt next to the dog and rubbed his head. "Nothing we do here is going to make any difference."

Axel swiped at Shaw's face with a warm, wet tongue, intense gaze unrelenting.

Shaw heaved a sigh. "A man shouldn't be pushed into action by his dog. It's not right. I'm the master, remember?"

Axel stood up, hearing the acquiescence underlying the words.

"I'm going to regret this," Shaw muttered as he got to his feet and took off for the edge, slipping on the muddy ground. He spotted two men—uniformed police—already at the bottom. He recognized them both; Josef and Roque, both of whom he'd paid to escape various delays and insane governmental red tape.

Josef spoke to an old lady with a young child clasped in her arms. The woman spoke so rapidly Shaw couldn't follow the Spanish. He caught enough from Josef to know the officer urged her farther away from the actively burning wreckage which belched out billows of acrid smoke. A few feet away from the woman, a man laid stretched out in the mud. From the awkward position of the body, Shaw could tell he was dead.

Josef looked up at Shaw's approach and flapped a hand at him. "Move away, please. It is dangerous here, señor."

Shaw nodded. It was more than dangerous; his own presence was ridiculous. He started to call to his dog, nosing around and tense from the constant noise. Roque had a small boy by the arm, intent on dragging him toward the tree line. The boy pulled mightily against Roque's grasp, shouting in a language Shaw didn't understand.

"Stupid peasant," Roque grunted. He yanked the child so hard that his feet left the ground, but still the little boy fought, sinking his teeth deep into Roque's hand. The officer dropped the boy and he scrambled away toward the wreck until Roque caught him again in a volley of curse words.

He hauled him back up the slope, the child flailing all the while, stuffing him into the police car and locking the door. Shaw waited until Roque turned his back before jogging toward the front end of the bus to retrieve Axel, trying to stay clear enough that he could jump away if the thing came loose and rolled down the slope.

He couldn't see a thing through the blackened space, the interior roiling with smoke. The vehicle would be an inferno in a matter of moments.

Axel nosed close, his body taut. He barked once and sat, face rigid. Axel had been briefly trained as a rescue dog before he'd wound up as a canine officer in the Los Angeles Police Department. Some remnants of the training must have stuck because now his body acted as a signal, pointing with laser intensity. Shaw ran to meet him and saw what he had missed amidst the choking smoke: a set of sandaled feet protruding from the smashed side window.

Shaw yelled to Josef and grabbed hold, pulling until the legs were visible up to the knees. Josef arrived and together they yanked until the body emerged up to the waist. The man's upper body was too big to come through. Shaw grabbed the metal framing of the window, burning his hands. Stripping off his jacket, he wrapped the fabric around his palms and tried again, heaving with all his might. The metal gave only a few inches.

Josef continued to pull until the body slid loose from the window, sending Josef tumbling down the slope a few feet. He scrambled upright and they carried the man away to the safety of the trees where Roque joined them.

Josef wiped the sweat from his thick black brows before he checked for a pulse. "Still alive," he said with an incredulous shake of his head.

Shaw peered down at the unconscious man; obviously poor with cheap, broken sandals and the fabric of his pants worn. Judging from his condition, he might have suffered permanent damage, perhaps enough to preclude him from ever driving a bus again. How many family members depended on this one broken man for survival?

A muffled pounding came from upslope, and the scenario came crystal-clear in Shaw's mind. "You'd better let that kid out so he can be with his dad or he's going to break your window," he advised.

"And you'd better retrieve your dog, Señor Wilder. The bus is going to blow," Josef said. "The drivers always keep extra cans of gasoline stored below."

Shaw called to Axel who was still sitting near the front of the bus.

The dog stood, turned around in a complete circle and sat again with a whine.

Shaw didn't bother to call him again. He knew. Deep down in his gut, he knew. There was someone else in there.

*Probably too late,* he speculated. The victim was likely dead from smoke inhalation or blood loss.

Try as he might, he had never been able to explain to Axel the rationale behind giving up. He went to him and put a hand on his collar, prepared to force surrender upon him. "You did well, boy, but it's time to go."

The dog resisted, pulling his eighty pounds against Shaw's efforts. A low rumbling sound echoed from the back of the bus. A tire, flung loose, hurtled over their heads, crashing into the trees.

"Now, Axel!" Shaw yelled, hauling the dog with all his strength.

Axel's whines escalated into barks as Shaw forced him away. Heat played on the back of Shaw's neck and he realized he'd left his jacket. Axel's contortions nearly knocked him off his feet but he was able to twist his body to keep his balance. As he did so, he looked once more at the tiny space where they had pulled the man out.

To his utter astonishment, his jacket was fluttering back and forth in the window opening like a dilapidated signal flag. Once, twice, and then it stopped and settled to the ground.

# CHAPTER 3

Shaw released his grip on Axel's collar, and the dog shot back toward the bus, which was now crackling ominously.

Josef spoke into his ear above the noise.

"Dumb dog," Josef said. "He will get his master killed."

Shaw didn't answer. The heat surged from the wreck in waves, beating against his skin. He made it to the window and pushed the dog aside. Snatching at the jacket, he shoved his hand into the opening. "Here. Grab on."

He felt no answering grasp so he flattened himself on the grass. Face pressed to the muck, he could make out a smoke-filled space no bigger than a closet, a dark shape silhouetted on one side.

Ignoring the pain from the broken glass lacerating his fingers, he thrust his hand in farther until he felt something soft and pliable. Grabbing as big a handful as he could manage, he pulled it toward the opening. A woman's slender arm fell limp, covered in a filthy cotton shirt. Her body lay across the space, causing her to wedge sideways in the opening as he tried to free her. He'd have to push himself farther in to reorient her, but his shoulders were too wide to fit through the opening, no matter how hard he tried.

Scrambling to his feet, he yanked at the metal frame as he'd done before, but he succeeded in accomplishing nothing except scorching his hands. He looked around for some other way in, but the bus had collapsed and no opening presented itself. He raced around to the other side, feet clawing for purchase on the slippery ground. Axel followed. The folding door on the passenger side was smashed and twisted. Try as he might, he could not get it unwedged. He kicked at the door, ramming his foot into the hinged middle again and again until he felt it give way. Sweat soaked into his shirt and ran down his face, stinging his eyes.

Without warning, the bus lurched and he fell forward, slamming hard against the metal side. Roque appeared around the front, his forehead creased in worry.

"You must stop, Señor Wilder," he called over the rain. "It's going to give way or the fire will cause it to explode."

Shaw yelled back. "There's a woman in the front. She's unconscious."

"Probably dead," he shouted. "Too late. Come away before it is too late for you as well."

Shaw ignored him, eyeing the bus uneasily. It seemed to have stopped moving, but the fire mounted, flames now shooting through the broken windows. He kicked at the door again, hoping he wasn't merely speeding the woman to her death at the bottom of the ravine. Roque shrugged and disappeared, muttering something Shaw couldn't make out.

A half dozen ferocious kicks later, Shaw's strength began to ebb, the heat sucking his energy. He summoned the stamina for one more blow, aimed at the weakest part of the door. It gave way with a shriek of metal, the two halves of the folding door splitting neatly down the middle.

He leapt through, blinded by the black swirls of smoke. Getting as low as he could, he felt his way along until he touched something soft and tangled, a woman's long hair. Prostrate on her stomach, head near the steering wheel and knees curled underneath, lifeless as far as he could tell.

Probably dead, like Roque said. But just a few moments ago, hadn't he seen her wave the jacket?

*A few moments*, he thought grimly. Plenty of time for a life to slip away. God did things like that, ended a life when help was so excruciatingly close.

He eyed the slender woman again, her small hands and graceful fingers curled just underneath the cloud of hair that covered her face. Taking hold of her waist, Shaw pulled, but something stopped his progress. Peering closer, he saw that part of the dashboard had collapsed, pincering a section of her hair underneath. He could probably work it free given enough time, but that was a luxury they didn't have. The floor continued to shudder uneasily and the flames marched toward their position, reflecting madly in the shards of broken glass. Axel's barks from just outside the vehicle had increased to near-manic levels.

*I know, buddy. Get out and get out now.*

He took the knife from the sheath and sliced through a chunk of hair. The strands separated easily, surprisingly silky to his touch. As he straightened, her eyes suddenly opened, gleaming in the flickering light.

He took a step away as she jerked to a sitting position.

The woman went rigid, sprang to her feet and scuttled back, slamming into the side of the ruined bus.

* * *

Nina quickly assessed the surroundings within her nightmare: her back pressed against a section of hot metal, black smoke pouring in from every direction and a knife-wielding man standing over her.

"*Cálmese,*" he commanded. "*No se mueva.*"

The man who commanded her to stay still was a foot taller, arms strong and muscled, nearly shaved head matching the dark stubble just visible on his chin by the light of the dancing flames. She could not make out his features clearly, other than to recognize that he was powerful and angry and armed.

As nightmare and reality merged, Nina looked around wildly. No escape offered itself. The space where she remembered shoving the driver was now engulfed in flames. She wondered how the boy had been able to pull his father's bulk through the small hole.

Her choices were desperate: Obey the man bent on slitting her throat, or crawl through the flames and hope she could make it before she burned to death? Fear whipped her pulse and caused her legs to shake so badly she wasn't certain she could move, but somehow she did. Dropping to her knees, she launched herself through the debris toward the hole.

She heard the man swear but his exact words were lost in the groaning of the bus which seemed to have come alive. With nothing to grab on to, she felt herself tumbling until a pair of big hands wrapped around her waist. She tried to peel the fingers away but found herself dragged to the opposite end, the bus shuddering around her.

Beating at the arms did no good either as he tossed her over his shoulder. There was no time to scream as metal and glass hurtled at them and tongues of flame erupted from the front cab. Shadows and destruction tumbled before her eyes.

What had once been the door of the bus now took the shape of a curtain of flames, and in that moment of horror she realized they headed directly for it. She tried to kick out.

They hurtled out the door, propelled by what must have been a giant leap on the part of her abductor. Her body collided with the ground, his heavy weight torqued slightly, preventing him from crushing her with his bulk. Nonetheless, the impact drove the breath straight out of her.

A high-pitched screech split the air, and the rocks shook underneath them. A wave of intense heat enfolded everything until she thought it would burn her lungs to cinders. Seconds later, the noise and ferocious heat faded away. The man rolled to the side and she became aware of something warm and damp snuffling along her face. She sat up and a dog's muzzle swam into focus. She tried to push him away with a shaking hand.

"*Él no té va á morder,*" came the man's voice, heavy with some emotion she couldn't grasp.

*Maybe the dog won't hurt me*. Nina's reply came in unspoken gasps. *But you've got a knife.*

She didn't think her legs would support her long enough to run to the blurry figures she saw at a distance under the trees, so she began to inch backward in a reverse crab walk while his attention remained fixed on the bottom of the ravine.

He still stared down, hands on hips, the knife now sheathed on his belt. Something about his defiant posture struck her as familiar.

"We almost went to the bottom along with the bus." He turned toward her, strong chin and drawn brows angry. "I told you to stay still."

She froze. "Maybe you should have put down your knife first."

His head jerked, eyebrows raised in surprise, probably at the fact that she spoke English as well as he did.

"My knife?" He scowled and then sighed. "Your hair was stuck. I had to cut it off."

Her fingers flew to her head, finding the frayed ends of the chunk that he'd hacked away. The bus belched out a cloud of acrid smoke. Suddenly, Nina felt every cut, every scrape and burn. The horror and fear and pain rushed in together as she fingered the severed strands. Tears began to slide down her face.

The man stared at her, dumbstruck. He rubbed a hand over his stubbled chin. "It's just hair." He pointed to the burning bus. "You could be there with your hair intact."

She pressed her face to her knees to avoid the dog's determined licks to her soot-glazed cheeks.

*It's not the hair*, she wanted to yell at him. *It's the soldier with the gun, the bullets that killed Juan Carlos and struck the driver.*

It was the boy who would never forget the terror of trying to free his father who might never recover. It was almost burning to death in the country she'd served for years, a place that now felt strange and hostile. It was her inability at that very moment to feel God's presence amidst the horror. She couldn't say it, and he wouldn't understand anyway. Squeezing her eyelids together, she willed the tears to stop.

"Señorita Truman?" A uniformed officer she knew approached.

She tried to struggle to her feet, but her legs would not cooperate. "Hello, officer."

He came to her and put a concerned hand on her shoulder. His partner joined them after releasing the little boy from his car. She watched him run down the slope to his father, lying at a safe distance from the fire.

Josef looked into her face. "Are you well? It is a surprise. We believed you were to leave town."

"I am not hurt, not seriously." She rubbed a hand across her eyes. "How did you know I was leaving?"

Josef exchanged a look with Roque and shrugged. "We hear of these things."

She was in the process of giving the two officers a detailed account of the gunman when she noticed her rescuer staring with open animosity at her.

"Is something wrong?"

"You're Nina Truman?" he asked, eyes boring into her face. "I didn't recognize you."

"Do I know you?"

He shook his head. "Not as well as you knew my sister Beth. Last name's Wilder."

Nina felt a cold shiver start in her belly and work up toward the nape of her neck. Beth Wilder's brother Shaw. Even if he hadn't confronted her years ago after Beth's death, she would recognize the condemnation in his expression now.

"I'm . . . sorry," she said.

He opened his mouth to reply and then snapped it shut. "Come on, Axel," he said as he turned away.

"You must come with us to the hospital, Señorita Truman," Roque said. "To have the lungs treated."

"No," she said, eyes still on Shaw's wide back. "I'm okay. You need the doctors for the critically injured." Now that the clinic was officially closed, the nearest hospital was a good four hours distant, and woefully small.

Both Roque and Josef protested vigorously, but she shook her head. "I will go back to the clinic and rest. I'll leave when I'd planned to."

She waved off another round of argument.

"Let us take you then," Josef said. "It is too far to walk."

The way her legs felt and the rhythm of her pounding head almost inclined her to agree . . . until she looked toward the victims huddled near the shelter of the trees. "They need help. Do you have a first aid kit?"

Roque provided one and she trudged away. The boy knelt next to his unconscious father, chafing his hand and singing softly. He offered a shy smile when she joined him. Nina felt encouraged by the bus driver's regular breathing and the color pushing up to his cheeks. She said a prayer for the man as she bandaged his wound and checked him as best she could for broken bones. As she struggled to her feet to move on to the next patient, the boy grasped her hand and pressed a scrap of paper into it.

"Woman," he said, pointing to his eyes then gesturing to the trees.

She understood. The note was from the woman who had made her escape into the trees, but not before she'd written a message. What reason could she have had for sticking around to write a note? And what could she say to explain the strange smile she'd given the shooter? As much as she wanted to read it, the desperate call from the elderly lady crouched near the trunk of a sprawling tree made her pocket it instead.

Nina struggled for nearly two hours to treat the critically injured survivors, though there was little she could do to ease their pain. For Juan Carlos, who had faithfully helped at the clinic with everything from patching the roof to holding flashlights when the generator failed, she could only offer a prayer. Even as she spoke the words, her mind tumbled in dizzying circles.

Why? Why? How could this nightmare have happened?

An ambulance—actually a van with the backseat removed —

finally wheezed up the path and Nina assisted the driver in loading the two most seriously injured victims into the back. Another six, including the boy and the old lady, still grasping her child, crammed into the seats.

Roque took two more in his car, and Josef was left the grim task of wrapping Juan Carlos in a blanket and bundling him into a Jeep that had arrived after the ambulance.

"Where . . . ?" Nina tried, her throat thickening.

"To the hospital, for an autopsy."

"His family. He's got a sister and two brothers in Mexico."

"*Sí, sí*. We will notify them. Please, señorita, come with me. We will take you to the clinic, yes? It is nearly dusk and you should not walk alone now."

Because something bad might happen to her? She felt the insane desire to laugh. What she needed, what she craved, was some time alone, to order in her mind the disastrous minutes that felt like a lifetime. An odd sensation rushed over her, as if she were no longer the same person who had boarded the bus with camera in hand, flush with tender feelings for the work she'd accomplished.

"No, thank you," she answered him. "I'll contact you tomorrow."

"We will send a car for you then, when one is available." With a sigh, Josef joined Roque and they drove away into the watery afternoon sun.

The van followed, leaving a few men behind to survey the mangled bus, pointing and calling out plans to each other, phoning for tow vehicles from larger towns outside the Petén.

Left alone with only the sound of the mud pulling at her feet, Nina stayed to the side of the road pondering how long it might be before the police sent a car. She suddenly felt almost frantic to get away from the smells and sights of the horrendous crash and get back to the clinic, so she started walking. After a few yards, a sharp pain in her side made her stop. She pressed a hand there, coughing violently, and the reality of her decision to hike back came fully home.

The sky darkened and the clouds rolled, speeding the sun's departure. Another storm. Perhaps it would last for minutes, perhaps hours. She heard the click of night insects as they began to awaken for their nocturnal feeding and pictured the tarantulas common to the Petén creeping out to feed.

She heard something over the noise of jungle life, a powerful engine churning to life from somewhere behind her. For a moment, she wondered if the soldier had come back to finish his grisly work. Muscles tense, she whirled.

Her breath caught as the big truck pulled to a stop next to her. Pressed right to the edge of the path, her only escape would be to flee into the untamed jungle behind her.

Shaw stuck his head through the open window. "You can't walk. Get in."

She sucked in a breath and couldn't suppress a fit of coughing. "I thought you were leaving."

His eyes were unreadable, but the coldness on his face was clear. The dog watched her from the passenger seat. "Police blocked my truck. Couldn't get out until they left."

She studied him for a moment as he drew his full lips together and furrowed his thick brows. There was only a hint of his sister there; in the cheekbones, she supposed, and in the way his mouth quirked slightly at the corners. "Thank you, Mr. Wilder, but I can walk." She turned and continued gingerly down the slope.

The truck edged next to her. "You nearly burned to death. What do you think you're proving by walking alone through the jungle? Are missionaries superheroes or something? Last time I checked, you all bleed and die just like anyone else."

She stopped, spine stiff, and turned back to face him. "I know that, Mr. Wilder. I just saw one of my missionary superhero friends die in that wreck. He was a fine man; a very fine man." Her lip trembled a little but she held the grief in check, chin high.

He shifted in the seat. "Then why don't you get in," he said, in a lower tone.

"Because I am the last person you want to help. You believe I brought Beth here to her death and I can see the rage in your eyes. I appreciate the offer, but I'll spare us both and decline."

His eyes narrowed and he let out an enormous sigh. She got the feeling he might have added a string of profanities if he wasn't face-to-face with a woman. "If you don't get in, I'm going to have to follow you in the truck with Axel barking the whole way until I can't stand it anymore. Then I'm going to have to get out and toss you over my shoulder again and haul you in here. You don't want that, do you?"

She was so startled that she could only shake her head.

"Fine," he snapped. "Then do us both a favor and get in the truck."

There was not a flicker of humor in his face. She recalled the strength in his back when he'd yanked her out of the burning bus. Her cheeks warmed. The rain began to patter around her in thickening sheets. Axel barked three times, the sound echoing through the moist air.

With as much dignity as she could muster, she walked to the passenger side and got into the truck. Axel obligingly moved over after licking her under the chin.

Shaw guided the truck down the path without so much as a glance in her direction.

She ran her fingers up and down Axel's thick fur; a distraction from the exquisite awkwardness of the situation. The dog gave her a pleasure-soaked stare.

*He'll drop me off at the clinic and it will all be over. Just a few more miles.*

Axel began to sniff at her tattered pants. Though she pushed him away, he jammed his nose at her pocket, tickling her side until she squirmed.

"Give him a shove," Shaw said, without looking at her. "If you don't show him who's boss, he figures he is."

She tried to fend him off, but the wet nose still pressed into her side until she remembered with a start what was in her pocket.

She pulled out the scrap the boy had given her and unrolled it, holding it away from Axel's prying nose. The words were hard to make out, blurred and hurriedly scrawled.

A cry escaped her lips.

Shaw looked at her. "What's wrong?"

Trying to still her shaking hands, she couldn't answer. Instead, she stared toward the jungle, into a world gone suddenly dark.

# CHAPTER 4

Shaw resisted the urge to glance over at the woman beside him, but his brain hummed at her strange behavior. He diagnosed a form of delayed shock in her. And why not, after what had happened to her on the bus? He'd seen it before during his five years as a bomb technician for the LAPD. Victims could seem perfectly calm and in control, and then fall apart when the realization of what they'd survived settled in. He shot her a quick glance to see that her hands were shaking, eyes fixed on a spot somewhere out in the darkness.

*Perfect.* His ridiculous notion to see her safely to her destination and vanish immediately afterward looked unlikely. Why him? Why her? He'd somehow become responsible for the woman who had led his sister to the place where she would be murdered. He should open the door and leave her, drive back to his place and forget all about Nina Truman.

In spite of Axel's persistent sniffing, Nina stared out the window. Unsure whether the failing light was at fault or whether her emotional abyss had already closed in, he couldn't miss the unnatural color of her complexion. Something wasn't right, and he wondered why she didn't just pray herself out of the mess or sing a hymn or something. If any singing started, he determined to get out immediately and leave her in the truck to do her thing.

"You okay?" he finally managed.

She didn't answer, just crushed the paper in her hand.

"You're probably in shock. I'll take you to the hospital," he snapped, knowing it would be hours before they reached the marginally equipped hospital.

"I don't understand," she whispered, so low he almost missed it.

He thought about explaining the particulars of shock when he remembered that she was a nurse of some kind. She should have covered that topic in whatever training she'd had. He looked closer and realized Nina Truman's issues surpassed simple shock. On instinct, he wrested the paper from her cold fingers. The scribbled message was in Spanish, but he knew enough to translate.

*Run or you'll die. I will contact you soon. —A*

He fingered the filthy paper. "Who gave it to you?" When she didn't respond, he repeated the question. "Who gave this to you?"

"A woman on the bus. She tried to get me to run away from the crash with her." Nina's eyes slowly swiveled to his. Her lips moved but no words came out.

He killed the motor and looked at the note again. "You don't know her?"

Nina shook her head. "A stranger to me, but inquisitive about where I was going, what stops I would make. She . . . had green eyes."

The night fell like a cloak over the tree line. A tingling started in his gut, a feeling Shaw couldn't define. He shifted. "Probably nothing. She saw it as a way to score money, maybe."

Nina seemed to turn the matter over in her mind, but she didn't comment.

Shaw shrugged. "We can bring it to the police, but they're transporting the victims right now so it will have to wait until tomorrow sometime."

She squinted her eyes as she seemed to bear down on his words. He noticed her hair gleaming in the watery moonlight when she interrupted. "I'd better go to the clinic."

He nodded, relieved. For a while, the only sound was the creak of the old vehicle as Shaw maneuvered it over the bumps and occasional potholes. It didn't bother him in the slightest that she remained silent. He preferred it to forcing out meaningless pleasantries. He'd never been particularly good at small talk, and his skills had deteriorated even further after his years in the jungle with only a dog as his constant companion.

They skirted a thicket of broad-leafed palms and turned off into the minuscule village of Pajarito. It wasn't really a badly appointed place, as far as Guatemalan jungle villages went. The clinic was the only modern-looking building in the area with wood-planked walls and a tiled porch. Farther away was a small market which he visited from time to time, a corn mill, and even a crude electrical plant that supplied the nearby towns with power until eight at night, unless it experienced one of its frequent *off line* incidents. He checked the luminous dial of his watch. Eight-fifteen.

The village was completely dark. Nearby houses rose in the distance, not one flicker of light showing in their shuttered windows as Shaw took the gentle slope to the clinic.

"Is there anyone here?"

She shook her head. "We closed yesterday. Dad and I are on furlough. There's another team of missionaries set to arrive and take over."

"Where's your father now?"

Shaw had seen Dr. Bruce Truman, his tall form almost bent double as he stopped to talk with the littlest villagers who called him *El Monte*. The mountain. Shaw understood what it felt like to be over six feet tall in a country where the average man barely topped five feet, but Dr. Truman commanded respect by more than just his stature.

"He left yesterday."

"And you didn't go with him?"

"My uncle had a stroke. I stayed behind to close up properly and take a side trip and greet the new missionaries before I flew home." He heard her breath catch and she jerked convulsively.

"My passport. It was in my bag." She looked at him. "It's gone now."

"You'll have to go to the embassy." That meant a trip to Guatemala City. A fifteen-hour trip. Probably more, considering the reliability of the buses. "Best thing is to hitch a ride with the police when they return, or the next batch of missionaries to arrive."

Her lips twitched at the touch of sarcasm he hadn't intended.

"The next *batch* will be busy." She looked away. "I think I have a copy at the clinic. I'll figure it out."

He grunted. "You can show the cops the note, anyway. See if they can make anything of it." Shaw pulled up at the front, a sudden onslaught of rain spattering the windshield. She got out and he followed her up the tile walkway.

At the door, she turned to him. "Thank you for your help. I appreciate it."

He nodded. "I'll come in and get the generator started for you."

She held up a hand. "I can manage."

"It's no trouble." He wasn't sure why he made the offer. His whole body screamed at him to get out of there, but she looked very small standing on the dark porch, rain-dampened hair clinging to her face. His sister would not have wanted him to abandon her without so much as a flashlight. He started to push by her, but she gripped his arm with surprisingly strong fingers.

"You don't believe in this clinic. You think we're meddlers, offering medical treatment as an enticement to convert people."

He jerked. "Did I say that?"

"You did, to Beth."

He stared, suddenly angry. She didn't have the right to know his personal views, certainly not when acquired through his sister. It felt like a betrayal. "Don't talk to me about her."

"She was my friend. My *best* friend."

"And she was my sister, flesh and blood, and you're the reason she's dead," he spat before he could think better of it.

She took a step back as if he'd struck her.

He wanted to erase the ugly words but his anger kept them alive, simmering in the humid jungle air.

"Good night, Mr. Wilder," she said, vanishing into the cool interior, closing the door behind her.

He stood on the step, staring at the sturdy wood door, regret and rage coursing alternately through his body. He stayed there, teeth clenched, hands balled into fists, until the falling rain began to soak him thoroughly and Axel's impatient bark rocketed through the partially open passenger window.

"Coming." He stalked back to the truck and threw himself into the front seat. A soft glow illuminated a window of the clinic. She must have gotten the generator going, or lit some lamps.

*Good luck getting home, Nina. Or maybe this is your permanent home now.*

Permanent. Like Beth's.

*Was it worth it?* He flashed on an image of his mother, her face lit by some strange inner fire, a passion stronger than her love for her children. Would she say it had been worth it after what awaited her when she followed her God into disaster? Would Beth?

Trying to smother the tumult of feelings, he pulled the truck down the path and made it nearly a half mile back to the main road when his phone rang.

* * *

Nina's whole body trembled as she lit three kerosene lamps. Three was excessive and wasteful, but she hoped the light would push away the darkness that seemed to fill her up inside. She went to the ancient rotary phone, her only option since her celi was in the bottom of the ravine along with the bus.

Her father would answer, his quiet voice calm and steady as he listened and contemplated. A careful planner, an unflappable physician . . . and a liar.

The word buzzed inside her heart, the ugly truth of it still grating at her. He loved her, she had no doubt.

But he'd lied to her.

She shook her head to clear away the tears which had begun to fill her eyes and choke off her throat.

*Not now. It's not the time to think about that.*

Suddenly all she craved with every sinew in her body was a chance to wash away the past few hours, the soot that clung to her, the smell of fear that seemed to permeate her hacked-off hair. Her hands shook, sent crazy shadows spiraling around the room as she moved a lamp to the tiny bathroom; the mildewed shower curtain hung crookedly on the rod. A lackluster stream of water poured down.

She should collect her passport copy and phone her father, like it or not, to decide her next step. As confident as she'd tried to sound in front of Shaw, the thought of getting on another bus to start the journey toward the embassy seemed abhorrent, even though she knew it was the only option. A bus trip from Pajarito to the tiny Flores airport where she could catch a flight to Guatemala City would mean eight or ten hours of travel, barring delays, mechanical failures or any number of impediments that multiplied exponentially the farther away a person was from the city. And then there was the rain which turned many of the jungle roads to an impassible muck.

All these concerns chased one another around in her mind, but overriding all was the desire to get clean—to wash away the horrifying crash, the death of Juan Carlos, Shaw's cutting words. The cold water elicited a shiver as the weak stream rinsed the grit and smoke from her hair. She lathered as best she could with the rough ball of soap, scrubbing until her skin stung, and then letting the cold water whisk it away.

A memory of Beth caught her by surprise.

She pictured her friend washing her hair in the *pila*, the outdoor sink, shortly after her arrival in Pajarito. Her blonde hair curled into ringlets, and water coursed down her face as she laughed, her face tipped toward the sun. Beautiful and so fair, she attracted the attention of everyone in the town. Everyone, including a certain Colonel Fuentes. The people called him *Padrino*. Father.

The irony still bit at her along with the guilt. Shaw had been partially correct. She'd encouraged Beth to come to Guatemala for a visit. It was supposed to last only a month. It was supposed to be life-changing. Instead, it was life-ending.

When the cold water became too much, Nina padded to the tiny bedroom, careful to avoid the skittering cockroaches, and wrapped herself in clean clothes—the warmest shirt she owned, sneakers, and thick socks. She still felt chilled as she returned to the battered desk and contemplated the relic of a phone.

She had to call. Her father would have arrived at his brother Paul's house in Wisconsin, taking charge in that unflappable way that saw them through their on-again-off-again years of service in the Petén jungle. She'd never seen him unsettled about anything, except when he spoke about her mother's death from cancer.

"If she'd only told me sooner, we would have returned to the States."

They both knew she hadn't revealed the seriousness of her condition because she didn't want to curtail their mission work. Nina thought of the tattered picture she carried in her wallet, the picture of her father, tall and straight, his arm around the shoulders of her mother, short and voluptuous with a wide and genuine smile.

People said she had her mother's smile. But she'd learned very recently that people lied.

Even people she had never imagined could do so.

Again, she moved away from the phone. She would call in a moment. Ahead of her was an arduous trip to Guatemala City. Snatching a backpack from the shelf, she threw in what she could fit. The small medical kit, some snacks and water, about seven thousand quetzals—roughly equivalent to one hundred US dollars that she'd have to replace for the incoming missionaries—her Bible and a flashlight for reading during the inevitable waiting time at the Embassy.

She caught a glimpse of one last item she wanted to squeeze into the backpack, and her eyes grew blurry. She fingered the soft material of Juan Carlos's old crushed hat before tenderly tucking it inside.

Would they ever know why the soldier had fired on a bus full of innocent people?

She wiped her face as she sat down at the old rotary telephone to call her father. With icy fingers, she turned the dial and breathed in. The exhale that followed blew some notepaper to the floor.

She waited for the connection, but there wasn't one.

She tapped the cradle and called again with no better result. A tiny flicker of panic started up her spine, but she shut it down. Phone problems were nothing unusual. Even though Guatemala had found its way into the modern age of satellite phones and internet, the jungle could play havoc on any man-made technology. She replaced the receiver and heaved a few slow breaths before she tried again. It took a moment more for her eyes to fasten on the cord that traveled from the phone and disappeared behind the desk. Some prickle of unease that she couldn't explain spurred her to give it a gentle tug. It sprang easily from behind the desk, the end neatly severed.

She stood so quickly that her head spun, the chair falling to the floor with a crash.

Someone had cut the phone.

They must be here. Hiding.

She quickly reasoned the thought away. Where? Where would they hide? There was simply no place anyone could hide.

Even so, she tiptoed to the doorway of her bedroom. Just two cots, no linens, no closet . . . and no one hiding there. The other bedroom which normally housed her father, Juan Carlos, and any other male missionary was the same, the precise columns of *centavos* stacked on a makeshift table, exactly as her meticulous father had left them.

She went to the window. Standing to one side, she peered out. Was someone there? Hiding in the fringe of oil palms or behind the tangled hibiscus?

Why would they be? The clinic held nothing of value except a few basic supplies that would be replenished by the arriving missionaries. The people of the Petén were poor, but they were honest. The quetzals she'd taken for her backpack had not been touched.

So who had cut the phone line? And why?

She'd get away. One of her friends in Pajarito would let her stay the night. She didn't know what reason she would give for abandoning the clinic, but at the moment she didn't care. Stomach tight, she retrieved the key to the desk from under the floorboard where her father recently insisted they keep it. Odd, she'd thought. They never locked the doors of the clinic, or the Jeep when they were fortunate enough to borrow it; just the desk drawer. Because her father insisted.

It took several tries to get the key in the lock, several tries before she realized there was no need for the key. The lock was broken. The wooden drawer slid open and she peered inside.

She thrust her fingers into the space and felt around.

Her breath came in harsh rasps. Mind spinning, she tried to quell the rising sense of panic.

The copy of her passport . . . *Gone!*

# CHAPTER 5

Shaw asked Otto to repeat the story for a second time. The man's thick Spanish accent was normally not a problem, but at the moment, agitation and a bad connection made some of his words hard to make out.

"There is talk. A man I know, he comes to tell me he sees a truck in Pajarito early this morning, very early, before the sun rises. The truck parks away from the clinic in the bushes, you see, but two men, they go inside and come out a short time later."

"What men?"

Otto paused. "Perhaps soldiers."

Shaw's heart slammed into his ribs. "What soldiers?"

"This he does not know. It is dark and he does not wish to stay around."

"And why did he come and tell you?"

Otto sighed. "He is troubled by this. He is very fond of Señorita Truman who has saved his baby girl when she gets the parasite so he is concerned for her, yet he does not wish to go with this information to *la policia*."

No doubt. The indigenous people stayed away from anyone official, but Otto was different. He helped the locals when he could, and the locals repaid the kindness by turning a blind eye when Otto broke the odd law or two in order to push his business interests forward. Otto wasn't an honest man, but he held to his own code.

"You see my confusion," Otto continued. "We have a shooting

of the bus and then I am told there were men at the clinic. No police have returned to town yet."

Nor would they for many hours still.

Shaw regarded the clinic through his rearview mirror, quiet and serene in the watery moonlight.

"There's no sign of trouble here."

Otto laughed. "And when does trouble send out a signal ahead of time? Listen, though I am not wishing to entangle myself in trouble, even for a pretty señorita, I tell you this because . . ." He trailed off.

"Because she was my sister's friend," Shaw finished with a growl, picturing Otto's indifferent shrug. "Well, my sister's dead."

Another pause. "Perhaps not so dead in your heart."

Shaw ground his teeth as he felt the flood hit him again, fresh as the driving rain. "I don't owe this girl anything except blame for convincing Beth to come to this . . ." He stopped himself before he added something that would insult Otto's homeland.

"You would say 'godforsaken'?" He laughed softly. "I would not repeat that to your little missionary girl."

"She's not my missionary girl. I gave her a ride, that's all," he snapped.

"I am simply the man who gives you the information. What you do with it is your business, but perhaps it is best if you are bringing her to me, no? This way you are saving her life and getting her out of your hair at the same time. *Adios*."

The connection ended with a soft click.

Shaw stared again out the rearview mirror. Nina Truman could take care of herself. She was on God's side, after all.

His own mother had believed such a thing when she left them to go on her Christian crusade to that oh-so-needy Mexican border town. Where had her belief in God landed her? Parked in a hospital bed, with people to cleanse and clothe the shell of a body that no longer held a mind. Her belief had cost her her life and destroyed their family.

He pictured his father, sitting at his wife's bedside, helping with everything from brushing her teeth to changing her diaper. Where there should have been anger—even rage—toward God and his wife for crippling them all, Shaw's father expressed only sadness, and an odd sort of acceptance that Shaw could not endure.

Acceptance even when God took his daughter, too.

"They were doing what God called them to do," he'd said.

If that was God's call, Shaw had vowed, he had no intention of ever answering.

*Ever,* he thought bitterly, acid churning in his stomach. His father's attitude disgusted him.

Shaw drove the truck away from the clinic for the second time that night, the wheels crunching rocks underneath the tires. With one more quick glance back at the clinic—nothing out of the ordinary—he decided Nina was fine. Not his concern.

*Let go and let God.* The bitter memory of his mother's words brought the realization that the expression had been passed down to Beth.

*All right, God. She's all Yours.*

He made it half a mile before he stomped on the brakes so hard that Axel almost slid off the seat.

God didn't take care of His own. He let innocent and guilty die right alongside each other. There was no justice from Him.

Before he could think through his actions, Shaw yanked the truck around and barreled up the road until he found himself in front of the clinic again. He pulled the truck to the back, something whispering in his ear about the wisdom of anyone seeing his vehicle parked there at such a late hour.

He got out, resisting the urge to slam the door. The lights glowing softly inside indicated she was still awake. He heard no cries for help, saw no signs of disturbance. Otto's informant had made it up, told Otto a story to curry favor, a way to garner some palm-greasing dollars, no doubt.

Shaw stood, hands on hips, defying the rain that drummed on

his head. Axel sniffed around with no particular sense of urgency, his paws pressing into the damp ground.

"Stay out of the mud, dog. I don't want it all over my truck." He missed paved roads and long stretches of freeway where a man could drive without stopping unless he wanted to. Maybe it was time to go home in spite of the grief that lingered there in a hospital bed.

"This is insane. Come on . . ." He broke off as he spotted the gash in the ground. Two deep gouges left by the wheels of a heavy vehicle.

The doctor's ride out of the jungle?

Shaw noticed that the tracks didn't lead to the clinic at all, but rather away, out into the flat area fringed with bushes that partially covered a sturdy wooden shed roofed with corrugated tin. He walked slowly, avoiding the muddiest patches of ground, but dirtying his boots nonetheless.

The shed showed no sign of tampering. But then again . . . two rusted handles with no locks hardly constituted a tough barrier to what might be inside. He shone a flashlight at the mud to check for footprints. Nothing but puddles.

*Hang on.* He bent closer and saw the imprint of a boot heel at the edge of a small mirror of water.

With a growing sense of urgency, he grasped the handle on the shed.

Axel stood alert, curious, ears rigid and tail erect.

Standing to the side, Shaw braced to jerk the door ajar. Could be the soldiers hadn't all retreated into the jungle. There might be one who stayed behind. Waiting.

The dog picked up on Shaw's tension, his eyes fixed on the door.

Shaw gave him a signal to stay before the silent count to three. He yanked the door open, and Axel strained forward but stayed put. The inaction told Shaw that no men hid inside. Axel, command or no command, did not react calmly when he came upon men he hadn't met. Every male was a potential threat according to Axel.

Many a time, Shaw felt like he should explain to the dog that women posed as big a threat, if not bigger, but Axel remained unconvinced. Shaw gave him a hand signal, Axel's cue to bound forward, and they both entered the dank space. It smelled of mold. Something brushed his face and he batted at it. Just a web of some insect, but he couldn't seem to rid himself of the sensation. Dilapidated cardboard boxes jammed the place, and a broken pair of pruning shears and several rolls of plastic sheeting rounded out the mess.

One of the rolls got serious attention from Axel. He pressed his nose to the opaque bundle, snuffling and snorting as he inched his way along.

"Someone been in here recently?" Shaw wondered aloud.

He knelt next to the dog and found the edge of the plastic, secured with duct tape. Clean, he noticed. Freshly cut and applied. He used a fingernail to peel at an edge until the tape gave way.

"Okay," he said, taking hold of the edge. "Let's just take a look, shall we?"

Like the old trick where someone tugs off a tablecloth without upsetting the plates, Shaw stood and jerked at the plastic, sending the contents settling neatly to the floor.

* * *

Nina searched, tossing everything from the desk. No sign of her passport copies anywhere.

She tried to steady the hammering in her chest.

She knew that, once her father sent copies from the States, the embassy would reissue her a passport, but it didn't ease away her bigger concerns.

The cut phone line. The broken lock.

One of the lamps flickered out. She'd forgotten to refill the kerosene.

*Get out!* her mind screamed like an animal ensnared by a trap.

She grabbed her pack and ran to the door. Just as she reached out for the knob, a heavy hand pounded on the sturdy wood and she leapt back.

"Señorita Truman," a deep voice called. "*Es la policia. Abre le puerta.*"

The breath surged out of her. The police had returned. Finally. Her fingers grazed the dead bolt as someone grabbed her from behind and a calloused palm pressed over her mouth. Struggling did not loosen the grip of the strong man who held her fast. Panic sizzled through her body.

"Quiet," Shaw whispered in her ear. "They're not here to help you."

Nina fought to breathe, clutching at the fingers that pressed into her lips. He marched her backward a few paces and spoke again. "Tell them you're getting dressed. You'll open the door in a minute."

She spun around the moment he released her. His face was barely visible in the meager lamplight, but his eyes were two embers in the gloom. "What is going on?" she whispered.

"There's no time to explain. In a few minutes, they're going to get tired of waiting and break down your door. You have to get out."

"I have nothing to hide," she hissed.

His eyes narrowed. "Has someone been in here?"

She nodded, wondering how he knew. "My passport copy's been taken and the phone line's cut."

Another fist hammered on the door with a louder request for her to open the door. "*Abre le puerta, por favor.*"

"Tell them," Shaw snarled.

Nina looked from the door to the ferocious man staring at her. She had done nothing. There was no reason to lie to the police.

But the phone line . . .

The passport . . .

The deadly serious tone in Shaw's voice.

Run or die.

Another whack on the door.

"*Un momento, por favor,*" Nina called. "*Me estoy vistiendo.*"

She'd just done it. She'd lied to the police on the advice of the man who now grabbed her wrist and yanked her toward the back door.

"I've got to talk to them," she hissed.

"That's the last thing you need to do," he said, continuing to haul her swiftly over the tiled floor until they reached the heavy wooden door. He moved the curtain a fraction and peered out. "They haven't found my truck. Get in fast because once I start the engine they're going to be all over us. Ready to run?"

"Why? What is going on?" She tried pulling at his arm, but he shook her off. "I'm not going until you tell me what's happening."

His lips pulled into a scowl. "Fine. Stay here and explain it to those guys then." He eased open the door and ran out into the night.

She heard pounding on the front door. A small scraping noise sounded from the side of the structure; someone heading around toward the back? Her breath froze in her lungs.

She had only a moment to decide.

Shaw? . . . Or the police?

The rain pattered softly on the leaves outside. Inside, the glow of the kerosene lamps transformed the familiar interior into a strange place of odd shadows and flickering silhouettes. It was no longer a place of refuge, the spot of light in the jungle. Her heart beat louder and louder, along with the pounding on the door.

With a whispered prayer, she made her decision, and plunged into the night.

# CHAPTER 6

Shaw's heart hammered as he waited with Axel. Rain pelted down, and blood pounded in his veins as if he'd just run a marathon.

*Come on, Nina. Show some good sense.*

Good sense? Serving in the jungle, following her father in some fruitless endeavor in a country where some of the natives were just as likely to try *curanderos* before doctors? Where *campesinos* slaved for hours for a pittance, the poorest boys got a paltry schooling and girls none at all? Good sense would be to go where you could actually make a difference.

Rain fell harder, drumming with furious intensity on the windshield. Seconds passed into a full minute.

*She's not coming.*

With a bitter sigh, he reached for the gearshift.

A surge of relief went through him as Nina appeared, head ducked and running. When she touched the door handle, he shifted into neutral and allowed the truck to begin the glide down the short incline before she'd even managed to close the door behind her. He didn't hear any shouts, but he knew. They would figure it out, and they'd begin their pursuit in a matter of moments. When the truck reached the bottom of the slight incline and drifted to a stop, he had no choice. Shaw turned the key, jammed the truck into gear and drove as fast as he could toward the mucky path leading to the jungle.

She pushed the wet hair from her face. "Why are we running?"

He ignored her, focused on keeping the truck moving quickly, slowing only slightly for each slippery turn. "Do you see them?"

She reached over Axel and grabbed his upper arm. "What is going on?" she hissed. "Tell me right now."

He gave her a quick look, long enough to see the emotional storm building in her. There was no time for hysteria, and he didn't have the patience for it anyway. "Some guys posing as soldiers or police hid a stash in the shed."

"What kind of stash?"

Could she really be so naïve? "A kilo of cocaine."

He heard her gasp, followed by several seconds of utter silence. "Cocaine? Who would do that?"

He yanked the truck around a sharp turn. "I don't know the particulars, but the cops or soldiers or whoever they are were coming to arrest you. I'm thinking they got a tip about the drugs."

"How do you know that? Maybe they were coming to ask more questions about the crash."

"Yeah," he said. "I'm sure that's why they headed right for the shed before they knocked on your front door."

She went quiet.

He savaged her with the rest of the facts. "Wake up, Nina. You're a foreigner, a woman without a passport, who just happens to have a kilo of cocaine in your backyard."

"I can explain to them that it was planted there."

He shook his head. "If you'd like to try, I'll pull over. You are on a mission for God. Maybe that will convince them."

The look she gave him was so fearful that he felt a flicker of shame. "We've got to get away. I'll take you to my friend Otto. He has contacts and he'll get you out of this mess." He accelerated up a slope so bumpy it tossed Axel off the seat. "Do you have a cell phone on you?"

She shook her head. "Mine was lost in the bus crash."

"And my phone is almost out of charge. If I can lose them,

we can make it back to my trailer and I'll contact Otto from there. Unless they got a good look at my plates, we have a little time before they come looking for me."

She gaped. "How will you explain?"

"That I helped a missionary drug dealer escape from the authorities?"

She bit her lip and nodded.

"Good question." He couldn't even explain it to himself.

They rounded a corner and the truck lurched forward into a pit of mud. He gunned the engine and the wheels plunged forward just enough to pull them free of the muck. Shaw wiped the sweat from his forehead and opened the window.

He heard the vehicle following. Just one. They hadn't called for assistance. Not yet, anyway. The road they followed offered a marginal choice to avoid getting stuck in the mud or coming up on thickets of broad-leafed palm or banana trees that wouldn't allow passage. The better option provided the easiest avenue for capture.

Shaw's trailer sat parked in a little thicket well outside Pajarito, a quiet and relatively untraveled place where he had never entertained anyone.

Nina sat with her hands clutched together; praying perhaps.

Was she praying for God to deliver her from the soldiers? Or from him?

With gritted teeth, he turned off the headlights and guided the truck deeper into the foliage.

He handed her a flashlight. "Cup your hands around it so the light shines only out the front."

She shot him a questioning look but, to his relief, she remained silent and did as he'd asked.The flashlight provided just enough illumination for him to keep the truck from smashing into tree trunks that crowded them.

The rain had intensified, thundering down until Axel settled onto the floor at Nina's feet, ears down. Thick leaves slapped at the sides of the car, blackness seeming to swallow them up, along with the massive living jungle.

Farther in . . . two feet . . . three. A canopy of lacy branches enfolded them and the hum of crickets thrummed in the air.

"Turn off the light."

She did, and he killed the motor. The night closed around them in a moist fist.

"Will they follow?"

"I'm hoping the rain will wash any tracks away. They'll continue on the main road for a while before they figure out we took a detour. By then, we'll be at my trailer."

"Are you sure it will work?" she whispered.

*Sure?*

He'd just allied himself with a woman who'd led his sister to her death. A naïve, helpless woman who relied on the God who had destroyed both his mother and sister.

Was he sure? He'd never been less sure of anything in his life.

He let the downpour answer for him.

* * *

Nina shivered, in spite of the perpetually warm jungle temperatures. So many terrifying possibilities cascaded through her mind that she couldn't seem to pick out a thread of rational thought to follow. One recrimination rose to the top.

What had she done, running into the jungle with Shaw? *Pure insanity.*

Yet here she was, lost, like a small rodent pursued by the deadly puma.

She'd been wrong to run, to believe Shaw's outrageous conspiracy theories, the stuff of movies and thriller novels. She had always been an ordinary person who followed rules and obeyed laws. She'd come to the Petén firm in the knowledge that God meant her to minister to the people of Guatemala alongside her father.

But details knifed through her insides. The bus crash. The note. Her missing passport copy. Her father's strange behavior.

She tried to shut it all out and focus on the simple act of breathing. In and out, reminding herself that she was the same person and she was still alive.

For the moment.

The throb of the engine forced her eyes open. Shaw backed out onto the road, branches snapping against both sides of the truck, before he turned on the headlights and drove in the direction from which they had just come.

A half mile of silence followed until Shaw veered off into a slight parting of the trees, nothing resembling a road. She'd never have noticed it if she'd been on her own. Shaw followed it now, slowly, skirting sinkholes of mud as best he could. The vehicle jolted and bounced so badly she had to cling to the door handle to keep from being thrown into Shaw's lap. Shadows slithered by the windows, and once she thought she saw a boa constrictor roped around a sturdy branch causing her to gulp back air and swallow it hard. After who-knew-how-long of violent tossing, Nina couldn't help herself. "How much longer?"

He didn't look at her. "Forty minutes unless we blow a tire or get stuck in the mud. In that case we'll have to finish on foot."

She couldn't imagine hiking that road in the dark in the middle of a torrential storm. Especially with all the night creatures that roamed the darkness. Teeth clenched together to keep from biting her tongue, she held on, too harried to think or to do much of anything except send up fragmented, incoherent prayers.

*Please, Jesus. Help us, please.*

After an eternity, they reached a smoother path, still muddy but more level. He again switched off the headlights and slowed to a crawl as they came within sight of a metal-sided trailer. Axel leapt back onto the seat, staring out into the night.

She expected Shaw to park and head for the trailer, but he remained there, window rolled down in spite of the rain that dampened him. The smell of wet earth and the rich odor of rotting vegetation turned the inside of the truck quite pungent.

Nina burned with impatience to get to a phone to call the embassy or her father or both, and to straighten out the mess that had suddenly become her life. "What are we waiting for?"

Shaw looked not at her, but at Axel. "Roll down your window."

"Why?"

He didn't answer, but the grinding of his teeth and the ripple of his clenched jaw told her he didn't appreciate being questioned, so she rolled down the glass. The dog shoved his muzzle out and sniffed. After a moment he turned to Shaw, tail wagging.

Shaw's shoulders relaxed. "I thought maybe your friends with the cocaine might have figured out my involvement and sent a team to cut us off."

"They aren't my friends," she said irritably.

He ignored the remark. "Axel would let me know if anyone had been here."

"Is he some kind of telepathic dog?"

Shaw gave her a look. "He can detect a land mine buried one meter deep. I'd trust his nose over yours or anybody else's." With that, he got out of the truck and headed for the trailer, leaving Nina to let Axel out and follow along after him.

The area in front of the trailer was covered by a scalp of grass, soft and feathery under her feet. She stopped on the warped wood of the doorstep, as the rain pattered down around her.

She didn't know Shaw. Didn't want to know him. He was Beth's brother, yet he shared none of her precious qualities: grace, compassion, the ability to make anyone feel like an old friend from the first moment of conversation, a zeal for life and love. Nina had met Shaw once, years before, at a family picnic. He'd been quiet, constantly in motion, buzzing from the barbecue to putting up the volleyball net to adding ice and more ice to the coolers. She recalled how he'd enveloped his mother in a hug that swallowed up her tiny frame. Quiet, but there had not been the angry edge of hate in his eyes back then.

The leaves rustled nearby and her stomach tightened. Nowhere to go now, disoriented as she was by the night. A branch cracked off to her right in the dark velvet of the jungle. She jerked toward the noise but saw nothing. At that moment, she would have found the red gleam of animal eyes comforting, less terrifying than the eyes of the soldiers likely combing the area for her.

The whole situation smacked of insanity, like some of the bad movies she'd seen on the grainy television when they'd briefly lived in Mexico. Maybe she would wake up and realize it had all been a nightmare, except that her body was bruised and sore. And even in her wildest dreams, she never would have dreamed up someone as prickly as Shaw Wilder.

She looked back again into the shifting shadows of the jungle before glaring at the open doorway into Shaw's trailer. It was temporary, until she could contact the embassy in the morning and bring the whole nutty episode to a logical conclusion.

With gritted teeth, she stepped inside.

It was sparse and surprisingly clean, the worn linoleum tiles swept, the bunk neatly made. A faint scent of apples lingered in the air, spiced with cinnamon and sugar. Her mouth watered. "Mmmm."

He raised an eyebrow. "What?"

"I thought I smelled applesauce. The homemade kind."

"You do. I make up a pot whenever I can collect enough apples. The ones here aren't as sweet so I have to add more sugar."

She hid her surprise at his culinary expertise as he grabbed a bowl from the cupboard and ladled up a glistening mound from the Crock-Pot and handed it to her with a spoon.

"You're a chef," she remarked, and he snickered slightly at her astonished expression.

He shrugged. "My mother taught me a few things."

Then he gave her his back. Conversation over.

Well it was something, anyway. The subject of his mother was painful, she knew. Gratefully, she ate a mouthful of the sweet apples. Warm and absolutely heavenly. Shaw would be disgusted to know he'd blessed her at that moment, but she'd keep that to herself, she thought, hiding a smile. She began to gobble it up, throwing delicacy to the wind.

Axel lumbered toward a cushion with an indentation in the middle that sat tucked into the corner of the floor. The dog sat on it, staring pointedly at a set of aluminum bowls, obviously waiting for Shaw to fill them.

He did, emptying a cupful of kibble into one of the bowls and water from a bottle into the other. The dog set upon the meal with gusto, the crunch of his working jaws loud in the small space. Shaw grabbed his laptop and pushed a button to bring it to life before plugging in his phone to recharge.

She swallowed the last of the applesauce. Once she'd checked to be sure he wasn't looking, she swiped her finger around the bowl to get every remaining drop. She rinsed the bowl in the sink, wishing she could ask for another. Shaw didn't seem to notice. Nina thought he might ignore her completely until he grabbed a long-sleeved denim shirt from a miniscule cupboard.

"Here. It's not your size but it's dry." He eyed her waist, bringing a blush to her cheeks. "All of my pants will be far too big. There's a bathroom over there."

She escaped into the bathroom and closed the door. For a moment, she leaned against the wall and closed her eyes. She had to be imagining it all, this nightmare from which she'd awaken safe and sound in the clinic, listening to the sound of her father's snoring and the scuttle of cockroaches crossing the floor. There would be a little pile of gifts left on the kitchen table, a few eggs, a pineapple; some freshly made tortillas, still warm and tender, brought by the villagers who sometimes arrived before sunup and never came empty-handed.

She opened her eyes, confronted by her own ghastly reflection in the warped mirror. Several scratches adorned one cheek, and her whole face looked bruised as a punching bag. The section of hair that Shaw had hacked away to free her on the bus hung oddly over her right shoulder. She looked tired, filthy, like some of the little ones they'd treated at the clinic suffering from malnutrition or parasites. Her dark eyes were Guatemalan, not Mexican as she'd been told by her parents since she was old enough to remember.

Exactly when had her father learned the truth? And why had he kept it from her?

Blinking tears away, she splashed tepid tap water onto her face and cleaned the muck as best she could before she slipped off her wet shirt and put on Shaw's dry one. It was coarse and slightly stiff from drying on the line during sunnier days. She rolled up the sleeves and buttoned it all the way to the top. Her pants had dried somewhat from the car trip, though they still clung to her legs. Rolling the wet shirt into a ball, she took a deep breath and opened the door.

Shaw frowned at his laptop, his phone pressed to his ear, charger still attached.

He pointed to a cup on the table which emitted the comforting aroma of tea. She held it gratefully between her palms and went to sit in the only other chair propped against the window. A crate served as a sort of end table, holding a battery-powered lamp. She sipped tea and looked at a black-and-white photo that lay there, a slightly fuzzy copy showing a young man dressed in dark colors with a mane of long hair. She picked it up and held it close. The man was walking, caught mid-stride, slightly ahead of two others.

She gasped when Shaw snatched the photo from her fingers.

"That's private," he growled, returning to the table and again picking up the phone. "Otto isn't answering. He's probably gone to his plantation, so I'm trying him there."

"We should call the embassy right away," Nina said.

"That's the next call."

"It should be the first one," she insisted.

He let out a breath and scrubbed a hand over his face. "My primary concern is how to survive the next few hours. I doubt the embassy is going to be able to help us with that since they're all the way in Guat City."

Closing her mouth abruptly, she hopped up and paced the floor, feet squishing slightly in her wet shoes. A taller set of crates served as a bookshelf, housing a neat row of books. One about fly fishing, two technical manuals relating to the history of land mines, several Zane Grey novels and, much to her surprise, a King James Bible. She traced a finger along the spine.

"Beth's," he said.

Her name came out of his lips softly, more like a sigh than speech. Nina's heart squeezed as she looked at the worn cover with faded gilt lettering. Shaw was an angry man, bitter and hard, but on this subject they could agree: Beth had blessed them both. And she didn't deserve to have her life snuffed out. Not in the horrible, violent way that Nina tried hard not to think about.

On top of the rough crate, lay a precisely arranged set of gears and dials, the innards of a small clock, the shell of which sat empty nearby. She would not have pegged those rough and calloused hands as those that tinkered with clocks.

Shaw moved around the kitchen, staying close enough to keep the phone charger plugged in as he packed things into a knapsack. A packet of nuts, flashlight. Then he moved to the same cupboard where he'd gotten her dry shirt and began to pile in another shirt and something wrapped in plastic, a bowl and water bottles. He kept the phone pressed to his ear.

Did he imagine they could outrun the soldiers? Make a dash for the embassy or Otto's plantation? Folly! They should call the authorities and wait it out. She was about to share her thoughts when Shaw stiffened.

"Otto." The relief in his tone was palpable. "I've got trouble," he said, giving her an unmistakable look. Guilt trickled through her in icy rivulets. He had trouble all right. All because of her.

# CHAPTER 7

Shaw turned away from Nina. He wasn't used to having someone in the cramped space with him. There had been nobody except Otto and the silent Guatemalan mechanic who helped level the trailer and hook up the generator. Something about the way her eyes roved the photo, the clock project he worked on, his collection of books . . . She disturbed him.

About the only thing she'd done so far that he could even understand was licking her fingers when she'd thought he wasn't looking. He snickered at the memory as Otto's rumbling voice brought him back to the matter at hand.

"What is the problem?" Otto said, calm as ever.

He relayed the details about their flight into the jungle, and a long silence followed, drawing Shaw's stomach into a tight knot. "Otto? Are you there?"

"Yes, I am here. I am wondering why someone has taken the time to set this trap for Señorita Truman. It seems strange, after this accident earlier on the bus."

Shaw edged farther away from Nina. "What are you thinking?" He could hear the sound of Otto's breathing, the faint scuff of his shoes as he paced.

"This woman, she is nearly killed by a gunman. She is wanted dead by someone, this is clear."

"Unless she wasn't the target on that bus."

"Perhaps this is so, she was merely an innocent. Yet this innocent does attract trouble, are you not in agreement?"

Oh, he agreed all right. Nina appeared to be a magnet for trouble ever since he'd pulled her from that wreck. But what was the connection? Why take the trouble to hide drugs in the shed? Did the shooter need to label her as a smuggler? Or . . .

Shaw sighed. "It might be someone else, not connected to the shooter."

Otto paused. "This occurs to me, too. So we have two parties, no? One wants her dead. The other wants her in prison. And the reason for both is . . . unclear at this time."

One thing was abundantly clear. Nina Truman would be lucky to get out of Guatemala alive. And now—thanks to his unexplainable heroics—so would he.

Axel finished his kibble and trotted to the bench seat under the window. Shaw watched closely, but the dog showed no sign of tension.

"I am fearing for the time being, the trick is how to keep you both alive. Where are you now?"

"My trailer. We're okay so far, but it's a matter of time before they figure out I doubled back."

"Ah, yes. Even the soldier is capable of some small measure of reason." Otto whistled, a mournful song that Shaw knew indicated he had departed into thought.

Shaw cast a look at Nina, and she watched him intently. He tried to offer a reassuring smile that felt unnatural plastered on his face. It felt like a child's Halloween mask.

"Can you still get here, to my plantation?"

Shaw considered. Otto's new venture was reachable only by road that could be best described as treacherous, even in the dry season. He listened a moment to the rain pounding on the roof. Mud would make it all but impassable. On the other hand, what choice did they have? He didn't trust the police, and the only worse alternative he could muster seemed to be Colonel Fuentes, the self-appointed local, the only other person of power and means in this jungle nowhere. Fuentes, a man in his early fifties, had no business marrying his sister, and Shaw would rather crawl through shards of glass than ask him for a single *centavo*.

He glanced again at Nina. She would no doubt advise staying put until he got through to the embassy. Rain thundered hard against the metal roof. Axel shook his head and pressed his nose to the window glass.

"We need to call the embassy," Shaw repeated.

"You have not done so yet?" Otto asked.

"No. My first call was to you."

He laughed. "I am flattered by your faith in me."

"You can get things done here," Shaw returned, forcing a confidence that he didn't quite feel.

His mother danced across his thoughts just then, tickling him with the prickly memory of her raspy singing voice. She always saw the truth inside him, no matter how hard he tried to conceal his vulnerabilities. But his mother was unreachable in her current state. She'd left him and Beth and their father, turned her back on them to follow God. And look where it got her.

Her God told mothers to abandon their children.

Her God told wives to leave their husbands.

Her God would never be his.

Shaw blinked back to the conversation. "We'll go to the plantation as soon as I get a call in to the embassy."

"This, I am feeling, is not wise, my friend. You are being hunted. In the jungle, only the fastest or the most ferocious survive."

He looked again at Nina, small and schoolgirlish in his shirt which dwarfed her, her black hair curling slightly as it dried. She was not fast, nor ferocious, but this was her future at stake, as much as his. If she wanted to call the embassy, that's what they would do.

"We'll come when we can," Shaw said.

He listened to Otto's disapproving cluck. "And you are trusting in the government to help you? That is one thing the peasants here will tell you is a mistake, Shaw. And they have learned that lesson well."

A bloody war had put the indigenous people smack in the middle of a conflict they could not escape, with the government on one side and the guerillas on the other.

Yes, they had learned that lesson well.

"I—" he was about to reply when Axel stiffened, ears swiveling.

The decision came in an instant. He flicked off the phone and pocketed it.

"Grab your bag," he snarled to Nina as Axel pushed upward, legs stiff, hair on his scruff standing on end. Shaw risked a look out the window. The headlights of a vehicle were visible as it made its way down through the trees toward the clearing. They had only minutes before they were discovered.

Shaw snatched the laptop off the counter and kicked open the back door. He tossed a jacket at Nina, grabbed her arm and tried to push her out toward the truck, calling the dog to follow.

Something—just what, he didn't know—made him duck back in and take the photo and Beth's Bible, shoving it in the inside pocket of his jacket. He sprinted out into the rain toward the truck. Nina opened the door for Axel and closed it behind him without getting in.

"I'm not going," she said.

He blinked. "You're crazy."

She sighed. "You're not the first person to tell me that. I know this is just a misunderstanding, and I will straighten it out. Thank you for your help."

His jaw dropped. Could she really be so stupendously naïve? "They're not here to help you. Someone tried to kill you on the bus and those guys may or may not be a part of it. Best case is you wind up in prison, awaiting trial for drug smuggling."

"Then I'll have access to a lawyer and hopefully a phone. I'm innocent."

"It doesn't matter," he snapped. "Innocent people die."

"I know that," she said quietly. "Go, Shaw. Thank you for what you've done. I'll tell them you were trying to help me."

He watched in astonishment as the woman who was either spectacularly brave or completely insane, walked through the storm, around the trailer to meet the men coming to arrest her.

* * *

Nina felt somewhat surprised that she wasn't scared as she squished over the wet grass. She had even been calm enough to put on the jacket Shaw thrust at her before she headed for the clearing. She took up a spot away from the trees, hands half raised to show that she didn't intend them any harm. Silently, she whispered a prayer.

*I know You sent me to Guatemala for a reason, Lord. I know You won't let me die until I do what You meant me to. Give me the words to straighten it all out.*

A truck jounced into the clearing, black, double cab, with big yellow lettering on the side and a light bar on top. She relaxed a fraction. These really were the police. Shaw's theories that there were multiple groups out to get her were wrong.

She tried to smile as the headlights blinded her, forcing her to shield her eyes from the glare.

Car doors flew open and two men leapt from the car, guns pointed at her.

"Hands up," they shouted in Spanish.

She complied. "There has been a mistake," she said, also in Spanish. "I'm a missionary nurse."

They moved closer, guns still drawn until she could see their faces, serious under the soft berets they wore. Roque and Josef. They lowered their weapons and regarded her with a somewhat bemused expression.

"Señorita Truman," Josef said, shaking his head. "We have come to arrest you for the possession of cocaine."

Roque wiped water from his brow. "We would not have

thought this. Your father, he has been a good man to the people here."

"He is a good man. He has nothing to do with cocaine, and neither do I. That was planted in our shed."

"Who would do such a thing, and for what purpose?" Josef asked.

"I don't know," Nina said. "I don't understand anything that's going on, but I didn't know about those drugs."

Roque considered her words, his eyes wandering over the tree line. "People will wonder why did you run? Why did you go with this American into the jungle if you are innocent?"

Nina sought for the right words. "I was scared, after the bus accident. I thought you meant to harm me. Mr. Wilder offered to take me somewhere so I could call the embassy."

Roque became more animated. "The embassy. Yes, that is the proper thing. They will advise."

"So you believe me that I had nothing to do with those drugs?"

Josef shifted, hooking his free hand into the belt of his pants. "This is not for us to say. We must do our job and arrest you, but things will be put right in time."

He was right. They had no choice other than to do their job, but it was important to her that he knew she told the truth. "I didn't do it. You must believe I didn't do it. We've lived and worked right alongside you for four years. We are here for God, you know that."

He looked at her, rainwater running off his beret. He didn't speak, but she could tell in the lines around his eyes and the tension in his shoulders that he knew something more. "We must follow our orders. That is all."

Roque slung his weapon over his shoulder. Josef kept his ready, pointed alternately at Nina and the trailer.

She tried to keep her tone level. "Who told you there were drugs in the clinic shed?"

They were silent for a moment until Roque gestured irritably. "We do not need to disclose this to you."

"They didn't identify themselves?"

"I will not say," Roque said, a hint of petulance in his voice.

"But it's suspicious, isn't it?" she pressed. "This person, whoever it was who called you, happens to know what's in our shed?"

A quick glance passed between the two men. "The facts are these," Roque said. "We came to discuss the matter of this phone call, and when we look in the shed we discover a kilo of cocaine. What are we to think?"

"We should not stand here. We must arrest you and Señor Wilder," Josef said.

Nina started. "He isn't guilty of anything." She hoped Shaw had already disappeared into the jungle so he wouldn't have anything more to blame on her. It would be her gift to Beth to keep Shaw out of her troubles, if she could. "I asked for a ride. That's all he did, nothing more."

"It was evading the police," Josef interrupted. His eyes narrowed. "What was he doing at the clinic at such a late hour?"

She flushed. "Taking me home after the bus accident."

"Yet it is hours later when we arrived, so why was Señor Wilder still there?"

Nina felt a stirring of renewed fear. "He left and came back."

"Perhaps," Josef said, "he left and visited your shed? Perhaps he left a package there that he did not wish to be discovered?"

Roque nodded with enthusiasm. "Yes, perhaps this is what happened."

Nina didn't credit the story. Shaw despised her, but using drugs to discredit the clinic and her family? No.

Rain poured off her jacket, dripping onto Shaw's long shirt that hung down almost to her knees.

"If you'll just allow me to call the embassy in the morning, I'm sure they can help us straighten this out."

"You will come with us now," Josef said.

She was not going to talk them out of jailing her. At the very least, she'd be dry and fed and in close proximity to a working phone. And Shaw would have the chance to get away.

"All right."

Josef sagged in relief, clasped his hand around her upper arm and escorted her to the truck. He opened the back door and she scooted in. There was a pop, as if someone had pulled a stopper from a bottle. Suddenly, Josef jerked and she thought he might have stepped in a hole.

He slumped down over her lap, a bullet hole in his temple. She couldn't even scream as the shock overwhelmed her. She watched through the water-blurred window as Roque scuttled to the front of the truck for protection. A covered Jeep emerged in the clearing. Roque didn't wait, but began to fire his automatic weapon wildly at the Jeep. Nina hauled Josef's body into the car and pulled the door closed.

She dropped to the floor, hands covering her head. Oddly, she wasn't able to discern any return fire from the Jeep. Perhaps her own thundering pulse drowned it out. When she risked a look, she caught a glimpse of Roque's face in the windshield as he poked his head up. His eyes were wide with fear. Slowly, he began to inch to the driver's side and she realized he intended to get into the car and drive them out of the line of fire.

Her body went rigid with fright as she crouched on the passenger side, away from Josef.

Who? Why?

She had no time to think as Roque yanked open the door and slithered to the driver seat, barking at her to hold on as the vehicle surged forward into the night. Her stomach knotted and she looked behind at the Jeep. It didn't move, no doubt because Roque's shots had flattened two of the tires.

The sight calmed her enough that she was able to force out a question. "Who are those men?"

She didn't catch his hoarse reply except for one word. "Escorpion."

The word ignited horror deep down in her core. Escorpion was a drug runner, a man so powerful that people whispered his name. Some spoke of him with reverence, those to whom he had been beneficent. Those who had felt his sting, however, did not live to speak at all.

"What does he want?" she cried.

He didn't have to answer. For some reason which she could not comprehend, Escorpion wanted her.

She held in a scream of panic as their truck lurched around the back of Shaw's trailer. Shaw's pickup was gone. She ignored the strange flood of disappointment. Of course he'd gone. She'd told him to. With the storm thundering around them, he had probably not even heard the gunfire.

Their vehicle skidded on the wet ground, the back end swinging perilously close to the sturdy trunk of a palm.

"Slow down," she yelled.

If they wrecked the car, they would be easy prey. Besides, Roque had disabled their Jeep and she saw no signs of pursuit. She wanted to put a hand on his shoulder to reassure him, but his body was so rigid, his profile so electric with terror, that she thought he might shoot her out of instinct.

Forced to slow as the foliage closed in around them, she saw that the headlights illuminated only a few yards at a time. Roque's breathing began to slow as his dark eyes found no signs of pursuit in the rearview mirror.

Soft streams of words poured from his lips in Spanish, so quickly she could not decipher them. "I will call," he said, trembling hands reaching for the radio. He launched into a loud and animated explanation as he continued to guide the vehicle slowly along with one hand.

Nina tried to force her lungs to work in some semblance of a balanced rhythm. As she pushed the air in and out, she reached one hand over to check for a pulse on Josef's neck. There was none, as she'd known all along.

Eyes closed, she said a prayer for Josef and the family she

knew he had back in the town. Two boys who would not have a father, a wife left to struggle on alone. The senselessness of it sizzled through her. A small piece of flying metal, cold and inanimate, could snuff out the spark of life so easily. And why? For what purpose did Josef need to die?

Escorpion had his reasons, she thought grimly. He was an untouchable power who could operate by his own rules, unanswerable to anyone.

*But not to God.*

Her teeth ground together as she found a blanket on the floor of the truck and draped it over Josef's still form.

"And I'll tell him so, if ever I get the chance," she murmured to Josef's poor ruined body.

Roque risked a glance over his shoulder and grief flashed over his face. "*Dios este contigo,*" he whispered, turning his attention again to the road. He reached in his pocket and handed her something.

She stared at the hard metal of the clasp knife. "I thought I was your prisoner."

"*Si,*" he said, sweat beading on his forehead. "But if we are captured and killed, you should make them pay dearly for your life."

Make them pay. Defend herself by stabbing the people who meant to kill her.

Her body grew cold as she pocketed the knife. Could she use it if it meant a chance to save her own life?

A second Jeep surged out from the wet screen of leaves, so suddenly that Roque could not stop in time. Instinctively, her fingers curled around the door handle. *Get out, get out,* her mind screamed.

The truck collided with the Jeep, the sickening crunch swallowed up by the jungle.

# CHAPTER 8

Shaw fumed, his tension mounting as he approached the top of the slope, the incessant pounding of the rain on the truck roof keeping time with his pulse. Nina had thanked him for his service, as if he'd given her a lift to the market, as if he was some sort of hired hand. She hadn't displayed a moment of concern for the fact that his act of idiotic kindness had propelled him into the line of fire, too. The cops were coming after him next, he had no doubt about it.

So off she marched to deliver herself to the police. The sheer audacity of it . . . or was it naiveté? . . . floored him. It brought back a flash of memory. His mother, before her missionary zeal had taken her body and mind away in one horrifying flash, often greeted the world with that kind of cheerfulness, from the newspaper boy to the raving panhandler near the old grocery. He'd admired that incomprehensible ability in her to see the best in people, no matter how unpresentable their exteriors. She'd greeted every person she met with that smile, the same one that graced his sister's face.

But Beth was dead, and that smile on his mother's face was now a hollow grimace from lips that leaked drool and mumbled words he would never understand. He resisted a shudder. The truck crested the top and he kept as much as he could to the shrub-lined periphery of the makeshift road. The only reason the wheels weren't mired into the goo was that he'd painstakingly laid a layer of gravel during the dry season. Fast in, fast out for a quick departure.

It would have to be a fast exit, as soon as he finished what he needed to do. He felt the reassuring presence of the worn photo in his pocket. This little misadventure with Nina wasn't going to rework his plans. Axel sat up straight on the seat next to him, fur silvered in the moonlight that appeared and then disappeared behind trailing wisps of gauzy clouds. This time Shaw saw it too; a Jeep tucked at the edge of the clearing below, fifteen yards from his trailer. He took a pair of binoculars from his glove box. The vehicle wasn't police or army. He thought the tires were flattened on one side. No movement around the Jeep or his trailer, and the police truck had gone.

Could it be his gut had been right? It was more than just the police looking to get their hands on Nina Truman for some unfathomable reason? He kept the binoculars trained on the clearing without detecting any movement. He longed for the pair of night vision goggles that he'd ordered, but not yet received.

"I don't know what she's gotten into," Shaw said, "but she's in pretty deep." Maybe the naiveté was just an act. Maybe she really had willingly involved herself with the wrong people. She was convincing. And he was a fool. Plenty of women would stand in line to testify to that.

Axel flicked him a look.

"Nothing we can do now," he added. "We'll get to Otto and hole up until everything calms down. Then we do our thing and go home."

Axel stood now, attention riveted once more out the window.

Shaw raised the binoculars, nearly dropping them in surprise as he caught the slow movement below. A slight figure with long dark hair crept along the edge of the clearing, head low and shoulders hunched.

Moving toward Shaw's trailer.

His mouth fell open. Nina wasn't done messing with his life?

She'd somehow escaped both police and whoever drove the Jeep, and now she would return once again to his trailer to f urther drag him in? He flung open the door, shutting an irate Axel inside and charged down the slope.

This time he would make it clear.

Crystal.

*You've made your decision, now live with it. You're on your own.*

She didn't hear him make his ungainly way through the bushes, careening down the hill to bisect her path. He lost sight of her repeatedly, her small frame disappearing behind the dense leaves of the bushy hibiscus, straining to hear over the rainfall and the call of the crickets. There, down five yards and to his right, the slight swoosh of parting foliage. He moved faster.

She kept to the shrubbery, showing more good sense than he'd imagined her to have. He closed the gap by another three feet.

She must have sensed a presence because she ducked suddenly behind a plumeria and grew still. He took the opportunity to put an end to the ridiculous chase and make his point. "Nina," he hissed, voice low. "Stop running."

True to form, she took off, sprinting fast now, slapping away the leaves that blocked her, feet sliding on patches of wet ground.

*Crazy woman.*

He took off after her, skidding on a patch of decaying leaves that sent him down hard on one knee. With a grunt of pain, he clambered back up and resumed the pursuit. She was agile and more nimble than he, ducking away when he thought he'd just about caught her arm.

They'd reached the edge of the clearing. Another yard and she'd have a direct path to the trailer. And then what? Would she beat him there and lock herself inside? Waiting for the help which was about as likely to come as snow to the Petén?

The thought of her, ensconced in his trailer, surrounded by his things and the precious few belongings he possessed from Beth, poured fire in his belly. He surged forward and grabbed her arm.

The action made her lose her footing and she tumbled headlong into a muddy depression. Sucking in air and nursing his sore knee, he stood at the patch of muck, hands on hips, searching for a tone that was appropriate to use on a woman, even a selfish, religious nut like this one.

"Nina," he panted. "Whatever you think you're doing, I'm not a part of it." Lungs still working overtime, he pulled in another gulp of air to finish.

When she sat up, his breath came out in a gasp.

The woman, with long dark hair and eyes that seemed to glow, was most definitely *not Nina Truman.*

* * *

Nina felt the impact of the Jeep crashing into the police truck. A crunch of metal vibrated through the frame, and the front windshield cracked from top to bottom, spidering through the glass. Then the world kaleidoscoped again into some surreal sequence of bizarre events, like an old film, played backward in fast motion.

Roque reached for the weapon on the seat next to him, but his fingers didn't make contact before the door opened and he was wrenched from the car. There was shouting, grunting, the sickening sound of fists on flesh. She crawled to the passenger side, ripped open her own door and hurtled out, falling on hands and knees. Feet rasped quickly across the ground after her. She did not stop to look, surging, crawling, smashing her way into the shrubbery. Terror rippled through her in icy waves. Each brush of a twig or slap of a broad leaf on her face made her cringe, waiting for those cruel hands to catch her, to kill her.

If she could only disappear, wrap herself in that verdant cloak and hide. Her mouth was dry, teeth clamped together to still the chattering. The animal instinct deep inside gave her speed and agility which she'd never imagined of herself, but the sound of booted feet continued. One man? Two? She bolted toward the thickest pocket of green she could find and then sprinted in a direction perpendicular to her hiding spot. Her ruse worked. The sound of her pursuers changed as they began to paw through the branches to find her.

Body shivering, hands shaking, she pressed on as quietly as she could. Her father had escaped guerilla soldiers decades before, during his earlier mission trip to Guatemala. God had shown him a way, he steadfastly maintained. When the men left him unattended, he'd simply melted away into a nearby village, hiding in a patch of corn until he could walk back to the clinic.

Her father had always been steadfast in his faith; unshakable, unmovable. Perfect.

Liar.

*Stop it, Nina*.

She bit her lip so hard that she tasted blood. She heard a man shouting something in rapid Spanish, maybe six yards away. Through a screen of branches, she saw him only as a shadow, attaching and detaching itself from the larger darkness that surrounded her.

The buzz of a mosquito startled her as it whizzed by her ear. She jerked involuntarily, praying that her movement would not give away her hiding spot. She thanked God that it wasn't the height of the Guatemalan summer when the insects were so thick she could not escape them for any amount of spray, netting, or swatting. She didn't feel lucky just then as she ignored the prickle and hum of the bug life swarming around her.

Or was it slithering she heard now over the roar of her own pulse?

*Barba amarilla*. The name of the deadly snake coiled through her mind. She sat in a clump of shrubbery, the perfect shelter for a nocturnal hunter, the snake with the deadly venom. She'd seen it, victims who had made the arduous trip to the clinic from their remote villages, bleeding from the eyes, limbs swollen three times their natural size as the venom seeped through their veins and stopped their blood from clotting.

She tried to still the shivers which rolled through her body.

Snakes. She'd always loathed them, feared them to the point where she could do nothing but flee if she thought there was a snake in the proximity. Her muscles tightened, as she felt the panic begin to take over.

*There are no snakes here*, she told herself, but her body began to shudder.

Every rustle, every flicker of shadow was a snake, a horrible *barba*. A wet branch brushed her head and she clapped a hand over her mouth to hold in the scream. Her eyes scanned the overhanging branches for the glossy *bejuquillo*, the whip-thin green snake that coiled in the trees, dropping down with its enormous mouth gaping open. *Stay quiet or die, Nina.*

*Please, Father, help me*.

An image of her own strong, straight-backed father, *El Monte*, swam in front of her face. He would not be swayed. He would not be controlled by fear.

She forced a breath in and let it out slowly, still behind the cover of her palm in case a scream came with it. Forcing the oxygen in and out of her lungs became her only task. Seconds passed which blurred into minutes. Ten breaths, twenty. The man stopped thrashing through the bushes and fisted a hand on his hips. Then he turned and set out for the Jeep.

Her elation took the edge off her fear as she continued to breathe. In and out, as silent as she could manage.

Part of her brain noticed that the rain had slowed, and the man who now passed by her hiding place took off his hat and shook the beaded water from the brim. She could not see his face, but she heard his muttered Spanish. He was disgusted, that much was clear, and not at all pleased about having to return without the "crazy woman." He was dressed in fatigues, but he did not look like the government soldiers. His hat had a small, flat brim, not like the berets the army wore. Mexican? Guatemalan? She wasn't sure.

Shaw would probably know, she thought, but he was no help

to her now. Slowly, she lowered her hand as the man moved away, sloshing across the wet ground in the direction of the crash.

Forcing her mind to track the sound of the stranger, she listened as an engine coughed to life. Another creak of metal, probably from the Jeep disentangling itself from their police car. Wheels spun and the engine gunned again. A flicker of lights shone for a moment and then disappeared. Whoever they were, these killers did not want to attract any more attention than they already had by wrecking a police vehicle, killing Josef . . . and Roque, too? Her breath caught. Perhaps he was left unconscious. The thought cheered her. She would sneak back as soon as it was safe and help him.

Leaves parted near her right foot. Her scream split the air and she bolted from her hiding spot, running blindly, frantically, fleeing across the muddy ground until she nearly ran into the banana palm. Arms clutched around the trunk for support, she sucked in a series of frantic breaths. Had they heard her shriek?

She listened. Nothing but the wind in the leaves, the faraway rant of a howler monkey. Her knees shook so badly she could not take a single step. Instead, she concentrated on getting her bearings. The ruined truck was just past the cluster of trees. To be safe, she waited what she estimated to be fifteen minutes before she started uncertainly in that direction, swatting at a cluster of doctor flies that flicked in her face.

Every step seemed to make a ridiculous amount of noise as she crept along, heart in her throat. What waited for her at the truck scared her as much as the dark. Not death so much; she'd seen plenty of death before. Rather, it was the helplessness she knew she would feel if Roque was mortally wounded, the inability to be the doctor, to be her father. That ache of discontent had arisen more and more frequently in the past few months.

Mud splashed against her legs, caking her jeans in an even thicker layer of muck. She could see the truck now, pushed crookedly across the path from the impact. Stopping again to listen, she strained to pick up any sounds of the Jeep returning, but she didn't detect any. Breaking into a jog, she ran to the open driver's door, pressing her back to the cold metal, eyes scanning the black jungle. One long moment later and she forced herself to look.

The truck was empty. Roque's gun was gone too, not that she would have so much as touched it anyway. She thought about climbing inside and trying to start up the vehicle, but she didn't have much confidence in her ability to navigate the mashed-up heap through this unfamiliar part of the jungle.

She searched the interior on the off chance of finding a phone, but there was none. The long coiled cord that snaked from the radio to the dashboard was severed, the glove box gaped open. Allowing herself one quick look, she saw Josef's body still crumpled in the back.

She turned away and crouched down, the metal side once again at her back. The night enveloped her, invaded her, the humid currents of jungle air pressing inside her with subtle scents of decay. The only place of refuge, the tiny clinic, seemed so far away, and she couldn't even be certain in which direction. Besides, her father wouldn't be standing there waiting for her, ready to clarify the next move. She thought there might have been a slight chance of making it back to Shaw's trailer, but he wouldn't be there either, nor would there be a phone for her to call for help. Somewhere, perhaps a few miles out at most, a village awaited where she would find friends who would shelter her, but she had not the foggiest notion how to reach it.

She squeezed her hands together and tried to pray.

*Father, Father . . .*

The incessant jungle noises pricked into her mind, leaving her unable to finish, and the only thing she knew with any certainty was that staying planted there was not an option. The strangers would come back, and there were snakes on the move hunting alongside them.

She stood so quickly, it dizzied her.

*Go find the road that Shaw had taken to the trailer.*

A road meant people, sooner or later; the friendly farmers and fishermen who eked out a living from the jungle would arrive. They would help her, if the strangers didn't find her first. On shaky legs, she set out, following the ruts left by the police truck. Exasperatingly, her stomach growled, clearly the only part of her body unencumbered by the peril of the situation. The grumbling reminded her that her small pack was still in the ruined truck so she turned around, circling to the passenger side that still gaped open from her frantic dash to safety. She reached into the interior, fighting an irrational fear that a snake had slithered into the dark maw and lay there, waiting to plunge fangs into her wrist as she grasped the pack.

A quick movement sounded from behind her, followed by a sudden rush of air.

Something did capture her. The blow pushed her to the seat, expelling the breath from her lungs.

# CHAPTER 9

The shock set Shaw back a step, and the woman used the moment to surge to her feet. The moonlight picked out slivers of gray threaded through her dark hair and he now discerned she was near fifty, long and lean, wearing a man's shirt and black trousers. Her eyes, the exact color of which he could not discern, were lighter than they should be.

Green?

The facts fell together. She was the woman from the bus who passed Nina the note. *Run or you die.* She was about to run right now, he could read it in the tensed lines of her posture. He held up his hands.

"I'm a friend of Nina Truman's." *Friend* was no doubt too strong a word, but he didn't think he could be counted on the enemy side, and there didn't seem to be much middle ground where Nina was concerned.

The woman shifted, still ready to flee, but she searched his face, still silent.

"Where is Nina?" he said. "*¿Donde está?*" he said, hoping his gringo Spanish would prove sufficient.

Her eyes flicked to the jungle and then back to his. "She was in the truck," she answered in accented English. "There was shooting."

He stiffened. "What happened?" When she didn't answer, he took a step forward. Wrong move. It scared her and she scooted back a pace. "I'm sorry. I'm not going to hurt you," he said, palms up. "I know you tried to warn Nina with your note, after the bus crash."

Her eyes widened.

"What's your name?"

She hesitated for a long moment before she answered. "Anna."

"Tell me what happened. Please, Anna."

She told him a cop had been shot before the truck took off into the jungle, followed by men on foot. He considered. The cop knew the jungle well enough. He should have been able to get her out ahead of two guys on foot. She'd land in jail, but at least she'd be alive. He didn't really understand why the thought eased his mind. "How did you get here?"

"They brought me in the other Jeep, to help find her," the woman whispered.

He thought he'd misheard. "What?"

"There was a second Jeep. They ordered me to stay in the one with the flattened tires and they went after her."

The blood thudded in his ears and he looked toward the jungle where he thought he'd heard a shot earlier. "Who are they?"

The woman looked away.

He edged up the volume a notch. "Who are they? The men who are after her. I need you to tell me who they are."

She shook her head, still not looking at him. "I am afraid. They will kill me."

"You can stay with me. I'll get you some help." Had he really just said that? It wasn't enough to be chasing after one wanted woman? Beth always said he was a knight in cowboy boots.

*Not me*, he thought grimly. *Not by a long shot.*

He would give all the info over to the embassy and let them sort it out. It would be a place to start, anyway.

She began to cry, tears running down the creases around her mouth. Crying women were an unpredictable breed. He shifted. "I need to know," he said, more softly this time. "Who are they?"

She whispered the name.

The dripping of the leaves and the soft shush of wind over the grass tricked his ears. "Say again?"

She stepped toward him and put a hand on his forearm, her fingers cold and trembling. Leaning up so she could put her lips to his ear, she murmured the name again, as if speaking it aloud might be lethal.

There was no mistake this time.

"Escorpion."

Shaw's muscles tensed and something started to burn deep inside his gut. Escorpion, the most powerful drug smuggler in the region, and the one man that Shaw needed to find, was after Nina. If God was paying any attention, which Shaw doubted, He could not have concocted a situation richer in irony than this.

He realized he'd gone quiet for too long. The woman stared at him.

"You know of him?"

Shaw forced his clenched fists to relax. "Oh, yeah. I know of him." He blinked himself back to the present. "Come with me."

"Where are you going?"

"To get Nina."

"But the police . . . Escorpion's men . . ." She gasped as he turned and hurried back up the slope.

"I'll drop you at the nearest village," he said.

"He will kill you or anyone else who gets in his way."

"He can try," Shaw said through gritted teeth, "but I don't die so easily."

She nearly ran trying to keep up with him, entreating, begging him all the way to the truck not to embark on such a foolhardy mission. He ignored her, reprimanding Axel when the dog offered an eager bark as he opened the passenger door for her. She hesitated only a moment before she got in.

As they rumbled back toward the trailer, he kept an eye on the churned-up dirt, hoping the tracks would not dissolve into mud holes. He opened the window and stuck his head out to check every few yards once they'd made it down the slope.

He risked a quick look at Anna and found her peering out into the night, hands clasped firmly in her lap. "Why did Escorpion's men take you along? What is your connection to Nina?"

Her mouth opened, and then closed. "She does not know me."

"I got that, but you know her. You knew she would be on that bus and you knew she would be here with me. How?"

Her breathing grew quick and labored. She pressed a hand to her mouth and shook her head.

"I won't tell anyone," Shaw said as he passed his trailer, continuing to follow the indentations left by the police truck. The Jeep must have approached through the jungle. Someone knew the territory, and knew it well.

Anna continued to mumble to herself, eliciting interest from Axel who poked her experimentally with his nose. She didn't flinch. Shaw wanted to stop the car and face Anna, to question her thoroughly until he figured out how the pieces fit together, but he didn't dare take the time. Besides, she was terrified, that much was clear. She had reason to be, having almost died in a bus shooting and been pressed into service for Escorpion, the man who left his enemies hanging from trees minus their hands, feet, and, tongues.

They both saw it at the same time, the ruined police truck, door open, gleaming in the headlights. Shaw leapt out. The search only took a minute. They'd clearly been ambushed, and Josef lay dead in the back. No sign of anyone else. Though he trained a flashlight over the wet ground, he found no indication about which way anyone had gotten on foot.

*If,* he thought grimly, *anyone had escaped at all.*

His stomach knotted as he found the marks of the Jeep tires on the ground, leading north. He was back in the car in a moment.

"They got her," he said grimly.

Anna shook her head. "They will take her to Escorpion." She looked almost relieved. "There is nothing more we can do."

"What does Escorpion want with Nina?"

She didn't answer, but as he headed the truck in the direction the Jeep had taken, Anna once again began to cry.

* * *

Nina's face pressed into the Jeep seat as she lay facedown. The man who smelled of garlic and sweat tied her hands with a rope that scratched her skin every time she moved. They had been driving for what seemed like hours, though it had probably only been half an hour. In the past, she'd felt fear, like the time some drunken soldiers had shot out the windows of the clinic, or the very recent bus crash. In those cases, the fear had come in roaring waves, receding as quickly as it had come on. This time, the terror hung on, running through all the nerves in her body, repeating and recycling itself like a song put on endless loop.

*You're not dead, Nina. Not even hurt.*

The logic did nothing to stem the fear. Where was she being taken? Several miles back, she'd given up on the why.

"Where are we going, please?" she asked, her voice partially muffled by the vinyl seats. Both men in the front seat continued their chattering without notice. On the upside, they had not hurt or threatened her to be quiet either.

"I want to know where you're taking me." She tried again in a stronger tone.

That silenced their chatter. Now they began to laugh. The Jeep hit a rut or hole, and the impact made her slide off the seat onto the muddy floor. This set her captors to laughing even more uproariously.

She jerked herself awkwardly on the seat and sat defiantly upright, ignoring the hammering of her heart. The action surprised the two who turned to look at her. Though it was dark, the moon had revealed itself, just enough that she could get a sense of them. One tall and thin in a baseball cap, the other short and even thinner. Both wore jeans, long-sleeved shirts. Guatemalans. She felt the tiniest bit better. At least she wasn't being kidnapped as some part of a plan by the Mexican Zetas whose ruthless tactics were only whispered about.

"Where are you taking me?" she asked again, fixing them both with what she hoped was a stern look.

*"No hables ingles,"* the one in the passenger seat said with a wolfish grin.

*"No hay problema,"* she snapped off. *"Tambien hablo español."*

The driver laughed and set the Jeep rattling over the uneven path, and both turned their backs on her. In a fit of outrage, she kicked the seat in front of her. No response. She began to kick it harder, and harder, the motion releasing some of the frantic energy that had been building up since she left the clinic. "Answer me, answer me, answer me," she shouted.

"Enough," hollered the man in the passenger seat. He turned and aimed the muzzle of a wicked-looking gun at her.

"You won't shoot me," Nina said, panting. "You didn't go to all this trouble to kill me."

He cocked his head and pushed his face over the top of the seat, leaving her to shrink back into the far corner. "There are other things we can do," he said softly.

The glitter in his eyes stopped her voice.

"Now you will be quiet," he said, turning around again and lighting two cigarettes, one of which he gave to the driver.

Her bravado melted away and she pressed her knees together to keep them from shaking. What had happened to the Guatemala she knew? In days gone by, each village, each town had a person in charge—the boss, so to speak—and as long as he cooperated with the local drug cartels, and the villagers minded their own business, generally people did not die. But things had changed in the Petén as Mexican cartels arrived to muscle their way into the local drug trade, and violent crime became more prevalent, even in the jungle. The boss, though controlled by the local cartel, had been a stabilizing influence. The bosses remained, but the stability did not.

She'd heard the rumblings in the village, helped try to save some of the victims. Some, like the innocent laborers working on a farm, were beyond saving when they landed squarely in the middle of a territorial dispute. So many murdered, and now it seemed she was next in line.

The Jeep continued its awkward journey and Nina considered her options. They were slim to none until she remembered something that both cheered and scared her.

The knife!

The small clasp knife was still tucked in the pocket of her jeans. If she could somehow loosen her bonds, she might get access to it.

And do what? She swallowed hard. That small knife would hardly be a match for the two men, even if she did know how to use it properly to defend herself. Still, it might give her a moment, provide a precious second of surprise so she could flee into the jungle. She set to work wiggling her wrists as much as she could without attracting attention. The ropes were strong and tied tightly, but she detected a slight loosening as she continued to work in spite of the rough fibers that abraded her skin.

The path on which they traveled had flattened somewhat. She still had no idea where they were, but the foliage had grown sparse, as if the land had been cleared by the destructive slash-and-burn farming. The driver leaned forward. Looking for a marker, perhaps?

She pulled and tugged at the ropes more forcefully.

After a quick exchange, the driver turned the wheel sharply, and their journey smoothed out. Her heart quickened. Paved road, narrow and rough in spots, but definitely paved. She strained to see out the window, fogged by the moisture from her own panted breaths.

The long, straight road cut through the grass almost like a . . .

Her stomach clenched.

Landing strip.

She thought she made out a shed in the distance, its brown siding and metal roof camouflaged underneath a fringe of trees and painted with blobs of color borrowed from the hues of the jungle canopy. They drew closer, Nina working at her bonds all the while. For reasons she couldn't fathom, the thought of boarding a plane and flying to some unknown location terrified her more than anything else she'd experienced thus far.

The moisture on her fingertips pricked Nina's curiosity for only a moment before realization tumbled over her.

*Blood.* It dripped down her wrists from the friction.

*Hurry, Nina.*

The driver headed for the shed and let the engine idle while the other man got out and slid open the heavy metal door that shrieked on rusted hinges. Nina nearly cried out in frustration. With her hands still bound and in that battered condition, bolting out the open car door would surely result in no more than a few moments of freedom before they captured her again.

The man returned, slammed the Jeep door and gestured for the driver to pull the vehicle into the shed.

*Please, please, please . . .*

No last-minute reprieve thundered from the heavens, and the ropes around her wrists held stubbornly in place. Thick darkness swallowed up the Jeep as the heavy doors crashed shut behind them.

# CHAPTER 10

Shaw resisted the urge to bang on the steering wheel. Dawn peeked around the horizon as the thick cloak of sky gave way to a softer shade of gloom. The storm had ebbed into a lackluster drizzle that combined with the spattered mud to muck up the windshield.

"I must have missed them," he grunted. "They turned somewhere."

Anna's lips remained tightly pressed, and she looked tired, face drawn.

He felt a stab of pity. "There's some food in my pack," he said. "And water."

"*Gracias,*" she said, but she made no move to take any of it.

They rumbled slowly along a semi-paved road. Paved roads meant traffic, and traffic offered up the very real possibility that the police might arrive to investigate the disappearance of their officers.

He took note of the truck gas gauge, hovering somewhere around a quarter of a tank. Axel turned around on the seat, restless from being in the car for so long. Ahead of them, a man appeared on the shoulder of the road and walked directly toward them, a stick over his shoulder with a few small trout hanging from it. He wore muddy jeans, high rubber boots, and a small brimmed hat. At first sight of Shaw's truck, he averted his eyes and moved surreptitiously as far to the other side of the road as possible.

Shaw rolled down the window and called the obligatory polite greeting. "Good morning, sir. You've made a good catch."

He nodded and continued plodding along.

Shaw tried again. "Sir, I'm looking for a road, a turnoff around here. I wondered if there is such a thing."

The man paused, shrugged for a moment, and continued on.

Shaw ground his teeth and turned to Anna. "Can you ask him?"

She nodded and pushed Axel away before hopping out. Shaw drummed his fingers on the wheel as she engaged in the typical chitchat that led at a maddeningly slow pace to the question. He heard her laugh, saw the man flash a gap-toothed smile, and she returned to the Jeep.

"Two miles back," Anna said, pressing her lip between her teeth.

"What else?"

"He says there will be trouble soon and we are smart to leave."

"What kind of trouble?"

"They have found the body of a police officer in the river nearby. We should go from here quickly."

Shaw agreed. Trouble was on the march, and he felt it moving closer with every passing minute. He yanked the truck in a tight U-turn that still sent them splashing through mud not thick enough to capture the tires, and he drove into the opposite direction. A little more than two miles and he found it, the turnoff neatly screened by trees and tall shrubs. His heart sped up a fraction.

An airstrip in the middle of nowhere meant drug shipments. Drug shipments involved ruthless people with no scruples. He wondered why that bothered him. Had he maintained a generous supply of scruples himself? If so, wouldn't he be at home, tending to his stricken mother? And wouldn't a man with scruples have taken Nina immediately to the embassy, no matter what time of day or night? He'd done none of those things.

He willed the thoughts away in deference to the current priority: figuring out how to extricate Nina, himself, and now Anna from the disaster brewing around them. He noted the shed at the far end of the runway and the fresh tire tracks that led inside. Guiding his truck behind a pile of rocks covered with a skin of green moss, he parked and pocketed the keys.

"What now?" Anna asked, still in that soft tone that teetered right on the edge of panic.

"I'm going to go around the back and see if I can look in the window."

She began to rattle off a stream of tense Spanish, clutching his arm. "You will be killed. There is nothing more to do. We must leave her to Escorpion."

"That's not going to happen." He pulled his arm away. "I'll be okay, and you can stay here in the truck." He looked into her green eyes. "You've never told me how you got involved in this. How did you know Nina was in trouble?"

She sucked in a breath and shook her head, lips clamped together.

He would not get an answer from her, not now anyway. Opening the door, he gave Axel a stern command. Slow and quiet. The dog understood, body hunched, nose quivering. They picked their way through the foliage, keeping clear of the road, approaching the shed from the back side. Shaw made out one window, smeared with dust about four feet up. He trotted closer and put Axel into a *stay* before he poked his head up over the sill. It was hard to make out through the grime, but there a Jeep sat parked inside, and two men stood outside it, talking. He wished he dared rub a spot of the window clean, but he feared making any noise. One thing was abundantly clear, however. The dark shape in the Jeep had to be Nina.

* * *

Nina's knees had stopped shaking long ago. Her mind and body had crawled into some sort of strange state of timeless limbo. She had the nonsensical notion that if she stayed very still and silent, the men would not return and she would not face any further horrors.

It made no sense, of course. The men with the guns stood near the shed door, talking and smoking, the one with the baseball cap pacing in maddening regularity, back and forth across the cement floor. They clearly waited; for what or whom, she didn't even allow her mind to contemplate.

She forced herself to take stock. She was alive; relatively unharmed except for some scratches and bruises; her hands were tied, but she felt sure the bonds were loosening. And there was a knife in her pocket.

She swallowed hard, still not certain she had it in her to stab someone, anyone. Her eyes had adjusted to the gloom, and the light that filtered in through the one small window revealed old crates and an irregular collage of rusted engine parts. A shadow crossed the window and she froze. Had it been a human-shaped shadow?

She sighed. No, there was no one who knew she'd been taken by these men. Her father would report her missing eventually, a cursory search to follow, but no one—not the police or the soldiers or the people whom she had given her life to serve—would likely search very hard for Nina Truman. Suddenly, she felt very small, as if the fear had leached out parts of her body and left her tiny and as inconsequential as a puff of mist.

When she felt the tears crowd her eyes, she sat up straighter.

*God knows when you're going to take your last breath, Nina, and so far you're still breathing.* Her movement attracted the attention of Baseball Cap, so she bowed her head and forced her body back to stillness. When he looked away, she continued to struggle with the ropes around her wrists.

At the same time, she worked on formulating an escape plan. When she got loose, she'd let them take her out of the car. As soon as the shed doors opened to allow in whomever they expected, she'd make her break for it.

They would surely shoot her in the back, she thought, beads of sweat forming on her brow.

But she would have done her best to save her own life and if

God saw fit, He would see her safely to the bushes.

If not . . .

She tried to quiet her mind.

*I will not be afraid,* she told herself, yet the fright still clawed at her insides, edging up when she caught the sound of an engine approaching. Not a car or truck. She began to pull on the ropes with renewed vigor that bordered on hushed hysteria.

If she had any hope of survival, she had to get free. *Now.*

* * *

Shaw peered through the fogged window again. At least she was alive, from what he could tell. He sank down next to Axel. *Now what?* The guys were armed, no doubt. Shaw had no backup except a dog and a terrified woman, a victim herself.

He turned the details over in his mind as a thrumming noise caught his attention. A small airplane approached the airstrip, zooming lower and lower until he could see it clearly. Shaw didn't know much about planes, had never shared the passion his father had for anything with wings, but he could identify this one as a two-seater Piper Cub, painted a dull beige with no identification stenciled on the side. He'd bet money that somewhere on the fuselage was a rubber bladder—an extra fuel supply to keep the plane moving—and the inevitable cocaine tucked away inside from the hands of the authorities. A drug plane, for sure. Wheels squealed and the fixed wings shimmied as the Piper touched down on the pavement. Shaw hoped the pilot hadn't spotted his truck on his approach in its scanty place of concealment. If he had, he'd probably radioed the guys inside. Game over.

The plane rolled smoothly toward the shed and stopped in front, the propeller thwacking the air as it slowed down. The pilot appeared to be the only person aboard. That was one break in his favor. One guy outside, and two in. For what purpose? He still had no idea.

None of it made sense, but he knew one thing for sure: He couldn't let them put Nina on that plane. For some reason that his head did not seem to fathom, he'd decided they would not take Beth's friend away. Not while he was still alive.

Axel started up a low rumbling in his throat, but Shaw quieted him.

"For now, we wait."

They didn't have to wait long. The door opened and a man climbed down from the cockpit. He thought at first it was an older guy with his slow and gingerly movements, and he sprang into immediate action. Creeping up behind the man, Shaw snaked his arm around his neck in a choke hold.

He stiffened immediately, his hands reflexively coming up to grasp Shaw's arm. That was fine. With both hands accounted for, the pilot wasn't going for a gun.

"No noise," Shaw cautioned. Axel stood next to him now, tensed, growling in spite of Shaw's command.

The pilot gasped for air; surprising since Shaw's hold wasn't hard enough to choke him. Yet.

"You are making a grave mistake," he said in Spanish.

"Won't be the first time," Shaw returned as he frog-marched the man around to the side of the shed, away from the sliding doors. He pushed his back to the metal and let go, and Axel snarled, waiting—Shaw thought perhaps hoping—for the man to make a run for it.

He didn't.

His long black hair, shoulder length and straight, set off smooth mocha skin and an aquiline nose that spoke of Ladino heritage. He stood tall, close to Shaw's six feet, and it took Shaw only another quick moment to make the identification, matching the profile to the crumpled photo in his pocket. His heart iced over, hardening as the hatred swept through him.

Escorpion eyed Shaw through wire-rimmed glasses. "I can see in your face that you know who I am. Now perhaps you will return the favor?"

"Don't think so." Shaw struggled to keep his emotions in

check. Escorpion, the reason he'd stayed in this third-world country, stood before him; unarmed, as far as he could tell.

"Then, you are a coward," Escorpion said, his tone level.

Shaw felt his blood thundering in his ears. "A coward? You are a drug runner who has your people kill off anyone who crosses you because you don't have the guts to do it yourself."

Escorpion eyed him, head slightly cocked. "There you are mistaken. I have no fear of killing." He smiled faintly. "I will enjoy killing you at some point, in fact."

Shaw laughed. "Sorry. We'll have to postpone." He came closer. "I'm going to tell you what is going to happen now."

Escorpion reacted with only a small quiver of the lip. His voice remained soft, his breath fast. "Imagine, an American, a stranger to this country, threatening me on my own airstrip. It is true what they say about American arrogance. You may be a big man in your country, but here you are nothing."

Shaw didn't take the bait. "You're going to call your guys in the shed and tell them to send the girl out and toss out their weapons."

Escorpion considered. "And what is your interest in this girl?"

"What's yours?" he shot back.

Escorpion reached for his front pocket with one hand and Axel stood, growling louder. He froze and smiled. "It is times like these I wish I had not given up smoking. A habit, looking for my cigarettes. Do you smoke?"

Shaw didn't answer.

"Don't," Escorpion advised, still smiling. "It will shorten your life span."

Shaw nudged closer, the gap between them a mere six inches. He smelled the faint musk of cologne, and noted the dark shadow of a beard on full cheeks. "Call them."

"Or you will kill me?" Escorpion didn't look away, staring deep into Shaw's eyes. "There is something familiar about you. Faces I forget, clothes, cars, compliments." His eyes narrowed. "But

I never forget the eyes. That's where you find the truth. I know you."

Hatred ran hot through his veins, as did the temptation to choke the life out of Escorpion that very minute. If he did, he knew retaliation from the men in the shed would follow quickly, and he didn't want to risk it. Nina could get caught in the cross fire between Shaw and Escorpion's vengeful companions; not to mention Anna. No, Shaw would exact punishment later. He unclenched his jaw and hissed. "Call them now or I will take you apart piece by piece and my dog will deal with what's left."

Escorpion eased back and showed his palms. "I must get out my phone."

Shaw watched every movement to be sure he didn't reach for a gun instead. As he dialed, Shaw wondered again. Why had he flown his own plane? Unaccompanied? No guards to flank him? The hairs on the back of Shaw's neck stirred.

*What am I missing?*

Escorpion spoke into the phone in Spanish, telling the men inside exactly what Shaw had demanded.

Shaw once again wrapped his arm around Escorpion's throat and eased him to the front of the shed. The heavy metal door slid open about a foot before disembodied hands tossed out a rifle, then another. They kept some back, Shaw was sure.

Shaw pulled his knife from its sheath and pressed it to Escorpion's Adam's apple. He could feel the blood pulsing there, coursing through this man who had done so much damage, taken away something so precious. His fingers twitched. Escorpion had no right to be here, feeling the wind on his face, the smell of the wet earth circling in his lungs. No right to take up space on planet Earth.

Shaw jerked, forcing his arms not to tighten around Escorpion's neck. "Tell them if they try anything, you will die."

Escorpion called out, and Shaw saw an anxious male face in the gap. "You have made a mistake," Escorpion said, his voice perfectly calm. "You are a stranger and you have crossed a line from which you will not return."

"Get her out here," he grunted, knife pressing into Escorpion's flesh.

After a moment more, Nina appeared, her hands behind her, face white, eyes enormous. She blinked and took a stumbled step forward, as if she'd been pushed. Escorpion sighed, leaving Shaw to wonder again about his interest in Nina.

"Here's where you tell your boys to keep calm," Shaw hissed in Escorpion's ear.

Escorpion didn't reply. Instead, he simply laughed.

# CHAPTER 11

Nina found herself pushed into sunlight, which dazzled her eyes. She'd gotten her hands free, but she kept them behind her back along with her pack, which she'd managed to snatch before she was pulled from the car. As soon as her vision adjusted, she'd decide on a direction and take off. She hoped her knees, which were now trembling again, would hold her.

A voice she didn't recognize shouted to the men behind her. Had he commanded them to throw down their weapons? She must have misheard. She realized the shouted instructions had come from a long-haired man wearing nice clothes, standing stiffly under the shadow of the airplane wing. He spoke in a calm but authoritative voice, a smile on his face. And then—

Shaw locked eyes with her from over the man's shoulder. "Come to me, Nina."

Axel, barking now, stood rigid next to Shaw. She forced her dead legs to carry her toward Shaw, toward the plane that seemed so completely out of place against the bushy backdrop.

Nothing in her brain could explain how Shaw had gotten there, what he was doing with a knife to the man's throat, why the men in the shed had walked out onto the airstrip behind her and thrown their weapons to the ground.

She walked.

Shaw called out. "If you try anything, your boss dies. Got it?"

The men didn't answer.

Nina suddenly recalled a newspaper clipping she'd seen along with a poor quality photo, a similar photo to the one Shaw possessed. The man in Shaw's grasp . . .

*Escorpion.*

Her mouth fell open as Shaw jerked his head toward the bushes. "The truck's there. Hurry."

She made a move to go when Baseball Cap lunged for her, pulling a knife from his boot as he moved. At the same moment, Shaw snarled a command and Axel surged forward, clamping his jaws around the man's arm and sending the knife skittering into the mud.

He screamed and went down, Axel's teeth still sunk deep into the tendons of his wrist.

The other man watched in horror. Shaw kept his knife in one hand and took hold of Escorpion's long hair, using it as a way to shove him forward as he attempted to call off the dog. Axel didn't seem to hear. They stumbled toward the truck and Shaw yelled at Axel again. This time, the dog reluctantly let go, running after Shaw while checking over his shoulder to see if anyone else dared approach.

Nina could do nothing but follow, jerking free from the branches that caught at her clothing, pressing through mud that sucked at her shoes. By the time they reached the truck, Escorpion's pants were spattered with muck and he panted heavily.

Shaw looked inside the truck and surveyed the bushes. Nina wondered who he could possibly be looking for, but she was smart enough to know it wasn't the time to press Shaw for details. She got in the truck and Shaw tossed her the keys.

Over the engine noise, she heard Shaw lean close to Escorpion and whisper something in his ear that she couldn't decipher. Then he let go of him and jogged to the truck. Axel remained on the ground a few feet from Escorpion, tense, a completely different animal than the gentle creature who'd licked her face after the bus accident.

Shaw got in. "Drive," he said.

"What about Axel?"

"He'll catch up."

As she yanked the truck into gear and pressed the gas pedal, she saw Escorpion, motionless, staring at them, his expression a mixture of curiosity and hatred.

He didn't say a word, didn't make any move to escape even after Shaw told Nina to slow the truck when they'd traveled about fifty feet. He called out to Axel, who came running. Still, Escorpion watched, his white shirt catching the morning light. Something about his absolute stillness and the intensity of his expression chilled her.

After Shaw opened the tailgate and Axel hopped in, tongue lolling, Shaw returned and commandeered the driver's seat. Happy to relinquish it, her body still shuddered. "How did you find me?"

He told her about Anna. "She must have taken off."

Nina didn't blame her. Even as they skidded onto the main road, the shock still coursed like electricity through her body.

"I don't know how she was privy to the information," Shaw said, his glance darting to the rearview mirror every few minutes, "but she knew Escorpion was pursuing you, and she tried to warn you."

*Run or die*. Nina bit her lip, hoping Anna had made it to a safe hiding place. She clasped her hands together to keep them from shaking. "Why did you come after me?"

He stared at her for a long and frozen instant before darting his eyes away. "Escorpion. He's not going to do it again."

"Do what?"

Shaw gripped the wheel. "Never mind."

"Don't brush me off. Tell me what's going on here between you and Escorpion. You carry his picture."

"I don't have to tell you anything," he said. "You're alive, isn't that enough?"

"And I'm grateful for that, but you didn't risk your life for me. You don't even like me."

He didn't answer. Before she could think better of it, she put a hand on his arm, and Shaw tensed.

"Please tell me why you came for me, Shaw."

He turned blazing eyes on her. "Don't read anything noble into it. I know you'd rather I was some missionary guy who rode in on a white horse, calling on the name of Jesus, and saved you like some kind of Rapunzel from up in your tower. Sorry, honey, that's just not true. My reasons are my own. You're alive and so am I for the moment and, whether we like it or not, our only chance of escape is to stick together." He pressed the truck to go faster.

His words were harsh, but he didn't shake off her touch. She allowed her fingertips to remain there on his muscled arm for one more moment, hoping it might ease some of the anger that raged inside him. Then she moved her hand away.

"You're wrong, you know," she said quietly.

"How's that?"

"I'm not Rapunzel." She picked a branch out of her hair and held up the ragged section for his perusal. "You cut it off, remember?"

He blinked at her, eyes round as if examining a new species of animal he'd never seen before. Then, perhaps as much to his surprise as hers, he smiled, the action lighting the blue-gray depths of his eyes. He shook his head. "This is crazier than a low-budget film."

She nodded, grateful for that small smile in the middle of the ugliness she'd seen in the past twenty-four hours. "Where will we go now?"

He eyed the fuel gauge. "Not far. I think there's a village about an hour from here. Maybe we can get some gas there."

They pressed on in silence. Not quite sure of the time, Nina guessed at somewhere in the neighborhood of late morning. Mercifully, the rain had given way to a bright yellow sun. Her socks were still damp from the previous night's drenching, her wrists sore from working against the rough ropes. The village resembled Sayache, where she and her parents had stopped before visiting the Mayan ruins of Ceibal in years past. Crowded along the banks of a wide river, she noticed several two-story buildings perched on mud lots set back from the water. Small boats traversed the surface, some of them paddled expertly along by children no older than eight or nine. A small hotel sat across from a small store, and Nina felt cheered at the sight of the paltry pocket of civilization after a night spent fleeing through the jungle.

Shaw stopped the truck under a spreading coaba tree and got out. "I need to call Otto."

"And I need to call my father."

He agreed, scanning up and down the road. "They may have police here somewhere."

A question hid underneath the casual statement. Were the cops to be trusted? Nina twisted her shorn strands of hair. She still believed Roque and Josef had not meant to harm her, but they had been dispatched by someone to put her under arrest. "I don't think I should try the police again right now."

He seemed to relax a little as he let the dog out of the car. Axel sniffed around and relieved himself before returning to Shaw.

Nina's stomach rumbled. "I'm going to go into the market and get us something to eat."

He shook his head. "I've got supplies."

"So do I, but I need something more than a handful of nuts."

He huffed. "Let me get it then."

"It's better if I do it. You're going to attract attention."

"And a pretty woman won't?" His cheeks colored as he realized what he'd said.

"Thank you for the compliment, but a pretty woman will still draw less attention in this town than a *gringo*, especially outside of tourist season."

With that, she turned on her heel and headed for the *tienda*.

* * *

Shaw couldn't believe he'd made that *pretty woman* remark. Her silky hair and those wide brown eyes weren't relevant to their precarious situation.

And she was right, of course. He fit in about as well as a camel in the jungle, but then again they'd already been spotted. He noticed several men lounging on the hotel steps who had glanced in their direction. Shaw kept his head turned slightly away, but he tracked the men with his eyes. So far, they'd made no move to leave the steps.

Like it or not, he needed to inquire about a gas station in town. Strolling around the place would attract even more attention to the dirty outsider and his canine companion. On that count, he instructed Axel to stay in the back of the truck.

He kept one ear tuned uneasily to the distant sounds of children playing. The workers on the dock waited for the ferry to transport trucks probably carrying over-stacked lumber from the sawmill across the river. He tried again to get his bearings. In the Petén, the two major hubs of activity centered around the twin towns of Flores and Santa Elena, both southwest of the massive Tikal ruins. The main roads leading to and from were paved and frequented by buses usually heading for or leaving the airport in Flores, the only civil airport aside from the one in Guat City. He guessed their erratic escape from the clinic in Pajarito had taken them farther west. Otto's oil palm plantation was in that direction, and the only person they could trust at this point was Otto.

He looked as casual as a stranger could look sauntering over to the half dozen men wearing jeans and dusty long-sleeved shirts. Some wore broad-brimmed hats, and two of them sported cowboy hats and shirts with collars.

He nodded respectfully. "*Buenas tardes.*"

They bobbed their heads in return, but offered no greeting. He read suspicion in their eyes. Roles reversed, he would have had the same look in his own.

"Can you tell me where I might find some gasoline?" He tried English, not wanting to insult them by his American-accented Spanish.

One of the men in a cowboy hat looked him over. "What brings you here, señor?" he asked in perfect English.

Shaw smiled. "I was traveling, looking at the sights, and I'm almost out of gas."

"*Tourista?*" a man with a thick mustache said, sipping from a bottle.

"*Si,*" Shaw said.

"Your woman," the mustached man continued. "She doesn't look like *tourista.*"

Shaw didn't like the smile he saw on the man's face. It was a macho culture, he told himself, and Nina was lovely. "She is also a traveler, from Brazil. We're with a group, on our way to see Tikal, but we ran low on gas." He wondered if the story sounded as ridiculous to them as it did to him.

The man he thought they'd called Lico raised an eyebrow. "She does not carry a camera, nor do you. I do not see any fancy cell phones either."

"Camera's in the car," Shaw said, jerking a thumb in the direction of the truck. "So is there gas here in this town?"

"There is no rush, señor, to see Tikal. It has been there for thousands of years already. It's not going anywhere." He laughed, joined by his compatriots. "Sit down here and tell us what you've seen on your travels."

Shaw bit back a sigh. He wanted nothing to do with polite conversation or beer. He just wanted to get out of this town before Escorpion arrived. "Many thanks, but we're supposed to meet up with our group and they'll be worried. We're already so late having to stop for gas."

Lico's face hardened. "Even the bad ones, they stop to talk."

"The bad ones?"

"There have been people here, outsiders like you," he hissed.

"Not just outsiders, Mexicans; gangs, you see. They arrive and they tell us how things will be and what they will require. Even they take the time to talk."

Shaw felt a cold prickle slide up his back.

"Yes," the short man said. "They talk and ask us to choose."

Shaw resisted the urge to lick his lips which had suddenly gone dry. "Choose what?"

Lico put down his bottle with a clank on the chipped glass table. "We choose between helping the Mexicans or our own."

"Your own? Who would that be?"

Lico shrugged and looked away.

He didn't need the spoken answer. He knew that Escorpion was the homegrown drug runner. Who had these men chosen to serve? The brutal Mexican cartel or an equally brutal hometown criminal? No winning choice in either direction.

"All this talking has worn me out," Lico said, wiping the sweat from his forehead. "I need to go inside for another drink. If you will not be polite and join us, then we will say *adios* and you can find your gasoline two blocks down on your right."

"*Muchas gracias*." Shaw nodded. "Another time." He glanced at the door of the tiny *tienda* from where Nina had still not emerged. How long did it take a woman to buy some food and bottled water?

He found the gas station and Axel hopped out to sniff at a small dog that wandered the dilapidated property. The fuel poured in and Shaw felt some small confidence return. He paid his quetzals to the attendant, a boy of no more than thirteen, and he noted the irony that in this country of metric measurement, gas was still measured by the gallon. Returning to the truck, he kept his eye to the horizon, searching for Escorpion's plane; although there was really no need for a plane. A phone call to one of his followers here in town would fill him in on their status. The pressing urge to get away pricked at him. Still, he drove carefully down the paved road which featured potholes filled with rainwater. Small houses painted in garish colors lined the road, and tiny yards festooned with clotheslines full of flapping garments took advantage of the break between storms.

Still no sign of Nina. When he returned to his spot under the tree, he checked his watch. Even accounting for the polite conversation she'd have been required to make before her purchases, she should have returned by now.

He flung the door open and started to get out when his gut suddenly clenched.

Strolling down the street toward the store, a police officer pressed a cell phone to his ear.

# CHAPTER 12

Nina sensed the shop owner's reaction to her appearance. Women in Guatemala didn't wear jeans and baggy men's shirts, not to mention the fact that her disheveled hair ticked another strike against her. She tried to smooth it surreptitiously with one hand as she browsed the crowded counter.

When she offered a smile, he gave her a curt nod and disappeared into the back, leaving a plump lady in a rumpled skirt and blouse to mind the store. The woman wiped down the counter, her thick braid draped over one shoulder, but Nina felt her furtive glances. Best to make the purchases quickly and get back to Shaw. Who knew what kind of unwanted attention he might have attracted?

At over six feet, Shaw towered over most of the men, and his ferocious look probably made him the subject of speculation; not to mention Axel. Remembering how relentless the dog had been in his pursuit of the man in the baseball cap, she shivered. Axel and Shaw had more in common than she'd realized.

She gathered up what she could find that could be easily transported; cola, some small apples, the two bottles of water she saw. A package of dried fish struck her as the only thing that might interest Axel, and she picked it up as well. Skirts in lavish colors hung on the corner of the counter near the owner's wife. Tourists probably paid well for the gorgeous textiles, and Nina couldn't help but trail a finger over the perfect handiwork.

The lady moved to her elbow. "*Buenos dias.*" She pointed shyly to the skirts. "Do you like them?"

Nina looked into the woman's tired face and smiled. "They're exquisite," she said without hesitation. "They take my breath away."

The woman ducked her head. The man called from the back and she disappeared through the woven curtain. Nina continued her perusal, her senses diverted by an aroma that made her mouth water. She moved toward the pale treats, and long-ago memories rolled forward. She and Beth had gorged themselves on the *canillitas de leche*, the confections known as *milk legs*.

"They named them after me," Beth had said ruefully, showing off her lily-white legs speckled with mosquito bites as they munched the fudgy, melt-in-your-mouth creations.

How they had laughed. When Beth married Colonel Fuentes, the charming ranch owner, he had made certain that there were platters of *canillitas de leche* at the fiesta. They had both seemed so happy, the unlikely couple—wiry and dark Colonel Fuentes and his porcelain-skinned bride. Who could have known Beth would be dead a scant six weeks later? Drowned after her car skidded off a rain-slicked trail?

A soft touch made her jump. The woman had returned from the back room and she smiled again, drawing Nina away to the far corner of the store. "I know you," she said, her voice sweet and lilting.

A few days earlier, Nina would not have felt the twinge of concern in her belly from such a statement. Now she found herself unsure how to respond. Two days ago, Nina Truman was a missionary nurse; today, she was a fugitive from both the police and a drug runner.

"My name is Carmen," the woman whispered. "You saved my son."

Nina started. "Carmen? But . . ." Nina looked toward the man in back. The *Carmen* she had helped six months before had come to the clinic with a baby suffering from diarrhea that left the infant malnourished. She remembered the baby's tiny head, the fontanel concave, the small face pinched and expressionless. The woman said her husband was dead after having been unable to see a doctor for a tumor in his esophagus. She was visiting relatives near Pajarito and there was no money to take the baby to a county hospital.

"He is my uncle," Carmen said with a glance toward the curtain. "You made my baby well even though I had no money for the *consulta*."

*A small thing*, Nina thought. They'd treated the infant for dehydration and the parasites that sucked away the nutrients from his body, and she recalled teaching Carmen how to make her own electrolyte fluid using sugar, salt and fruit juices. All the while she'd treated the baby, Nina wondered what would happen to the woman with no husband to help support the little family. He could have been saved in the States. A restless discontent bit at Nina, who felt the familiar craving deep down.

If I were a doctor, perhaps I could have helped her husband. If I had the training, I could do so much more.

But God put her here, a nurse, to minister along with her father. She'd heard the calling early on, while in her teens.

She blinked at Carmen. "Is your baby well then?"

She nodded, beaming. "He is well. His cries are strong now, and he is nearly crawling."

Nina sighed. "I'm so happy to hear that."

She looked Nina over again and Nina could see the question building in her eyes. To keep from having to make something up, Nina fumbled through her bag and extracted money for her purchases.

With a hasty look toward the back room, Carmen walked quickly to the pile of textiles and selected a full black skirt, embellished with a glorious rainbow of thread work. She held it up to Nina.

"I can't," Nina said, ruefully. She had only a handful of quetzals. The money wasn't hers in the first place and whatever she had left should be carefully tended.

Carmen added it to the paper bag anyway. "A gift. To repay a kindness."

She started to protest, but she couldn't. It was a simple gift, friend to friend; a tender thank-you spelled out in the embroidered language across the fabric. Tears collected in Nina's eyes as she thanked the woman. Carmen wrapped up a batch of *canillatas de leche* in waxed paper and added it, too. Nina made no effort to refuse, her mouth already salivating. "I am so grateful," she breathed.

"I make the best in the town," Carmen said with pride. "You enjoy them and take some back to *El Monte*." She paused, lowering her voice even more. "Why do you travel here? Without *el doctor*? It is not safe for a woman alone," she whispered.

Nina opened her mouth to reply when a shadow crept past the open window overlooking the street. Her gaze riveted to the profile of a police officer, pudgy in the middle, the buttons around his belly straining to hold the cloth together. He held a cell phone to his ear with one hand and a lighted cigarette in the other.

Nina knew Carmen could read the fear on her face. She came close, pressed herself to Nina's side and breathed in her ear. "He came to town this morning because two dead police officers were found nearby. He has been asking about any strangers who have come."

Nina's heart rose to her throat. "I see."

Carmen pressed her elbow. "He wants to know especially if any women have come here. He has offered rewards to the men at the *comedores.*" She paused for a moment. "There are many hungry families here."

Nina looked Carmen in the face and grasped her hands. "I did not do anything wrong," she said, feeling again the wash of tears. "Please believe that." She squeezed the woman's fingers in her own, trying to tell her with her touch that things were not, could not possibly be, like they appeared.

Carmen cocked her head. Nina could see her own terrified reflection in the woman's dark pupils before she pulled her hands away.

* * *

Shaw ducked down in the front seat. The police officer paused under the shade of a sprawling tree, apparently waiting for the person on the other end of the line. Shaw scooted over toward the open window on the passenger side so he could eavesdrop in earnest, ignoring his erratic heartbeat. He hoped that maybe their luck would change and Nina would catch sight of the guy and sneak out the back.

A ridiculous notion. So far, the only kind of luck they'd had was the bad kind.

"I have been waiting for some time," the cop said peevishly. "I must go about my duties." He took a deep drag on the cigarette and blew smoke for another few moments, his back to the wooden side of the store.

The cop took the cigarette from his mouth and stood up straighter. "She is not here yet, but I spoke to a man who says there were two people asking about a landing strip. I found tracks there. A plane and some footprints, three pairs at least, and the dog."

Shaw grimaced.

The cop sighed. "I agree, but they could not have gone far. They will head for a town, the nearest village where they can get help. And then perhaps to Flores to catch a plane." His voice trailed off again.

Shaw's mind raced. It didn't sound like this cop worked with Escorpion's men. He pressed closer to the door, Axel poking him in annoyance.

"I will wait here for a while, make sure to let the people know there is a reward if they assist in the capture of Señorita Truman and the American *gringo*."

Shaw bit back a groan. The police knew they traveled together.

"*Si*, I will make sure she is taken unharmed," he said, toying with the cigarette. "The *gringo*, too*? Si. Adios*, Colonel Fuentes."

Shaw rocked back in shock. Colonel Fuentes? Beth's grieving widower? This cop worked for Fuentes to capture Nina? His brain couldn't process the shocking information quickly enough. He risked a look out the window and saw the cop click off his phone and take the last few drags on his cigarette before he ground it into the cracked pavement. Shaw watched in horror as he walked past the open store window and stopped in front of the door.

Options thundered through his mind.

*Drive off. Get to Otto alone. Alert the embassy and leave it up to them to extricate Nina. Storm into the store unarmed, except for his knife, and try to snatch her and make a break for it.*

Axel would help even the odds, but he couldn't predict how the townspeople would react. Turn their backs on the two strangers and let the police have them? Try to intervene to assist the shop owner and get their hands on some potential reward money?

In his days working bomb squad for the Los Angeles Police Department, he'd grown used to making decisions in the space of a moment, but he now found himself at a loss.

*You've grown soft*, he thought. *The jungle has worn away your edge.*

But not the edge that still drove him from deep down—the sharp, serrated edge of the anger that would only be satisfied by vengeance. The one still honed by hours of grief, stropped and ready for use against his enemy.

Now, it seemed, Colonel Fuentes had been added to that short list.

Shaw ground his teeth.

So be it.

He gripped the handle and waited until the cop had nearly crossed the threshold. Axel leapt out after him on silent paws; dog stealth mode. Shaw kept his head down and walked quickly, still without any sort of a plan. Winging it.

The term had always amused Otto, who enjoyed the Americanisms.

"Winging it just gets you dead more quickly," he'd said with a laugh.

*Probably right,* he thought now, but he didn't see another option at hand.

A heavyset woman with a braid greeted the cop at the door. He exchanged some words with her before she led him into the store, just as another woman waddled around the narrow alley and onto the street. The woman's pregnant, swollen belly pushed out the skirt she wore, and her bare feet pattered on the wet sidewalk. Shaw ducked to the side of the building as the cop looked out the window and nodded at the pregnant woman who kept her head down in customary humble fashion.

The cop headed deeper into the store and Shaw got ready to go after him until he noticed the pregnant woman gesturing wildly to him. Axel trotted right over before Shaw could restrain him.

It took Shaw a moment longer to make out the chopped hair and inch or two of pants protruding from under the woman's skirt when she walked. He blinked to make sure he hadn't conjured up something that wasn't actually there. Axel didn't need convincing. He gave her bag a thorough sniff and contentedly followed her back to the truck.

Closing his mouth, Shaw did the same, backing the truck down the road until they moved out of sight of the *tienda* and he could turn around properly. He took the road leading away from the river at a pace that wouldn't attract any more attention than they already had. With each mile that passed, he felt the tension in his stomach relaxing ever so slightly.

Nina turned away from him and dislodged the pack and shoes which had doubled as a pregnant belly. She slipped the skirt off over her jeans and smoothed the fabric, running her fingers lightly along the embroidery, half a smile on her face, before she folded it into a precise square and pushed it into her pack. She took a cola from the bag and offered it to him. "Do you want a soda?"

He simply stared. "What happened here?" he finally managed.

She opened a bottle for herself and drank thirstily. "I know some people," she said innocently, a glimmer in her dark eyes.

The unexpected hint of mischief somehow pleased him. He took a bottle and drained it in a few gulps as they drove and she explained about Carmen. He glanced often in the rearview mirror, half expecting a police car in hot pursuit as soon as the men from the hotel ratted them out.

"They wouldn't give us up," Nina said. "Carmen would tell them. They're good people."

He maneuvered around a water-filled cleft in the road. "They're hungry people. They'll do what they need to do to survive, just like we will."

She cocked her head. "You see the bad in everyone, don't you?"

"I'm a realist. I see things the way they are."

"Maybe you need glasses," she suggested with a lopsided smile.

"Maybe you should take off your blindfold."

After a moment, her gaze dropped to her lap and he wished he hadn't said it. "People are bad, I can see that. They lie . . ." Her voice caught. "But God put plenty of good on this planet, Shaw. You could see it if you looked harder."

She was wrong, of course—just like his sister, just like his mother—but all the same, something beautiful emanated from what she said, and he found himself wanting to take her hand, to offer comfort.

Instead, he cleared his throat and rolled up his window against a sudden spatter of rain while she sipped more soda. "What do you know about Colonel Fuentes?"

Nina coughed, mid-swallow. "Beth's husband?"

He hated thinking about the man that way. "Yeah."

"Why do you ask?"

"My question first."

She dabbed at her mouth with the hem of her shirt. His shirt, he reminded himself.

"I know Beth loved him," she said quietly.

*Loved him.* A man she'd known for only six months? A guy from a foreign culture, a completely different lifestyle, decades older than Beth? He didn't want to let the conversation go in that direction. "What do you know about his business?"

"He's a cattle rancher."

"And?"

She eyed Shaw carefully. "And he's wealthy."

"From the cattle?"

"What else?"

Shaw drummed his fingers on the steering wheel. "What do the people say?"

She shrugged. "Rumors, innuendo, nothing more."

He tried to remain patient. "Rumors about what?"

"That he lets people move drugs across his land."

"What people?"

She shook her head, her pretty face solemn. "I don't know. I didn't want to believe it. Beth said there was absolutely no truth to it because she flat-out asked him."

"He would keep her so far away from his business that she'd have no idea." He blew out a breath.

"Beth was a journalist at heart," she said. "If she suspected something, she'd dig until she found the answers."

Beth Wilder was indeed a journalist at heart, with her own column wittily entitled "A Walk on the Wilder Side" appearing in *Traveler Magazine*. She'd written about some gritty topics like child prostitution, and he'd always worried she'd stick her button nose into something that would get her into trouble. He hated being right about that one.

"I'm a cat, Shaw," she'd said. "I always land on my feet, so stop worrying like an old granny."

But she hadn't landed on her feet, had she? She'd landed in a rain-swollen river the night her car went off the road and she'd died there in the swirling water, alone. He blinked away the visual.

"Why are you asking me about him?" Nina said.

He told her about the cop's phone call, and her misty eyes glistened with surprise. "Why would Colonel Fuentes be after me?"

"I don't know."

She relaxed suddenly and shook her head. With a confident smile, she told him, "He's trying to keep me safe. He's heard about what's going on and he knows I was Beth's friend. He's sending people to get me before Escorpion's men do."

Shaw answered with a raised eyebrow.

Nina slapped a hand on her thigh. "Well, he told the cops to keep us alive, didn't he? That proves it."

"That proves nothing." Her naiveté was both infuriating and fascinating. At the moment, because he was tired, hungry and worried, infuriating won out. "All we know is he's got the cops paying the locals to snitch and we have to run."

"To Otto?"

"He's the only one I can trust."

She bit her lip. "How far?"

Shaw glanced at his watch. The afternoon clouds rolling in gradually squeezed out the daylight. "His plantation is west of here, near the Usamacinta River."

"That's near the Mexican border, isn't it?"

"Yeah. Otto might be able to get us across, and from there . . ."

"My father could help. He has missionary friends in Mexico." She sat upright. "Can I have your phone to call him?"

He fished the phone from his pocket and handed it to her. She dialed, frowning at the device after a moment. "It's beeping."

"Low battery." He plugged the charger into the cigarette lighter. "Wait awhile and then call your dad and the embassy."

She sat back. "What do we do in the meantime?"

He eyed the sky, then the road behind them. Vegetation seemed to thicken around them. The shadows trickled through the dense screen of leaves, shrouding the way in shifting ripples of darkness and light.

"We disappear."

# CHAPTER 13

She'd always imagined it would be easy to disappear in the vast Petén jungle. The civil war had displaced many people who had to leave their villages and go into the jungle to find land to farm. So many people. Such horrendous poverty.

As the road became more of a trail, they passed several small houses constructed out of vertical branches and thatched roofs. Heedless of the rain, a little boy played with a ball, expertly keeping it in the air with his bare feet while he examined their truck as it passed, along with an oriole that fluttered along a branch to eye them closer.

When they came to a place where the path split off in two directions, Shaw stopped and mulled it over.

"That one looks muddy already," Nina said, peering through the slapping wipers. "We might get stuck."

"The other leads to town, according to the kid at the gas station."

"So we should head there. Find someplace to sleep, maybe a church. They'd help us."

He shook his head. "The cop figured we'd head for a village, and from there to Flores."

"And you don't trust him? That's the big decision we need to make right now, isn't it? Whom to trust?"

"That's easy for me," he grunted. "The answer is no one." He turned off down the muddy trail.

"I think you're wrong," Nina said.

"Well we're both still alive and that makes me right so far," he snapped.

She huffed but didn't speak, instead snatching up the phone and dialing her father's cell number. She pressed a finger to her ear and jammed the phone to her cheek. One ring, two, three. Her spirit soared when somebody picked up.

"Daddy," she said, relief flooding her body. "I'm in trouble."

Her father's voice was low and urgent. "Nina, get . . ."

Then the call ended. She blinked and looked at Shaw who had stopped the truck and stared at her expectantly. "It was my dad, but something is wrong. We were disconnected."

"Try again."

She dialed again. One ring. Then five. Ten. No answer. Fear nibbled at her mind. Her father's tone, so tense, so unlike the easy-going voice that always resonated with confidence. "Why doesn't he answer?"

"Call the embassy," Shaw advised. "Tell them what's going on."

She did. After weaving her way through the various voicemail options that left her chewing her nails, she brightened with elation when a woman answered the phone. Nina breathlessly launched into her story. Silence met her from the other end. "Hello?"

"Ma'am, I'm sorry. Would you tell me your name again please?"

Holding back her exasperation, Nina repeated her name. "I need to speak to the American Ambassador."

"He's away from the office today."

"Please, can you contact him? I'm in terrible trouble."

She hesitated. "Have you called the police?"

"No, I think . . ." Nina stopped, realizing she sounded like a raving lunatic. "I can't go to the police."

"Perhaps the Tourist Office? If you've been the victim of a crime . . ."

"No, no," she all but shouted. "I need to speak to the ambassador. This is an emergency."

"Please calm down," the woman said.

"Would you be calm if murderers were chasing you? Two police officers are dead already and something has happened to my father," she shrieked.

Another pause followed. Something in Nina's hysterical rant must have hit a note. "I will contact the ambassador and inform him of your situation. Is this the cell phone where you can be reached?"

"Yes," she said, heaving in a breath before giving her Shaw's cell number.

"Where are you now?"

Nina looked helplessly at Shaw who relayed the GPS coordinates he'd gotten from the phone.

"My advice is to stay there, right there, until I call you back. Do you understand, Ms. Truman?"

"I understand," she replied faintly. "Thank you."

She ended the call. "She said to stay here until she contacts the ambassador. I think she finally believes me."

Shaw nodded.

Nina tried her father's phone again with no better result, just endless ringing and no answer. What could have happened to him? He was supposed to be back in the U.S. by now, visiting his sick brother.

She'd call her uncle. Activating the phone again, she tried to punch in the numbers but found she couldn't remember them.

*Think, Nina, think.* Her brain just would not produce it.

*Information.* She would dial them up and ask . . .

Then she remembered her uncle no longer maintained a landline.

*Daddy, where are you?*

She looked out into the tangle of green, swatting at a mosquito which had found its way into the car and stung the back of her neck. The action seemed to loose something inside her and she shivered with emotion. Shaw handed her a tissue. She hadn't even realized she was crying, but that gesture and that hard face with the soft gleam in his blue-gray eyes made her feelings boil over into a blubbery mess.

"I'm worried about my dad." She gasped between spurts of sobbing. "I can't remember Uncle Joe's number. Why can't I remember?"

Shaw kept handing her tissues as the tears continued to flow. "Hard to remember sometimes when you're under stress."

Stress was an understatement. It was one thing to run around the jungle waiting for help to arrive from the embassy. It was another entirely to imagine what had caused the awful tension she'd heard in her father's voice. Unflappable Bruce Truman had disintegrated into broken and worried in just a few quick words. When Nina's mother died, he'd been the rock for his daughter, grieving with her, but sharing the comfort that Mariela was in her eternal home now, waiting for them. At the clinic, there had been moments—bloody, tense moments—where Nina thought the thrashing victim would not survive, but her father never flinched, moving with the calm fluidity of a maestro as he performed miracles in the tiny, under-equipped clinic.

Her father, her hero.

"We didn't part on good terms. He lied," she found herself babbling. "I don't know why."

Shaw stopped, tissue in hand. "Lied about what?"

She broke off, realizing she didn't want to share this shame, particularly with Shaw, who already thought her a fool. "Never mind," she said, wiping her face. "My dad is a good man."

Shaw handed over one last tissue. "So is mine, and he's a liar, too."

She looked up from her soggy tissue. "What did he lie to you about?"

Shaw leaned his head back against the seat. "I was away at a training when my mom had her so-called accident while she was in that Mexican border town. That's exactly what he told me when he called. There was an accident and she had a head injury. She'd recover fine, he said. No need to come home. So I finished out my class and, when I got back, I heard the rest of the story."

Nina knew some of the particulars from Beth. Her mother had been attacked by bandits while walking on a dusty road near town. She was robbed, beaten and left for dead. Her heart squeezed for Shaw as he continued.

"Even after I got home and figured out the truth, that she'd suffered major brain damage, my dad insisted God would make her well, but I could see it in his eyes. He knew she was going to be a vegetable for the rest of her life."

"Was it a lie?" she asked gently. "Or maybe something he wanted to believe?"

"Just more religious pap." He shot her a look. "No offense, but something along the lines of 'God will heal her in this life or the next.'"

"And you don't believe that?"

"It would be nice, but I'm the guy that believes what I see. My mom is brain damaged and doesn't know where she is. There was never the slightest chance she'd be well again. My father can say he believes in her healing until the earth stops turning, but he's lying to himself, and he lied to Beth and me." He stared out the front window. "So you can see why I didn't want Beth to go to Guatemala in the first place. Bad enough what happened to Mom. But Beth went. You convinced her."

His tone made her flinch. "I didn't convince her. I told her the truth about my experiences here and she wanted to come. You know that."

"I also know," he continued, words hitting hard like the raindrops on the glass, "that at the end of her vacation, she should have come home, but she didn't, did she? You talked her into staying and she wound up falling in love with Fuentes." He looked at her now, eyes boring into her as he spat out the words. Nina felt her cheeks grow hot.

"Shaw, I asked her to stay longer, which was selfish of me. I loved having her here, and she relished every day, every moment." Her throat thickened suddenly. "Don't you think I feel guilty? If I hadn't invited her to stay . . . don't you think I regret that decision?"

He blinked. "You don't regret it as much as my family does."

"I'm sorry. I'm truly sorry, but Beth . . ."

He held up a hand. "Don't. Don't tell me she died doing what she loved, realizing her God-given dreams and all that. Point is, she's dead, and my mom might as well be, and I don't see how the world is one iota better for their sacrifice."

"Sometimes we don't get to see," she whispered.

"And you still think that? That God's in charge?" He gestured to the rain-soaked jungle. "You're in trouble, deep trouble, and let's be real. It will be a miracle if we both survive. More likely, there are going to be two more dead Americans buried here. Are you going to die believing you made a difference for God?"

She thought about the little baby with the sunken head, the terrified mothers and malnourished children who would forever fight against the bonds of poverty. "I will die knowing that I tried to do what He wanted me to do."

He sighed, a long heavy sound. "And what about your father? You talk of him like he's your idol, but you said he lied."

She nibbled her lip. "Yes, he did. And when I get back to him, I'm going to ask him why." She sucked in a breath to keep from crying, anxious to get away from Shaw's probing questions. "Have you visited your parents since you came to live here?"

"No," he said, and she saw the flicker of shame on his face. "My dad is a liar, but I'm the coward."

Nina's mouth opened in surprise. "I wouldn't think you were afraid of anything."

"No, you wouldn't, would you?"

"Shaw, why did you come here? To live in Guatemala?"

He huffed. "The fabulous scenery."

"You don't like the jungle and you didn't come here for the

people. This place reminds you about Beth, and that hurts. So why did you come? And why do you stay?"

He looked at her and pushed a strand of hair away that had fallen in her face. "I could tell you what I say to everyone else, but I don't want to be a liar, too."

What she saw in his face scared her; a mixture of deep sadness and longing and the hot flush of rage that glittered in his eyes.

He let his fingers trail through her hair before he moved his hand away. "We'll wait awhile for the embassy call, but not too long. We've got to get to Otto's before Escorpion's men catch up. Try to sleep if you can."

He closed his eyes and leaned his head against the window, arms folded across his chest. Nina found herself not one bit closer to understanding the enigmatic man next to her.

* * *

Shaw jerked awake. Nina was curled up in a ball, head resting on the glass, darkness and drizzling rain on the other side. She looked impossibly small and young, her face smooth and untroubled in sleep. He wanted to reach out and cup that satin cheek, to feel the softness of it against his calloused palm.

Shaking away the ridiculous thought, he checked the time. Nearly seven p.m. No return call from the embassy. No contact from her father, but plenty of time for Escorpion's men or the police to trace their movements.

He dialed Otto's number and got his voicemail. Not surprising. Otto, the devoted gastronome, was probably enjoying his evening meal. Nothing short of nuclear catastrophe would make him leave it, least of all a ringing cell phone.

As far as Otto knew, Shaw was making his way steadily to his oil palm plantation.

*And that's exactly what we should be doing*, he thought, angry at himself for agreeing to the delay.

Nina woke up when he started the motor.

"Did they call?"

"No calls," he said, gruffly. "We're going to Otto's."

She wrapped her arms around herself to fend off the chill which had settled over the jungle. He heard a most unladylike growl from her stomach, and she pressed her hands to her middle.

"I'm starving."

She reached for the paper bag and pulled out some sweets, handing him one.

"What is it?"

"Milk legs," she said, stuffing one into her mouth. The look that came over her face, as if she'd just awoken from a luscious dream, forced a smile out of him.

"Why are you grinning?" she said around a mouthful.

"You look like you just tasted a little piece of heaven."

She smiled blissfully. "I did. Carmen was divinely inspired when she made these, I'm one hundred percent sure of it."

He laughed at the utter sincerity in her tone as he started the engine and devoured his own share of the candy. It was good; not rib-eye-steak-and-baked-potato-with-sour-cream good, but satisfying.

"You'll have to wait a bit for your kibble, buddy," Shaw said to Axel.

Axel drooled as he watched Nina unwrap the dried fish, and she slipped him a big chunk. The dog chewed the hard nugget between his back teeth, his eyes rolling in satisfaction.

"Now he's going to follow you around and he won't listen to me," Shaw said.

"Sometimes he doesn't listen to you now."

Shaw chuckled. "That's why he flunked out as a police dog. He developed a mind of his own and wouldn't obey his handler. I took him when I heard he'd washed out as K-9 officer. I trained him myself to be a detection dog when I quit the force."

"Detect what?"

"Explosives. He finds land mines."

Nina shivered.

"Sore subject?"

She shook her head and reached for another candy. "Land mines are hideous. Before we came to the Petén, my father treated a child who lost his leg when he stepped on one while herding cattle. The boy didn't survive." She shook her head. "After thirty-six years of civil war, the people are still being hurt."

"That's why Otto hired me. He needed some land cleared so he could start his oil palm plantation."

She remained quiet, staring out the window.

"What's wrong?"

"Nothing."

"Not nothing. You're a lousy liar."

She lifted a shoulder. "I've just heard that people get rich off those plantations by forcing the locals off the land. They ruin the ecology with fertilizers, strip the soil, and pay the workers a pittance."

"You sound like Beth. She grilled Otto the same way."

"And what was his reaction?"

"He laughed and laughed. He said he was giving jobs where they were needed and that a pretty woman such as Beth should be home raising a dozen children and cooking tortillas instead of worrying about palm trees."

Nina looked aghast. "I'll bet Beth didn't take that well."

Shaw smiled at the memory. "Nope. She nearly blew a gasket, which made Otto laugh even harder. Otto is a chauvinist of the worst order and Beth made it her mission to point that out every time they met, which only amused him more of course."

The truck headed down a slope sticky with mud. They made it through and continued on, stopping when an ocellated turkey darted alongside the road before vanishing into the trees.

The jungle had begun to come alive with the sound of night animals, the shouts of the howler monkeys, the click and croak of insects of all kinds. The smell of smoke from a distant cooking fire, or perhaps a residual odor from slash-and-burn farming, tainted the air.

Nina had rolled down her window a few inches.

"Better close it," Shaw advised. "The insects are waking up."

Nina reached for the handle to roll it up when she froze, fingers still inches from the handle. Slowly, she turned to Shaw. "Did you hear that?"

# CHAPTER 14

The sound of a small aircraft engine thrummed in the moist air. He craned his neck until it cracked, pinpointing the plane's location somewhere behind them. At the moment, the road they traveled crisscrossed an area between the trees. The break in the canopy would make them easy to spot by a determined pilot.

And Escorpion was determined.

Shaw pushed down the accelerator, urging the vehicle forward faster than was safe on the soggy road. "Going to get to the trees, or they'll spot us."

The tires skidded on the slick ground, protesting as they crept closer to the sheltering grove, the plane seemingly keeping pace.

"Is it Escorpion's?" Shaw asked through gritted teeth.

Nina rolled down the window and stuck her head out, heedless of the rain. "I can't see yet. I think it's small."

Shaw found himself angled forward in the seat, willing the heavy truck to cross the open ground and make it to the tangle of trees some fifty yards away.

"It's beige," she said as she pulled back into the truck. "Yes, I think it's him."

Her face had gone slack with fear, and he risked a moment to grip her fingers, still sticky from the candy she'd been enjoying a moment before. "We're almost there."

He depressed the gas pedal until it hit the floorboard, and the truck shot forward, bouncing and jostling like a wild horse until they careened across the gap and into the canopy beyond. The overgrown branches smacked against the sides. He pressed on for another few yards until the greenery closed around them, virtually swallowing them from sight.

Heart beating fast, he grabbed a pair of binoculars from under the seat and climbed out. The waning sunlight helped him to make out the plane. It was indeed the same one he'd encountered on the landing strip. The question was, had they been spotted?

Nina appeared next to him, followed by Axel who sniffed around, unperturbed by the rain and their sudden stop. They stared at the sky as the plane crept by, daringly low.

"If he circles around again, we'll know he saw us," Shaw said.

"But there's no place for him to land anyway," Nina said. "How would he get to us?"

"He can radio his people down here."

Shaw continued to watch the plane, which seemed to move in slow motion, wings cutting through the dusk, the engine causing the leaves around them to vibrate.

Inch by inch, the plane eased by and Shaw allowed himself to exhale.

Nina sagged against the side of the truck. "That was close."

He didn't answer. Now that the threat had passed for the moment, he realized his boots were nearly stuck to the ground. Dread in his gut, he took a look at the tires and confirmed the suspicion that they had sunk several inches into the ooze.

He groaned and jumped in, starting the engine and easing onto the gas. The wheels spun, spattering mud behind him and earning him a glare from Axel and Nina. He slammed the truck into reverse and tried to back out of the mud.

It didn't move and he quit trying immediately to prevent the wheels from driving themselves in any deeper.

He slapped a hand on the steering wheel as Nina came around to the driver's side door.

"Stuck?"

"Like a fly on tar paper."

She frowned. "My dad always carried kitty litter and some planks around for traction."

Shaw got out and moved past her. "This isn't a mud puddle. It's more like a swamp, so I don't think your father's kitty litter would work anyway." He unsheathed his knife and began to cut small twigs from the overhanging branches. Nina used her hands to snap off more until they had a sizable pile.

She worked right alongside him there in the muck, shoving the branches as much as she could underneath the rear tires. Petite as she was, Nina Truman didn't shy away from physical labor, nor did she seem to mind a thick layer of mud all the way up to her knees. She examined the branches carefully before she broke them. "Just making sure there are no snakes around. I don't like snakes," she explained.

When she finished her tire, she looked up at him, rain-slicked hair stuck to her face. "What do you think?"

He had to admit, she'd done well. "Let's see. Stay away so you don't get hit by debris, and keep Axel out of the line of fire if you can."

"Of course I can," she said, taking the packet of dried fish from her pocket and waving it at him with a crooked grin. Axel trotted away with her to a safe distance.

He started the engine and hit the gas. The wheels spun and rocks and twigs flew out from under the chassis with poor results.

Nina signaled him to cut the engine and she began patiently harvesting more branches. He joined in and they'd collected enough to try it again. The sky had grown dark, stars appearing between patches of clouds, and the rain temporarily slackened.

Nina drew Axel away again and Shaw started it up. For a moment, they accomplished nothing besides flinging debris in every direction until the truck gave a sudden lurch and jerked free.

He saw out the rearview that Nina was doing some sort of ridiculous victory dance; either that or she was having a seizure.

No, the smile on her face marked it a celebratory dance. It was sort of a cross between a John Travolta move and a ballet twirl. All Shaw could do was chuckle at the crazy woman who ended her jig with a pat for Axel before she joined Shaw in the truck again.

* * *

Nina gathered her soaked hair into a loose ponytail and tried to keep it from dripping down her back. It didn't really matter much since she was crammed into the truck next to a sopping wet dog and an extremely muddy man. She sent up another thank-you to God for extricating them.

The little cell phone screen still indicated no messages had come in from either the embassy or her father, which dampened her spirit, but she resolved to call again when she dried off a little. She didn't want to chance ruining the phone by dripping into it.

Shaw reached over the backseat, leaning close to her face as he did so. Her stomach jumped as his mouth came close to hers.

*Your nerves are on edge, Nina.* She scooted a smidge farther toward the door as he swung around again with a towel and handed it to her. She pressed the dry cloth to her face, blotting her hair as best she could. "Do you always travel this well prepared?"

He settled back into his seat, beads of water glistening on his close-shaven hair. "I would have done better if I'd known how things were going to turn out." He listened out the window. "I don't hear the plane. Wish we could keep moving just in case."

The road ahead stretched into the darkness, crowded by poinsettia bushes and plumeria. Whining mosquitos hovered in clouds, so he hastily rolled the window shut.

"Can you drive safely in the dark?"

"No," he said flatly. "But if we stay here and the pilot did radio to the ground, we're sitting ducks." His eyes darted in thought. "I'm going to check the path. Be right back."

Nina dried her hands and tried her father's cell phone again. Ring after ring accomplished nothing except racheting up her anxiety. There had to be a reason, a logical story to explain the strange tone in his voice, and she hoped she might laugh about it later. Forcing in a breath, she clasped her hands together and prayed for her father and for Shaw, and she lifted the deluge of worry and fear up to Him. When she opened her eyes again, she saw Shaw standing outside the car, staring at her.

When he got in, he wiped his neck with his palm. "Mosquitos."

"Why didn't you just get in?"

He shrugged. "You were praying."

She nodded. "I thought you didn't hold much stock in that."

"I don't," he growled, slamming the door. "But it means something to you. Road is tolerable for the next half mile or so, then I'll have to use the machete."

Shaw drove slowly, so slowly it seemed as though they weren't even moving. The scenery didn't change; thick branches, low-lying shrubbery, an occasional break in the vegetation that allowed them to see the sky and the sliver of a luminous moon. The bumpy path rose and fell in irregular fits and starts.

It would have been romantic, Nina thought, if you read it in a novel. Pushing through a tropical jungle with a handsome man.

*Handsome?*

Her own thought surprised her. Not in the traditional way of movie actors and models, but there was something appealing in the strong lines of Shaw's face and full mouth, even though usually fixed in a scowl.

The flicker of a memory tickled the back of her brain. She recalled thinking Shaw handsome once before, years ago, when she'd visited the States and Beth introduced them. They'd all been riding together in a car, and the light outside the window had shrouded him in a soft yellow glow. His blue-gray eyes had flickered with amusement—mixed with something else besides—when he caught her staring at him, and he'd smiled at her.

But this was definitely not a joyride, considering she couldn't get in touch with her father and some very bad people sought to catch up to them. It seemed like an eternity ago that the soldier stood on that grassy knoll and strafed the bus with bullets, killing poor Juan Carlton, and who knew how many others?

This was not a game or an adventure, and she knew a deadly outcome hovered on the horizon, for both her and Shaw. She let that thought sink in for a moment. As a missionary, she'd assumed certain risks, knowing God had the little clinic in His hands, but what about Shaw? He had some mysterious mission of his own involving Escorpion, but it certainly hadn't included signing on with a woman who seemed to have a giant target printed on her back, and certainly not with someone he blamed for Beth's death.

Shaw remained focused on easing the truck through the green maze, and he didn't seem to notice her stare. She wanted to stop him and say again how much she'd loved Beth and how sorry she was that she'd urged her to stay for another few months. If she hadn't . . . if Beth had left . . . how would Shaw's life be different now?

The truck took a bounce that tossed her against his hard shoulder and caused Axel to slip to the floor.

"What . . . ?" she started, but Shaw had already flown out of the truck to survey the damage. She joined him, eyeing the rapidly deflating tire.

"Must have hit a rock," Shaw said. "Tires were worn to begin with." He huffed with aggravation. "There's not enough room here for me to put the spare on. Get in," he said. "I'll push it toward that clearing."

"I've got a better idea," Nina said, following him around to the rear. "I'll help you push."

His look said he clearly didn't have much esteem for her strength, which made her all the more determined to show him. Missionary work wasn't for wimps and she'd done her share of maneuvering supplies and patients who outweighed her by a hundred pounds.

They pushed and heaved until the truck rolled free, and Nina assumed the role of alternately pushing and then hopping in to steer.

It was an awkward process, but the exertion did serve to warm her. It also served to allow the hordes of circling mosquitos to access the flesh of her neck and arms. She resisted the urge to swat at them, instead working alongside Shaw until they got the truck free of the trees. The clearing ahead ended abruptly, tapering steeply into a gorge spanned by a wooden bridge stretching in either direction for some distance. Quickly moving water filled it, maybe a mile across.

She could hear the water rushing below and the scuttle of creatures, rats perhaps, that traversed the rocks. Her disorientation grew, and she wondered if it was an offshoot of the Usumacinta, or the river itself. The bridge, though narrow, seemed a pretty good sign to Nina. Bridges meant people, and surely a village in the Petén might provide some help for them.

One more push and the truck crunched neatly onto a relatively flat area. Nina wiped her hands in satisfaction.

Shaw's mouth quirked in what she deciphered as a smile, though perhaps it was a trick of the moonlight.

"Good team effort. Thank you."

She smiled and flexed her biceps. "They don't call me Muscles for nothing."

He grabbed a toolbox from the trunk. "I'll bet they don't call you Muscles at all."

She laughed and held the toolbox while he squatted down with the lug wrench. "You're right, but I've helped Dad fix plenty of flats."

"Yeah?" Shaw said as he unscrewed the lug nuts. "And I thought missionaries spent all their time praying."

"You can pray and change a lug nut at the same time, you know," she said. "You'd be surprised at all the things I've tried my hand at while we've been in the jungle."

"Could have done things back home, too," he said, attention fixed on removing the tire. "Beth said you wanted to go to med school at one point."

Nina waved away mosquitos with her free hand. "That was just daydreaming."

"Why?"

She blinked. "Why what?"

He stared at her now, wrench suspended in midair. "Why is it daydreaming? Why didn't you stay in the States and go to med school?"

"I serve with my father here. It's what God called me to do."

"Is it? Or is it what God called your father to do, and you're being the good daughter."

She frowned. "I'm serving out of obedience."

"To God or *El Monte?*"

Her stomach tightened. "My father never forced me to do anything. I was called to serve here."

He rolled the flat away and placed on the spare. "You know what? I don't have much regard for this God-called-me business."

"That's not a surprise," she said, unable to keep the edge out of her voice.

He didn't seem to hear. "My mother said she was following a call too, some God directive that drew her to that border town in Mexico where she got beaten until she was brain-dead. How exactly was that furthering the kingdom?" His eyes were riveted to her face now, as if he could find the answer to his suffering there. "Maybe she just made up that call in her mind because she wanted to be needed, to feel like she was changing the world." His volume dropped a notch. "Could be we didn't make her feel that way at home. Took her for granted, so she made up this calling to fill the void."

"Your mother helped many people." Nina considered her words very carefully, trying to filter out the anger his comments had awakened in her. "She was doing what God meant her to do."

Shaw stood so still he could have turned to stone, oblivious to the bugs that swarmed around him and the explorations of Axel sniffing around the rocks at the edge of the gorge.

"Maybe He meant you to go to med school, but you're too afraid to leave the safety of your jungle home." The sarcasm-rich tone didn't escape Nina's notice.

"Safety?" she squeaked. "It's a real safe place, all right."

"You stay here so you don't have to face med school because you might fail, right? Or disappoint your father by leaving him?"

She dropped the toolbox to the ground. "You don't know what you're talking about, and I really don't think this is the time for you to pick apart my life."

"What better time than this?" he said gesturing with the wrench. "We're being tracked by killers and eaten alive by mosquitos for some perfect, God-inspired reason aren't we?" His volume edged up a notch. "Because you're following that divine instruction from heaven that told you to come to this picturesque spot and encourage my sister to come, too. What better time to talk about it?"

*And now we come to the heart of it,* she thought. Shaw wanted God's accountability for his mother's tragedy and his sister's death.

"You don't want to talk about my life or the decisions I've made," she pressed. "What you really want is for God to explain Himself to you, isn't it?"

Shaw's mouth opened, but he didn't answer.

*To ease the terrible suffering you feel and tell you you're not alone.*

She looked at him full-on through the anger and the tough-guy persona, straight down into the essence of a man in pain, a man who blamed, and who—though she didn't fully understand why—was beginning to tunnel his way past her defenses and into her heart. She willed herself to speak the right words. "Shaw, please listen to me."

His eyes caught the moonlight, shining like melted silver before they abruptly rounded in shock as a Jeep pulled into the clearing.

# CHAPTER 15

Shaw flung the tools into the truck bed as Nina and Axel barreled into the cab. He gunned the engine and took off toward the little bridge. It looked sturdy enough and with the Jeep only fifty yards away, they had no other choice.

*Head for the jungle, lose yourself, hunker down and wait for your moment.*

They left the tense and painful conversation behind as they shot through the darkness toward the bridge.

"Do you recognize the driver?" he yelled to Nina who peered behind her, hands gripping the back of the seat.

"It's the two men from the airstrip."

"Escorpion's guys."

He heard her breath catch just before something pinged into the body of the truck.

"They're shooting," Nina cried.

"Get down." He put a hand on top of her head and shoved her to the seat. Bullets rattled against the sides. "They're trying to take out the tires." It wouldn't be hard at that distance.

A stray shot shattered the back window and glass exploded through the cab. He ground his teeth. If their job was to take Nina alive, they were going about it the wrong way. The pursuers must have realized the same thing because the shooting stopped.

Instead, the Jeep sped up, flying over the rocky ground to close the gap.

Shaw pressed the gas as much as he dared, the tires already losing traction now and again on the wet grass.

Though he kept the pedal nearly to the floor, the Jeep was lighter and easier to handle, and it inched closer and closer. The bridge beckoned from only a few yards away ahead. He wondered if the old wooden structure would support the onslaught of his truck. No time to second-guess it. The shooting had started up again, this time in single shots, from a pistol of some sort, more precisely aimed from the passenger in the Jeep.

The bridge shuddered as they skidded onto it, wood planks wobbling under the tires. The glimmering black water surged in dark swirling eddies beneath them, and the creaking and groaning under the tires inspired Shaw to clench the wheel tighter in expectation of plummeting into the depths below. Miraculously, the wood held.

One thing. One tiny thing had gone right.

He monitored the rearview mirror in sharp, quick intervals. The Jeep followed behind them, taking on the rickety bridge. The passenger leaned out the window, a gun in his hand.

Shaw had always thought the slow motion bits in movies were ridiculous, but it seemed that the next few moments unfolded in some strange sort of distorted time sequence. The shooter aimed and squeezed off a shot. Did he feel a pop or was it his imagination? Though he heard no explosion over the rattle of the bridge and Axel's barking, the bullet must have found its mark because the truck began to shimmy out of his control.

"Tire's gone," he shouted to Nina, who clutched Axel around the neck.

The truck bucked toward the railing, a frail affair, no more than a series of thick poles nailed on upright beams. Still, in the grip of that odd, diluted sense of time, Shaw fought the steering wheel to no avail. The crack of breaking wood preceded the crash through the railing, and the truck plunged over the side.

Shaw grew dizzy as the truck tumbled once, then twice before ripping into the water below with an impact that shoved the breath out of him. Forcing his mind to ignore his addled senses, he realized the truck had come to rest on the driver's side and the swift water eased it along downstream. Moments later, he was nearly underwater and the cab filled rapidly. Nina already fought to roll her window down as a means of escape, but the undulating water resisted her efforts. When she finally got it down far enough, she shoved Axel out through the window. The dog let out a pitiful whine as he splashed into the water. Axel had never been fond of swimming, but he was competent at least.

Nina looked at Shaw. "Will they shoot us?" she asked him, her voice tight with fear.

He felt suddenly sorry that he had added to her discomfort by goading her earlier. "I think they want us alive," he said, keeping his chin above the waterline. "Make for shore when you can." He reached out a hand to hers and gripped her fingers tightly.

He wanted to say he was sorry.

He wanted to take back the harsh words and the blame he'd heaped on her.

Instead, he said nothing more. He only squeezed her fingers once again before she grabbed her pack, ducked through the window and swam away.

He'd forgotten she was a strong swimmer, a fact he had learned after joining her and Beth on a family outing when Beth returned to the States on her last furlough. He had a flash of memory . . . Nina, her wet hair dark like velvet, her arms both strong and yet somehow graceful as she cut through the water, swimming faster than his bulky form would allow. His recollection spiraled into the feel of her hair in his hands when he'd cut her loose from the bus, like silk against his fingertips.

The slap of cold water brought him back to the present, and he grabbed his duffel before it floated out the window with the current. He snatched up his cell phone, quickly thrusting it into a plastic bag from the glove box, hoping the moisture hadn't already ruined it. Then, with only a small pang of grief at losing the bruiser of a truck that he'd actually named, though he would never admit it under threat of torture, he squeezed through the passenger window.

* * *

Nina swallowed only a few mouthfuls of water as she pulled herself through the water, her sodden backpack fighting her efforts. She saw the lights of the Jeep and heard the shouts of the two men standing on the bridge, the beams of their flashlights dancing across the water and playing over the surface of the truck which had now turned completely upside down, wheels pointing toward the dark, clouded sky.

Her pulse kicked up, wondering if Shaw had gotten out.

*He's strong,* she reminded herself. *And determined.*

She followed Axel's frantic paddling as he made his way toward the bank. She fought through the overhang of low branches, and something thudded against her leg. She immediately went still.

*A snake. A water snake. Circling. Ready to sink its fangs into* . . . Panic surged upward from her ankles to her mouth, a scream building. She clenched her jaws so tightly that her teeth ached. A scream would tell the men on the bridge exactly where they were.

She couldn't breathe through the thick fear.

Something flickered past her arm. She pulled back sharply as a wooden branch floated by.

It's a stick. Just a stick.

But was the snake still down there somewhere? Waiting to strike?

Axel had made his awkward way to shore. He shook out his fur and stood waiting for them to join him. She had to move, had to swim, or the current would carry her too far downstream, to where the water widened into a vast expanse.

But the snake . . .

They could sense movement . . . fear. She'd learned that early on.

It was waiting. Nina could feel it.

Axel stood, staring at her as if he felt the presence of the thing that circled in the water.

Another thump against her legs, and Nina opened her mouth to scream, her shriek cut off abruptly by a hand over her mouth.

Shaw kept his hand there, his face close enough that she could see the water droplets that spangled his thick lashes.

"What's wrong?" He slowly peeled away his hand.

"There's a snake," she managed, tears rolling down her face and mingling with the river water.

He shook his head, voice low. "There are no water snakes here, just fish."

"I felt it." Terror made her voice break.

He put both hands on either side of her face, his fingers pressed to the curve of her cheeks. "Listen. There are *no* water snakes here." She clasped her hands over his, holding the comfort close, her fear ebbing slightly.

He must have felt the trembling in her hands. His arms went around her and he pressed her body to his, as if daring the river to threaten her. She touched her cheek to his neck and stayed there against the strong pulsing of his heart, letting him tread water to keep them both afloat.

*No water snakes.* But how did he know? Was he feigning a wildlife expertise to calm her down?

"Are you sure?" she said. "What if you're wrong?"

He cleared his throat. "I'm not," he said, letting her go and glancing back toward the bridge. "They'll figure out we're not in there soon," he said. "Gotta move."

He grabbed her arm and began towing her to shore. It was a cumbersome process, not to mention humiliating, to be dragged along like an errant child. She felt her panic subside somewhat in the face of her pride, and she extricated herself from his grasp and swam on her own toward shore. Just a moment of panic, now passed, a moment of intimacy with Shaw that made her feel like she'd come up for air too quickly. She took a breath and kept on swimming.

They emerged dripping and breathless on the bank, receiving a thorough sniffing from Axel. Nina tried to wring some of the water out of her clothes and hair while Shaw did the same. He took a plastic bag from where he'd tucked in his belt and held it to the moonlight. He groaned. "Bag had a hole. Phone got soaked. Doesn't work now but maybe when it dries."

She groaned. *No phone?* Add it to the list. No shelter, no vehicle, not much food and no clear idea where they were. How would the embassy ever find them? How would she get to her father?

*Enough of that*. She and Shaw and Axel were alive and unharmed. *Thank You, Lord*.

"We should follow the river north. That will take us toward Otto," Shaw said with a confidence that soothed her somehow. "Maybe we can find a town along the way, some sort of shelter for the night."

He turned to go and she caught his arm. She saw none of the tenderness she thought she'd detected in him when he held her in the water. She supposed her strange thoughts were born of her need for comfort.

"Wait, I've got to catch my breath."

"I wouldn't advise it," he said. "There aren't any water snakes, but there are plenty of crocodiles."

She didn't give him the reaction he wanted. "I'm not afraid of crocodiles, just snakes."

He didn't exactly smile, but his features softened. "Okay. I'll let you know if I see any."

Suppressing a shiver, she followed. She wanted to stop him, to look into his face and find out the truth of Shaw Wilder. Was he the tender man who held her safe in the water? Or the hardened soul who would always blame her for Beth and believed she hid out in the jungle as a coward, to escape the uncertainties of the outside world.

Her skin chilled rapidly as they clambered over the exposed roots. He was wrong. God had called her here, to serve alongside her father, to minister to the needs of the people there.

A tiny doubt niggled at her.

*Maybe He meant you to go to med school.*

Her time in Guatemala had been God-guided, God-blessed. She'd always known it, and she believed it to her core.

But why did she feel the occasional magnetic pull of a different way, as if He called her to do something else? The few times she'd tried to talk it over with her father, he'd avoided the conversation and grown suddenly busy.

She slapped uselessly at the curtain of mosquitos that enveloped her, trying to concentrate on the chirping of the crickets and the soft whoosh of the water to take her mind off the troubling thoughts.

She wondered again why her father had lied. All those years, he'd told her she had been adopted from an orphanage in Mexico . . . until she found a paper only a week earlier indicating an unnamed baby girl with the odd birthmark on her lower back. Born in Guatemala. Nina's birthmark, a bluish flower-shaped patch called a Mongolian birthmark, had disappeared by the time she reached her teen years, but she had no doubt about the baby girl described on the paper. It was her. She saw the truth in her father's eyes when she confronted him.

"Why didn't you tell me, Daddy?"

He'd looked at her gravely, calmly. "I didn't know until recently."

"Why didn't you tell me right away when you found out? I asked you what was wrong and you kept telling me nothing at all."

"We'll go back home. I'll tell you the story. Now is not the time."

And that was that. No amount of urging or pleading on her part had moved him from his decision to delay the conversation until their return to the States. The topic had all but faded from her mind in light of the slew of traumas she'd experienced since the bus crash.

They stumbled on for another hour, listening to the croak of frogs and the grunts of the monkeys traversing the jungle canopy above them. Several times, Shaw pulled her to a stop and they listened for the pursuers, but Nina heard nothing outside of the slam of her own heart into her ribs.

She guessed it had reached and passed midnight. Her watch no longer worked after the swim, and a peculiar emotion kept her from asking Shaw. True, he'd kept her alive; but he'd also awakened in her a mixture of feelings that she couldn't manage to decipher.

*Just keep on going.*

The longer they escaped capture, the better chance of the embassy dispatching soldiers to retrieve them.

She stumbled over a knobby root for what seemed like the hundredth time, adding a new tear to her already tattered jeans. Her legs ached, along with her knee and some assorted muscles; injuries attributed to any one of her misadventures, from the bus crash to the truck going off the bridge, or maybe even enduring those seemingly endless hours trying to free her hands while kept prisoner in the Jeep.

She still couldn't quite believe all that had happened. And the irony of her traveling companion bit at her, too. Shaw was the last person she would have imagined helping her, and definitely the last person to volunteer for the job.

Shaw stopped again. She thought he was listening, but this time he ducked down and peered at something, Axel instantly on alert at his side.

"We need rest. Let's hide in here for a while."

She followed his gaze and saw the dark maw of a cave, nearly concealed by the tangle of growth. Her breath caught. Caves were considered sacred to the ancient Mayan people who had built the massive structures like those at Tikal and Xultan, drawing tourists from all over the world. Ancient Mayans and some modern-day ancestors believed them to be portals between the visible and invisible worlds, the birthplace of the sun and the moon, suitable locations for ceremony and, in ages past, the ideal spot for sacrifices. Nina didn't hold with such teachings, but she still respected the people she served and she didn't want to trespass on their sacred spots.

"Shaw . . ." she started, but he had already begun shoving aside the curtain of greenery.

"Axel and I will check it out."

She stood outside, shivering, trying not to scratch at the new welt of bug bites that trailed across the back of her neck. Every flutter of movement, each crack of branches made her jump. Adding salt to her fresh wounds, it had begun to rain again.

She had to laugh. "No rainbows without the rain," Juan Carlos had told her many times. A slice of pain rippled through her as she thought about her gentle helper. He always had a smile, even in the worst of times. Rather than cower from the downpour, she tipped her face up to the sky and thanked God for keeping her safe. Not comfortable, not with an easy spirit, but alive for the moment.

"It's okay," Shaw called, his sudden appearance in the cave mouth startling her. "It's not the Hilton, but it will do for a while."

She took his hand and he led her into the darkness. When her eyes finally adjusted, she saw two glowing spots of blue.

"I had a couple of light sticks in my pack. They'll only last for six hours or so, but we're far enough back that no one would see it even if they did figure out there's a cave here."

The surprisingly bright lights helped her to discern the oblong chamber with a low ceiling that caused Shaw to stoop, but her shorter frame had no trouble. Massive boulders rested in piles throughout the space like marbles dropped by a giant's hand. Stalactites dripped from above, the moisture trickling off their delicate spires into a river that bisected the cave, running swiftly and silently. To her relief, she saw no sign of cave paintings or ceremonial offerings to indicate the place had been used for any ritual purposes. She found the flattest rock she could locate, sinking down to it with a sigh.

Shaw moved around the cave, shining one of the light sticks into the narrow corridor that led away to the rear. “Cool air coming from back here. There must be an exit of sorts.” He let the light trail over the ground. “A little guano, too, but not enough to ruin the air quality. I think they roost somewhere deeper in the tunnels. The bats must be out catching their share of mosquitos.”

“Good for them,” Nina said. “I hope they devour millions of those rotten things.”

Fatigue roared through her with such force that she didn’t care if there were bats—or even bears—in the cave. She might be too tired even to care about a snake, though she didn’t want to test the theory.

She stripped off her shoes and set them on the rock next to her, rubbing the chafed and blistered skin, willing some warmth into her frozen toes. What a relief to simply sit down.

When she looked up from her feeble efforts, Shaw was gone.

# CHAPTER 16

Shaw weighed the options, snaking his way between the narrow walls of the passage at the rear of the cavern. It was raining; pouring, as a matter of fact. He heard the roar of the storm even through the rock walls. The breeze trickling by his face told him the air would drift back and away from the mouth of the cave.

Another factor: Hunger. He was starving, Axel was too, and he had no doubt Nina—though she'd proven far stronger than he'd credited her—was ravenous as well. They still had a long trek ahead of them to make it to Otto's, at least four to six hours, and a packet of nuts—probably crushed in the bottom of his bag—provided the only provision for them both.

He made up his mind; uneasy, knowing his decision could mean the end for both of them. It rankled him. When had he signed on to hold someone's life in his hand? When had she become his problem? Still, he didn't like the feeling that he'd only barely kept her from being captured. The airstrip . . . and now the river. He wasn't winning this battle for Nina's life against Escorpion. He pressed a fist to the damp rock.

"If You care about your missionary girl," he muttered, "maybe You could give us a hand here."

"He cares about you, too."

His head snapped toward her. "I didn't know you followed me."

"Didn't want you to get eaten by a bear."

“There are no—” he caught the smile on her face. “Right. Well, anyway, I’m going to cook us some dinner.”

Her eyes widened and she looked all of ten years old. “You have food?” Her face fell. “My candy got ruined. All those wonderful milk legs.”

He could hardly resist her mournful expression, and he wrapped an arm around her shoulders. “It’s okay. We’ll get you more candy soon. How do you feel about seafood?”

She sucked in a breath. “I’ll eat anything that doesn’t crawl off my plate.”

“No guarantees, but I’ll try.” He led her back to the front cavern and set her to work gathering up anything from the debris that littered the floor that looked dry enough to burn. Meanwhile, he fished the small metal bowl from his pack, the one he carried for Axel’s water. “Sorry, dog. I’ll get you another one when we get back.” He dumped the small bag of kibble on a stone and Axel gobbled it up in seconds.

The dog then lapped the river water contentedly, leaving Shaw hoping he wouldn’t ingest any of the parasites that made drinking Guatemalan water a risky venture. When Nina handed over the dry bits she’d collected, he put them on the cave floor toward the back of the cavern and extracted a match from the waterproof package in his pack. The first one didn’t light, but the second did, and soon he had a tiny fire going. He carefully placed three stones the size of softballs atop the flames.

“Can you keep this fire going?”

She nodded. “Are you going to the grocery store?” she teased.

He gave her a smirk and returned to the edge of the river. Belly down, he peered into the water which flowed over small piles of smooth, flat rocks. Scooping quickly, he caught his prey, two crawfish. Moving farther downstream, he snagged four more, and then added another ten. They were fine and fat, legs moving in every direction. He wrapped them in one wriggling mass inside a soggy bandana, filled the metal bowl with water and set it onto the stones.

It didn't take long for the water to boil. The fire blackened the bowl and licked up the sides as he dumped in the crawfish. "Could use some potatoes, onions, and maybe some corn on the cob, but we'll have to make do." Nina stared at him with open admiration, and it pleased him; although he tried not to show it.

"That's totally ingenious."

He shrugged. "As long as the smoke doesn't give us away. In that case, it was just a stupid idea."

She brought her shoes over and laid them as close as she could to the flames.

He shook his head. "They're just going to get soaked again, you know."

"I know, but a few minutes of dry will keep my spirits lifted for a long time."

Again her optimism made no sense, but it was so enticing nonetheless; like the fragrance of cooking food to a hungry man.

She sat with her knees drawn up, toes close to the flames, yawning widely.

"If you want to sleep, I'll wake you when they're done," he said.

"No, thanks. I want to watch this culinary miracle unfold."

They didn't talk after that, each of them gazing into the fire, lost in their own thoughts.

Shaw wondered why he'd prayed to God for Nina, grumbling request though it was. He didn't believe praying made any difference, certainly not from a black-hearted man consumed by the need for revenge. But the prayer had escaped in an unexpected rolling tide just the same.

Thinking about that mission of retribution made the muscles in his stomach tense. It wasn't complicated; a simple plan for cold, calculated vengeance. The police said his sister's death had been purely accidental. Her car slipped off the road, tumbling into the muddy river that filled her lungs to drowning. But Shaw knew the truth. Beth had died to send a message, forced off the road by another vehicle perhaps, or the tires were shot out. Colonel Fuentes, he'd learned, had been trying to cut in on Escorpion's business, lending his property to the Mexican cartels for transport. Her blood had been spilled to warn Fuentes. Shaw knew it. Otto believed it, too; and so did the locals who dared only whisper about it. Shaw despised Fuentes for allowing his sister to become that helpless pawn, but he wasn't the one who had to be punished.

One way or another, Escorpion would pay for Beth's life with his own. Payback, plain and simple.

He felt Nina's gaze and blinked back to the present.

"What are you thinking about?" she asked.

"Nothing."

"Your expression was so . . . *hard* just then."

She had no idea. Should he tell her that she'd caught him contemplating the best way to murder Escorpion? It would appall her, he had no doubt. And for some reason, he didn't want to see disgust for him in her eyes.

*Why do you care what she thinks, Shaw?*

He didn't know.

In the space of time between the bus crash and their crawfish feast, he had somehow grown to care what Nina Truman thought.

*She was Beth's friend. Of course you'd care.*

He twisted atop the makeshift seat. "I think they're done," he said, wrapping his wet jacket around his hands to take the bowl off the fire. He plunged it quickly into the river water for a moment to cool, then he placed it between them.

Nina paused for a moment before she reached out and took Shaw's hands. Surprised, he didn't pull away. Her fingers felt soft and cool as she said a simple prayer of thanks.

Though he hadn't said grace in years, it seemed to suit the situation. Food had appeared just when they'd needed it most, like Elijah and those ravens.

Strange thoughts.

"Let me show you how to tackle a crawfish," he said. "My

Mama was from Louisiana so I've eaten a few of these before." He twisted off the head and sucked out the juices. Tangy and sharp, the food danced across his starved tongue, in spite of a lack of seasoning.

To his surprise, she grabbed one and did the same, expertly squeezing each section of the crustacean's body to extract every bit of the meat. She grinned at him. "I served with a missionary from Mississippi. I've eaten my share of mudbugs, too."

He laughed loud and long and, for a moment, it felt as though the burden of his anger had lifted, let loose to fly away along with the smoke from their tiny fire. They divided up the pile of crawfish and gave Axel his share. The dog devoured the treats, shell and all. Shaw insisted they each drink the cooled water from the boil. It tasted fishy and some grit floated near the bottom, but it would help to stave off dehydration. They'd save the precious few bottles of water he carried in his pack until they needed it.

Nina flopped back on the cave floor. "That was the best thing I ever ate in my whole entire life," she moaned. "I wish I had a hundred more."

He chuckled and reclined against a rock, watching the firelight dance in a million flickers across her face. "I think the crawfish are on to me now. We'll have to wait if we want more."

She sighed and he allowed himself to relax slightly as well. Safe for the moment . . . fed . . . sheltered from the torrential rain. Killers and revenge could take a back burner, at least for a while. He allowed himself the luxury to savor the sounds and the smell of the river mingled with ancient stones. His eyes closed.

His body screamed for rest, but his brain knew they still faced a man who would not stop until he got what he wanted. Nina. The why was still a mystery.

He opened his eyes to find her watching him, cheek resting on her hand.

"What?"

"Do you still sing?"

He blinked. "Sing what?"

"Barbershop."

His cheeks warmed and he looked away. Singing. How could she remember that? He'd certainly never sung for her. He'd never revealed that nutty talent, had he?

"That was just a lark, in my early days as a cop. The guys needed a baritone."

"Beth showed me a video of you singing. You were really good."

*Great. A video.* His embarrassing past forever preserved on film.

"Oh that was a long time ago."

"How can there be any sin in sincere?" Nina sang in a painfully off-key voice. "I'm terrible, but you sounded wonderful then. You don't sing anymore?"

He shook his head.

"Why not?"

In a fast-moving current, he drowned in memories. He recalled singing for his mother as she sat on the kitchen stool, pitting cherries for his favorite pie.

"Sing my favorite one, Shaw."

He could never resist her request, warbling out a few measures of "Harvest Moon." Barbershop was sweet, simple, easy; so completely removed from real life, especially his life, especially now.

His mother used to love to hear him sing, and yet now she had no idea she even had a son.

Shaw sighed. "I just don't sing anymore."

She sat up, pulling bits of grit from her hair. He tried not to stare as her fingers appeared and reappeared in the lush curtain. He reached over and removed a twig tangled near her temple. His hand lingered there in the soft warmth, grazing the smooth skin of her cheek. Her mouth opened slightly and for a crazy moment, he wondered what it would be like to kiss her.

*You're losing your mind.*

He stood abruptly. "Let's talk about your father."

* * *

Nina still felt the tingle where his fingers had brushed her face, sorry that he'd removed his hand so quickly, curious about the strange sense of loss. His singing, his sweet and tender voice on that video, just didn't jibe with the man she saw now, pacing, shoulders tense.

"What about my father?"

"What was the lie?" Shaw said.

"That's not important. It's private."

"It may have something to do with the people trying to hunt you—us—down. Let's have it."

Reluctantly, eyes on the remnants of the tiny fire, she told him. "They told me all my life that I was adopted in Mexico, but I recently discovered I was born here."

"In the Petén?"

She nodded.

The muscles in his jaw worked as he digested the information. "So you're a Guatemalan."

"Yes, but I don't see how that changes anything."

"It does if you're the daughter of someone powerful. That might explain some things." He started. "Fuentes was married twice, wasn't he?"

Nina shrugged. "At least. He had no children though, except for a girl that died from a fever as a newborn."

"What if he had one that survived and he sent her away for some reason? For safety, or the child was the product of an affair . . ." He looked at her. "Perhaps he didn't want a daughter."

Nina stood then. "This is silly. Guatemalans are very family-centered, and Colonel Fuentes has plenty of money to support a child, even an illegitimate one. Why go to the trouble?"

"I don't know, but if Escorpion figured out you're his daughter, you would be the perfect bargaining chip to get Fuentes to cooperate, turn his back on Escorpion's Mexican competitors."

"If Fuentes gave me away in the first place, why would he care if Escorpion got me or not?"

"He won't want Escorpion to have the power over him."

Her mind reeled. "Who would believe I'm Fuentes' child anyway?"

"Escorpion must have proof of some sort."

She drew as close to the embers as she could, willing some of the warmth into her skin. Her father was not her father? She could be the child of a man she'd known marginally, a thing to be used and exploited in the massive drug war that raged around them like an incurable disease. She'd come to Guatemala to serve God, to help His people. What was happening to her mission? To her life? She hadn't realized she'd begun to shiver until Shaw's arms circled her from behind.

"I'm sorry," he whispered in her ear. "This is a lot for you to take."

She leaned into him, strong against her quivering shoulders. "I don't know who I am," she whispered.

His arms tightened around her waist. "You're Nina Truman. You're the girl who can fix a flat tire and eat crawfish. The girl who craves milk legs."

She started to cry, tears flowing from the well of fear and despair. He turned her around and she pressed her face to his chest, her grief soaking into the fabric of his shirt.

"I want to find my dad. He'll explain everything. He'll always be my dad, won't he?"

"Yes, he will."

Shaw pressed his cheek to the top of her head then and sang in a voice so low it came out as almost a whisper; a song about summer picnics and bicycle rides and the innocent love of a young boy for his girl.

She listened until her flow of tears ceased, savoring the tenderness in his song. Somehow, she found herself tipping her head up to his face, his mouth grazing gently over hers. Tender emotion shot through her body until he pulled away, his face troubled.

"Nina . . ." Her name seemed to catch in his mouth and stop there, imprisoned, until he stepped away and gently released her. "We'd better get some rest. We'll have to get moving before sunrise." He threw some dirt over the fire. "Can't risk letting this burn much longer. It will be cold, but there's nothing we can do about that."

She watched as he bustled around rinsing out the bowl and returning it to his pack.

What had happened? What could explain the wild beating in her heart? The need she felt to comfort him, to hear him sing those silly songs again? The desire to kiss him?

She could find no answers as the fire went out with a hiss.

# CHAPTER 17

Nina had grown accustomed to sleeping in a variety of conditions; wrapped in mosquito netting, on the floor of a host church, in the backseat of various dilapidated vehicles. She found that her current situation prohibited much sleep, even though her body hummed with fatigue. As she lay on the cold ground, the moisture seeping into her clothes and Axel curled up against her back, the cave seemed to come alive, echoing the sound of the monkeys outside. The endless drip of water from the stalactites reverberated throughout the cavern. Part of her remained on a state of alert, listening for the sounds of the two men from the Jeep. They had not given up, she knew it deep within her.

Grateful that Axel provided a warm spot on her back, she wondered if Shaw had fallen asleep on the spot he'd chosen atop two flat rocks. Come to think about it, she wondered a lot of things about Shaw Wilder.

Beth had idolized her brother, but she wasn't blind to his faults.

"He's the guy who will cut off his own arm before he asks for help, but he's also the guy who will climb a mountain for a friend in trouble."

They hadn't encountered any mountains yet, but Shaw had already endured everything from gunfire to a chilly night in a jungle cave for her. Why? Because she was Beth's friend.

The timbre of his singing thrilled through her again, threaded with such tenderness. Her mind relived the feel of his arms around her; comforting, strong and solid. She curled into a tighter ball, shivering now. The situation that unnerved her, she decided. Nothing to do with Shaw Wilder.

She determinedly closed her eyes and willed herself to relax.

Moments later, Axel stiffened and jerked upright. She heard it, too; the crush of hundreds—No! More like millions—of wings. The light sticks were enough to illuminate only a roiling cloak of darkness that clogged the mouth of the cave, sweeping in like a thick cloud of smoke.

* * *

Shaw leapt from his makeshift cot and grabbed Nina's shoulder, holding her down to the floor with one hand and keeping the wildly barking Axel still with the other hand clutching his collar.

"Bats, coming home," he called in her ear.

He caught only blurred glimpses of the animals; grayish-brown fur, paler undersides, pointed ears. They appeared only about three inches across, but they were mighty in number. Whirling and jerking, the cacophony of noise and movement enveloped them. He supposed he should have been worried, but he found himself awed instead by the swirl of life that filled every corner of the cave. The bats chittered and danced, pouring in a constant tide over their heads, funneling into the back of the cave. In a few moments, the last of them had disappeared to darker recesses, leaving an eerie silence in their wake.

Shaw forced Axel into a *stay* to deter him from pursuing the departing bats.

Nina sat up. "That was incredible."

Shaw brushed off his hands and stood. "Yeah, and I'd say that's as good an indication as any that it's nearly sunup. We have to move." He pulled out the phone. "Not working, but that could be the cave walls. We'll try again later."

He tried to stretch out the stiffness from his hard night on the rocks. Several new sore spots had developed and his clothes were damp, prickling his skin with goose bumps that had to fight for space with the spattering of mosquito bites. At least there was no rain as they stepped from the cave into the predawn air. Unsettling feelings from the night before lingered in his heart. No time to think about that.

The air felt thick with humidity, the sun nowhere yet to be seen. Fortunately, the mosquitos hadn't awoken to begin their hunt for blood. Shaw listened and checked carefully before he set off toward the riverbank.

"Won't they be looking for us there?" Nina asked.

"We'll stay back somewhat, but that's the only way I'll be able to tell which way we're traveling, unless you happen to have a compass on you."

She shook her head. "No, and I have no sense of direction at all."

Shaw smiled. "Yep, Beth mentioned she'd had to come find you when you got lost at the mall back home."

"Malls are ridiculous." Nina sighed. "Who can tell one store from another? I can't imagine why anyone would need so many in the first place."

"Me neither," Shaw said, his stomach growling. The crawfish dinner hadn't stuck with him to the morning. He fished a battered package of nuts out of his pocket and shared it with Nina.

She took them with a smile and wolfed them down, pulling a packet from her own bag. "Look, Axel. At least your dried fish survived."

Axel accepted the gift with a vigorous tail wag, and they went on their way. When they'd hiked for a good half hour, he pulled out the cell phone and tried to dial. Nothing. Not even a flicker of light or an encouraging beep.

He tried to force his face into an encouraging expression. "It's okay. We can't be more than half a day from Otto's plantation. We can call the embassy from there."

He could tell by the crestfallen look on her face that she'd been hoping to speak to her father.

The sun touched the tops of the trees. It awakened both cautious optimism and new anxiety in Shaw. They'd survived the night unscathed except for the loss of his truck and phone, but the daylight would make them easy targets, two white strangers covered with grime, trekking through the jungle. They worked their way parallel to the river until they came to something that passed for a road; or at the least, a trail.

Another decision to make. He saw that Nina was already contemplating.

"The closer we get to town, the more likely someone might have a phone we could use," she commented.

"Or they might have already been instructed by Escorpion's men to capture us."

"I think we should go see if anyone can help."

"And I think we should continue on to Otto's."

Nina sighed. "How about a compromise? We'll head that way for fifteen minutes and check it out. If it looks unsafe, we turn around."

Shaw stared up the road. Fifteen minutes? He supposed it wouldn't be the end of the world.

*I hope.*

They walked through the dense foliage, avoiding the pockets of thick mud as best they could. Axel took time to bark at a plump tinamou that poked its beak among the fallen leaves in search of edible morsels. Shaw imaged that Axel pondered the same thing he did; how would such a bird taste roasted? Shaw swallowed hard and kept moving.

Nina, he noticed, kept to the middle of the road, no doubt to avoid the potential of a snake encounter. They moved quickly, slowed only when a coatimundi, a large raccoon-like mammal, skittered halfway up a tree and glared at a surprised Axel.

"Not worth it, buddy," Shaw advised. "They probably taste like squirrel."

The coatimundi reeled and, with a swish of his long tail,

disappeared back up into the tree.

Turning a corner, they found themselves facing a small house made of neatly bundled stick walls and a luxuriously thatched roof.

Nina pointed excitedly to a small rectangular box on a pole. "See? Photovoltaic panel. They've got electricity."

She hurried forward just as three children emerged with a scuffed soccer ball. The two boys wore tee shirts and baggy shorts, and the girl's skirt nearly swept the ground. All three had thick black hair and glossy dark skin.

Nina smiled. "Hello," she said.

The children didn't respond, so she switched to another language Shaw guessed was Kek'chi, and then she moved on to Spanish.

The little girl smiled and took a step toward them, fingering her thick braids.

A heavyset woman emerged from the house, hollering something neither of them could decipher. It didn't matter; the universal sign of maternal distress was unmistakable. A small man barreled across the threshold with a machete in his hands and fury on his face.

Nina backed up, hands raised until she landed next to Shaw.

"What did you say to them?" he whispered.

"Just hello, but I forgot about the rumors."

"What rumors?"

The man waving the machete barked something at the children, and they all ran back into the house and closed the door.

"There were rumors that foreigners were kidnapping Guatemalan children and taking them to the States. They're very sensitive about people approaching their children."

"So I see," Shaw groused. "Should we back away and get out of here?"

Nina didn't answer. In another one of her illogical moments, she stepped forward and smiled. "*Misionero. Enfermera.*"

The man with the machete cocked his head a bit, eyeing Nina

closely before shifting to Shaw. He poked the machete in Shaw's direction. "*Que es?*"

Nina launched into a long dialogue. Shaw only caught flashes of it. Something about their truck crashing in the water after some bad men shot at them. Shaw noticed the door to the house open and the woman's round face pressed to the crack.

The man's expression grew even more wary, but Nina didn't give him time to consider. "We just need to make a phone call. Please."

Perhaps he responded to that same sincerity in Nina's eyes that had struck Shaw, but the man stepped back into the house and began a spirited conversation with his wife.

Shaw began to suspect that time had been wasted, time they should have spent getting to Otto's. He was about to say so to Nina when the door opened again. The man with the machete gestured sharply for them to enter.

"I don't think . . ." he began, but he found himself talking to no one as Nina scooted forward into the house.

* * *

Nina blinked against the dim light in the windowless interior. A small electric light hung from the wall, courtesy of the panel outside. The space was tidy, wood floor swept. Pots and pans hung from the rafters overhead along with ears of dried corn. A rag doll with a missing eye sat perched on a small bed where Nina surmised all three children slept.

At the father's command, the children scurried from the house, but they hovered just outside the doorway, listening.

Their host, Arturo, sat with his machete in his hands while the woman seemed oddly shy now that Nina and Shaw had come inside. Nina was grateful that the woman knew enough Spanish that they could communicate.

Nina introduced herself and Shaw again, and she made polite comments about the house and the handsome children who tittered behind their hands.

“I am Marta,” the woman said. “And you are a nurse? You said so?”

“Yes. I am a missionary nurse.”

The woman shot a look of triumph to her husband as if she had just been gifted with a prize. She gestured for Nina to join her in a corner of the house, pulling a ragged-edged yellow curtain to screen them from the men. Slowly, she raised her skirt up to knee level.

Nina peered at a swollen, reddened wound on Marta’s calf. “You’ve had stiches. Why didn’t the doctor take them out?”

Marta sighed. “We had no money left to return to the doctor.”

Nina looked closer. “It’s infected. The stitches need to be removed.”

Marta nodded solemnly. “We have very little money. Will you do this, please?”

Nina took her hand. “Of course. I’ll get my bag.”

She fetched her pack, ignoring Shaw’s questioning look as the two men sat in silence. Outside, she heard Axel barking as he frolicked with the children. Thankful for the pristine condition of the medical kit protected by its own plastic bag inside her wet backpack, Nina washed her hands in a bowl of water Marta offered. She sterilized with hand sanitizer before tugging on a pair of rubber gloves.

Marta winced as Nina swabbed the inflamed wound and applied a topical painkiller before she set to work removing the stitches. It must have been painful in spite of Nina’s gentle touch, but Marta bit her lip and turned her face to the wall. When it was all over, Nina applied a heavy layer of antibiotic cream and bandaged the wound, giving Marta instructions on how often to change the bandage and reapply the salve.

She never had the chance to suggest that Marta rest for a while before the woman popped up and headed for the wood-burning stove. “You are hungry. We will eat together.”

“You don’t have to . . .” Her words were lost as Marta snapped into action with the assistance of her daughter. To Nina's relief, Arturo put down his machete to join them at the table.

"You will pray?" Marta asked.

Nina did, and they sat at the table while the kids nestled on the bed to enjoy the meal of black beans boiled with garlic, salt and chili peppers. Each person at the table received one perfect piping hot tortilla. Nina tried not to gulp down the food, praising Marta and her cooking until the woman's face shone.

Arturo sat back from the table, hands laced across his stomach. "Now, we have eaten. You will tell me who is after you."

Shaw cleared his throat and shot a quick look at Nina. She turned her dark eyes on him. "They've allowed us into their home. They have a right to know the situation."

Shaw looked reluctant, but he told a terse version in passable Spanish of how Escorpion's men pursued them.

The atmosphere in the room became electric. Arturo shot to his feet. "You must leave. Escorpion has been good to us. His men helped us to dig a well."

"He's a drug runner," Shaw snapped in spite of Nina's grimace.

"He helps his people. This is better than the government does." Arturo shot Nina a look. "He is still here after the missionaries have gone home. He is one of us."

Shaw's face darkened with rage as Marta broke in.

"She fixed my leg," Marta said. "She is doing God's work."

Arturo's thick brows drew together. "You must go now."

"But the phone . . ." Nina started.

Arturo moved backward so quickly his chair fell over with a sharp crack. "Now."

Marta's worried gaze flicked from her husband to Nina and Shaw.

"We'll find another phone," Nina said softly, her heart squeezing under the disappointment.

She thanked Marta again for her kindness and the food, and Marta nodded. Nina knew if things were different, the woman would help her in any way she could. But Arturo was the head of the household and Nina could not entirely blame him for his views. To the poverty-stricken people Escorpian helped, his drug dealings didn't matter. This breathtaking country was steeped in such need that idealism took a backseat to food on the table and clothes on the children's backs.

She had to hurry to catch up with Shaw as he strode angrily out into the yard, calling to Axel. The children stared at them as they went, and Nina waved to the little girl. She did not return the gesture, but a small smile played across her round cheeks just before Arturo called them sharply back into the house.

"They'd rather protect a drug dealer," Shaw spat as he strode down the road.

"He helps them. They are poor," Nina said.

Shaw whirled on her, fury sparking his eyes. "Escorpion is a murderer. Just because he does some good things, don't ever forget that."

Nina knew in that moment that Shaw's hatred of Escorpion was personal. It burned in his face and electrified every syllable. "Tell me what he did to you."

Shaw's jaw worked and he blinked. "Never mind. We have to go."

"Tell me," she said, catching up his arm as he started to walk away, but he snatched it away.

"He had my sister killed to send a message to Fuentes."

Nina's mouth fell open. "No, no, it was an accident."

Shaw shook his head.

"How do you know?" she whispered.

"Not important."

The awful truth came home in that moment. Nina suddenly understood why Shaw was here with her then. It wasn't a nod to his sister's friendship. Nor was it a noble gesture from a man who wanted to help.

"You're here . . ." She stopped and swallowed. "You're here in

Guatemala because you want revenge on Escorpion. You're planning to have him arrested."

Shaw's pupils widened then narrowed into hard black points which extinguished the light she'd seen in them before.

"No, Nina. I'm planning to kill him."

# CHAPTER 18

It had been the right thing to tell her, he muttered to himself. It was better now that he'd come clean with the whole business. He felt a razor-sharp pain somewhere under his breastbone. There would be no more tenderness between them, no more shared laughter. No more moments to revel in the softness of her hair or the lightness of her spirit.

Shaw Wilder was going to be a murderer, just as soon as he could arrange it.

Now Nina knew the truth about him. And she no doubt despised him for it.

She didn't speak and he was partly relieved; and uneasy at the same time. He wished he could think of something to say, but his brain wouldn't supply anything to take the sting out of his revelation.

*You never pretended to be anything except what you are. Get her to safety and go do what you were meant to.*

An unsettling thought circled his brain. Maybe she wouldn't follow him anymore. Perhaps she would take her chances on her own, or return to Marta and Arturo and try to persuade them to help her. It would be her choice and there was nothing he could do about that.

"Come on, Axel," he said, turning toward the river once again.

Gravel crunched under the wheels of an approaching vehicle. He grabbed Nina's arm and pulled her into the bushes, Axel following, just before a Jeep appeared; the same Jeep that had fired on them from the bridge. Even before it halted, Arturo's children streamed out of the house and jumped up and down in front of the vehicle.

Nina and Shaw watched through the screen of branches as the two men got out. Shaw's skin prickled when he realized there was one more man with them now. His long dark hair partially screened his face and his eyes were hidden behind sunglasses. Shaw bit back an oath.

Escorpion sat in the passenger seat, head leaning against the headrest, one slender arm propped on the open window edge and his delicate profile silhouetted in a patch of sunlight as he gestured for his men to go into the house.

Shaw's body went cold and then hot. So close. And all alone, unprotected for the moment.

He felt Nina watching him. He could not risk taking action with her there.

The children ran up to the Jeep and chattered to Escorpion. He appeared to listen with interest. Then he tossed some coins to them and they all cheered. Escorpion flashed a smile to the little round-cheeked girl and gestured for her to come closer.

Shaw's nerves prickled and he drew deeper into the branches, hand tight around Nina's wrist. "She's going to tell him about us."

Nina's eyes were huge as she shrank back against him.

Arturo interrupted Escorpion's conversation with the little girl when he appeared with the men, hat in hands, and approached Escorpion while his daughter returned to her mother's side. Shaw could make out Arturo's loud Spanish.

Arturo began with a string of pleasantries before he got to the crux of the matter. "The strangers, a man and a woman, they said they were running from you, that you wished them harm."

Escorpion paused, a rueful smile on his lips. "This is false, of course, my friend. I desire to talk with them only. I tried to explain, but Americans are always in such a rush. Very poor listeners." He laughed and Arturo did the same.

"The woman," Escorpion started. "She is guilty of hiding cocaine at her clinic. She is . . . *not trustworthy*, and the police wish to speak with her. It is a shame for a woman who says she serves God. Still, I wish to help her out of her situation. Her father has given assistance to the people, you see, and I have respect for him."

Arturo nodded. "They left not ten minutes ago," he said, pointing a crooked finger south toward the river. "That direction." His head dropped, bare feet shuffling in the dirt. "Forgive me, I did not know you wanted them, señor, or I would not have let them go."

Escorpion reached out a hand and patted Arturo on the shoulder. "You did the right thing by calling me. There is nothing to forgive. I was nearby, you see, so fortunate. They will head for the river and we will encounter them there." He paused. "You did not let them use your phone, I am sure."

Arturo shook his head. "No, señor."

"Excellent." Escorpion coughed. "Could I trouble you, my friend, for a small drink? My throat is very dry."

Arturo ducked his head. "Of course, of course." He trotted toward his wife, calling for her to provide a *refresco* for their guest.

Escorpion talked to his men in a lower voice. "You checked his phone?"

One of the men nodded. "Yes. He is telling the truth."

Escorpion sighed. "Good. There is no need to hurt him then."

Arturo returned with a cola and a relatively clean glass which he held up to Escorpion who took the can and waved away the glass. "This will do. Thank you, Arturo. We must be going." He scanned the little house, one hand shading his eyes. "I will send a gift, a little something to repay your kindness. A new coop and some nice chickens."

Arturo broke into a big smile. "*Gracias*, señor."

Marta watched from the doorway, her face grave, unlike her husband's.

Shaw held his breath as the Jeep drove by them, not more than four feet from their hiding spot. He saw Escorpion pass the soda can to his driver and wipe his hands on a napkin.

Close enough that Shaw could see the gloss of sweat on Escorpion's brow, his muscles tensed as Escorpion looked in their direction as if he could feel the hatred that streamed out at him from the dense thicket of jungle.

He heard Nina's sharp intake of breath and Axel's panting.

Another second more and the Jeep continued on, disappearing around a bend in the road.

The children began to play with their ball once again and Arturo returned to the house, the smile of satisfaction still on his face. They moved as quietly as they could manage back into the jungle, away from the path, and out of earshot of the children before Shaw picked up the pace, wishing he had a machete to slash at the branches that slowed their progress.

"We'll head upriver as far as we can. That's still the best chance of getting help or someone to loan us a cell phone. They won't find us as long as we keep to the trees."

Nina cried out as a branch struck her face.

He turned and saw a trickle of blood on her cheek. They both stopped, breathing hard. He wanted to offer comfort, to erase the anguish and fear shining in her eyes, but he turned away without saying a word and pressed on through the leaves.

* * *

She fell again, the wet ground soaking into her jeans. Shaw offered her a hand up but she didn't take it. He'd been plotting murder all along. Helping her was just a way to thwart the man he intended to execute.

Her head whirled along with their dizzying flight through the forest. Vengeance was wrong, killing was wrong, and murder definitely topped the list. How could he be the same man who held her gently in the cave and sang a sweet tune that circled in her heart even now? She'd seen the hatred on his face when he stared at Escorpion and she wondered if his accusation about Escorpion arranging for Beth's death could be true. She no longer felt certain of anything, except for one fact: God did not create Shaw to be a murderer.

If she got the chance, she'd prove it to him.

They stumbled upon a small clearing bristling with sixty-foot sapodilla trees, the trunks crisscrossed with thick gouges.

"Chiclé farmers," Shaw mumbled.

In the Petén, some of the natives supplemented their meager earnings by harvesting the sticky latex from the sapodilla trees which would be used as a base for chewing gum. She admired the agility of the workers who could easily traverse the trunks, working their way over them and tapping the bark with machetes to loosen the flow of sap and direct it down the gouges to be collected at the bottom.

Shaw snatched up a rusted machete which lay half buried in the dirt. "Now we're talking," he crowed. As quickly and quietly as they could manage, they skirted the little pocket of sapodillas and reentered the forest. Shaw swung the old machete in vigorous arcs which helped their passage.

Nina saw a flash of movement in the distance, something metallic.

"A Jeep?" she hissed.

Shaw followed her pointed finger. "Couldn't be Escorpion this soon. Someone else."

They watched, barely breathing, as a police truck pushed along a muddy trail not six feet away. The fat cop from the village where they'd stopped for gas looked out the window.

"He works for Fuentes."

She wanted to scream. This part of the Petén was home to relatively few people, yet it seemed everyone had a vested interest in capturing her. The cop stopped frequently to check along the sides of the trail.

Nina held her breath and prayed that he wouldn't look in their direction at the swath of mangled vegetation that would give them away. Shaw tensed beside her when the cop stopped the truck and got out, peering closely at the ground.

"I've got to do something," Shaw breathed into her ear.

"No," she whispered back, but Shaw was already moving. He grabbed a softball-sized rock and hefted it. Nina almost screamed as he hurled it several yards away from the cop. The ruse worked and the cop readied his gun and headed away from the truck.

"Keep Axel here," he commanded before he took off running.

Nina held onto Axel's collar, barely able to restrain him from charging after his master.

Shaw crept up to the driver's side and eased open the door. Nina could no longer see the cop, but he hadn't had time to get far. Axel growled and she shushed him.

The door opened with a squeak so loud it made her blood run cold. Shaw disappeared inside the truck and she imagined him rooting around searching for a cell phone. The scruff on Axel's neck rose under her fingers. The cop returned along the road, gun still readied in his hand. He approached cautiously, and she knew he'd heard the sound of the door opening.

Her nerves screamed silently. How could she warn Shaw? Axel pulled harder now, nearly ripping himself from her grasp. Images flashed before her; Roque and Josef, the people on the bus, the little boy and his bus driver father, so many people injured since the start of her disastrous adventure. The thought of Shaw being added to the list left an ice-cold stone in the pit of Nina's stomach. She found herself rising to a standing position, still barely holding onto Axel's collar.

"Here," she said, her voice starting off unsteady as a spring breeze and gaining strength. "I'm here."

The cop stiffened and eyed her closely as Axel whined for release.

"Señorita Truman?"

"Yes, I'm Nina Truman."

His eyes narrowed in thought. "And the dog?"

"He belongs to someone who helped me."

"Where . . . ?"

She cut him off. "Why are you after me? I have done nothing."

The cop's gaze still sifted through the trees, looking for Shaw. "I will take you someplace safe. There are bad people looking for you."

She saw a shadow of movement from behind him. Hurriedly, she blurted out, "Are you working for Señor Fuentes?"

He started visibly. "Why do you say that?"

"Answer the question," she said, forcing an authoritative tone.

The corner of a smile revealed tobacco-stained teeth. "I am not the one who needs to be answering questions. You should be concerned about your own answers, señorita."

*Little girl.*

She felt exactly like a little girl, helpless and unsure, wondering if she had just handed herself over to the Big Bad Wolf. Axel surged forward and Nina had to use both hands to restrain him.

The cop aimed his weapon at the dog. "If he gets loose, he dies."

Nina held on as best as she could, but she was no match for the dog who ripped from her grasp, causing her to fall hard on the ground.

"No, don't shoot him," she screamed, just as Shaw exploded from behind the man, bringing him down as Axel churned forward. Bullets punched through the air and drove into the mud around her. Fear twisted her body into a ball and she tried to roll out of the way, but the bullets kept firing, pocking the tree trunks and nearly deafening her.

Shaw.

Axel.

Please, God. Please, God.

The cacophony seemed to go on forever until finally the shooting stopped. Heart thundering, Nina forced her eyes open. Facedown in the mud, she covered her head with both hands. Cold sweat beaded her face as she willed herself to look.

Shaw straddled the groaning cop while Axel yanked viciously at the man's pants.

*Alive.* They were alive. Profound relief followed the course of the fear, and she got shakily to her knees.

Shaw cuffed the cop's hands behind his back and stuffed a rag into his mouth. He hauled him to his feet and shoved him toward the truck where he found another pair of cuffs and locked him to the steering wheel.

"We'd be too easy to spot if we take his car." He tore out the ignition switch, snatched the handheld radio, and lobbed it far away.

She took the cell phone Shaw removed from the cop's pocket. Axel had finally calmed to the point where he released his mouthful of pant leg and sat back, calmly licking the mud from his paws.

"Let's go," Shaw said, stopping one moment longer to retrieve a brown bag from the officer's front seat. "Here."

"What is it?" Nina managed, voice cracking.

"Milk legs. Apparently, you're not the only fan."

The sheer lunacy of the situation brought her to the brink of hysterical laughter. Milk legs. She peered inside the bag and inhaled the sweet fragrance.

"I suggest you save them for later," Shaw said over his shoulder. "As soon as those bullets left the gun, Escorpion and his men knew our exact location."

"What do we do now?" Nina said.

"Now, we run."

# CHAPTER 19

Shaw swiped at a cut on his chin. He wanted more than anything to use the cop's phone, to call Otto or the embassy, the cavalry or whoever in this cesspool of a jungle wasn't trying to kill them, but he couldn't spare the time. They might as well have deployed a signal flare to alert the enemy to their position. His plan hadn't worked and its failure made him angry.

At the same time, part of him shivered, recalling the spray of bullets that wrapped around Nina and Axel, the only two creatures he cared about at that moment. If one of those bullets had found its mark, puncturing Nina's slight form . . .

He swallowed hard.

*Going soft, Shaw.*

Axel remained oblivious to his close escape, but Shaw would expect nothing else from the dog he'd seen drag an armed man from under the train where he attempted to hide. Axel had received a deep gash that required stitches in that escapade, but he had paid it no mind; a testimony to the power of the dog's focus.

He wished he could maintain such laser vision. Right now, his mind rolled over itself in frantic fits and starts.

*Get to the river*, his gut told him. They wouldn't be able to hide in the jungle, not with the natives on Escorpion's payroll and yet another storm rolling in. Their best chance might be comandeering a boat and putting some distance between them to buy enough time to contact Otto and the embassy.

The first splat of rain bounced off his forehead. He reassured himself again that both Nina and Axel were unharmed before they took off for the water. He'd had the presence of mind to retrieve the machete from where he'd dropped it before his tussle with the cop and he used it now, chopping at the palms and bushes until they reached the riverbank. His heart dropped to find that they had emerged at a rocky ridge where the river pinched and twisted into a narrow ribbon.

"We'll have to climb past this," he called to Nina.

No choice. Going back was not an option, and the water raced too forcefully here to attempt a crossing . . . even if they weren't already weakened and exhausted.

Nina nodded and began to scramble up the rocks beside him. Axel shot him a look that clearly communicated to Shaw, "You must have me confused with a mountain goat." But the dog managed to keep pace as they clambered over the tumble of stone.

When they reached the apex, Shaw looked out over the vast sprawl of trees that carpeted the mountains that rose on both sides. The trees provided excellent cover for their pursuers. He caught a glint of movement a half mile down the river, but he couldn't be sure it was Escorpion and his men. Best to assume it was.

Nina panted now, sweat glistening on her skin. She didn't ask to rest, and he didn't offer. They began the descent, the rock now slick with the rain splatting in fat droplets. Nina fell, and Shaw heard her cry out as her knee struck the hard stone.

He helped her up and they made painfully slow progress, feeling their way from foothold to foothold. With only a few feet to go, he helped Nina down. She looked past him at Axel and raised an eyebrow.

"I think he needs a motivational talk."

Axel sat perfectly erect, rain sheeting over his thick coat, refusing to look at Shaw.

"Come on, Axel. Only one more big jump, and you're there," he said.

The dog held his refusal.

"Axel, come now." Nina giggled.

"Listen, you big hairy ape. You're coming if I have to carry you."

Axel studiously avoided eye contact. Finally, Shaw climbed up, hefted the dog in his arms and made his ungainly way down, muttering all the while.

When they finally reached the bottom, Nina laughed unrestrainedly. Although he wanted to maintain his scowl, Shaw found it impossible.

"He looks so embarrassed," Nina gasped.

Axel did indeed have a sheepish look as he slunk away to sniff the river which had widened into a span of gray water.

Nina's laughter still came in spurts.

He pretended offense, but he wanted to gather up each one of those giggles as if they were gems spilled on the ground, precious somehow, to be saved and savored.

She wiped her eyes. "Sorry, but that was funny."

He forced down his own smile. "If you're done laughing, we'd better move."

She wasn't done, and he listened to her peals of occasional laughter as they picked their way along.

Perhaps if he hadn't been such a fool listening to her throaty chuckles, he would have heard the Jeep approaching earlier. He didn't. Suddenly, there it was, appearing through the trees as if it had emerged from underground like a burrowing toad.

"Run," he shouted.

They raced ahead into a fluorescent green area of riverbank where the grass grew so high it reached Shaw's shoulders. Nina was all but concealed by the greenery. Their feet sank ankle-deep in the swampy ground, and he hoped it would be enough to slow down the Jeep, but he heard shouts right behind them.

One man stood yelling directions as he watched their progress through the grass. A blue heron startled by their intrusion surged upward, long legs trailing down under a canopy of huge wings.

They had no choice but to run. Panting, soaked by sweat and rain, they charged along the water's edge, frightening birds and insects into flight. The sound of an engine revved behind them, undermined by shouted directives, and something else out on the river. The soft splash of a paddle being applied to the water?

A boat!

He grabbed Nina's hand and they ran with renewed energy, Axel keeping pace, the three of them working to resist the mud that sucked at their feet. They exploded from the dense pocket of swamp grass to see a surprised man in a small wooden boat, the paddle suspended in his hand as he stared at the strangers.

"We need help," Shaw called in Spanish. "Please give us a ride in your boat."

The man didn't move.

"There are bad men after us," Nina pleaded. "Please, señor."

Her words seemed to break the spell and he plunged the paddle into the water and pulled toward shore.

Shaw and Nina splashed out to close the distance. They were knee-deep just as the Jeep exploded through the grass, rifle shots pinging around the boat.

The man immediately reversed course.

"Wait," Shaw yelled.

The boatman completed an expert turn and paddled away as rapidly as he could, taking their only avenue of escape with him.

* * *

Nina couldn't blame the boatman. As he disappeared around the river bend, the Jeep barreled down on them. Linking hands with Shaw, she half-ran-half-splashed through the shallow water as the Jeep kept pace on the ground.

Axel barked wildly, climbing in and out of the water in a frenzied effort to stay with his master while protecting them from the men in the Jeep.

She knew they would be taken soon, but it wasn't Shaw's nature to give up. Nor hers. She forced herself over the rocky bottom, wet clothes weighing her down.

"Stop," the man in the Jeep called. "Or I will shoot."

They kept going, stumbling along as a ripple of bullets hammered into the water near them.

Too near. Shaw pulled her to a stop and held up his hands. He didn't look at her but she could see fury and helplessness warring in his expression. Axel barked viciously as the Jeep parked.

The man stepped out and aimed at Axel.

"Don't shoot him," Shaw shouted.

The man looked from Shaw to Axel and smirked as he took aim again. Nina's heart dropped. The next few moments seemed to unroll in slow motion.

Shaw lurched toward shore. Nina screamed, her cries swallowed up by the sound of a motor.

A small white boat roared toward them, the driver hunched down in front, firing his own weapon. The men in the Jeep retreated to the trees; likely in an effort to keep Escorpion safe.

"Get in," called the man in the boat, water churning around the helm.

"That's Tito," Shaw hollered at her. "He works for Otto," he added as he pulled her toward the boat.

Bullets erupted from the tree line as Escorpion's men regrouped. The shots zinged around them but Nina noticed they didn't come close to hitting her as they staggered toward the boat. Tito took her arm and hauled her in. She landed on her stomach on the worn wood, Shaw hurtling in next to her.

"The dog," Shaw shouted at Tito as he scrambled to his feet. "Axel, come."

Nina struggled upright and saw Axel, still uncertain, alternately lunging toward the trees and then the water.

"Come!" Shaw roared.

After one more moment of uncertainty, the dog sprinted toward the water and splashed into the river.

"That's it. Swim, boy."

Another spray of bullets sliced his words in two. They ducked behind the wooden sides of the boat as Tito steered into a tight circle.

"We're not leaving without the dog," Shaw yelled at him.

Tito shook his head. "Dog is dead."

Shaw opened his mouth to reply, but Tito pointed to the water. Axel hadn't resurfaced.

Bullets continued to rain down as Tito steered the boat upriver, waves churning around them in a foamy white lather.

Heedless of the shots, Shaw continued to stare at the water, eyes combing the frothy surface. Nina searched the surface too, praying there would be the sudden bob of a head as Axel reappeared with a comical shake of his ears.

Seconds crept into minutes.

The men ashore had piled back into the Jeep in an effort to track the boat, but the marshy terrain slowed them.

They saw no sign of Axel as the little boat left the shooters far behind.

* * *

Tito guided the boat upstream for a few hours that felt like days. Nina tried to talk to Shaw, but he sat in silence, his face so still it might have been etched in stone.

"Maybe he made it," she whispered, trying to take his hand. He snatched it away.

"Don't," was all he said, his voice breaking. His eyes burned as they stared at nothing, hard and glittering with danger.

Nina said a prayer for Shaw and for Axel, her own heart aching. Protector and friend, Axel was much more than a pet to Shaw. Maybe Shaw's only friend.

She wanted to circle him in her arms and whisper words of comfort as he had done to her back in the cave, but he sat like the cliffs that rose along the river, immovable in his grief and his silence.

Throat thick, she moved next to Tito who seemed impervious

to the rain that continued to fall, leaving not one dry spot in the open boat.

"How did you find us?"

Tito was a wiry man she guessed to be somewhere in his thirties with a thick fringe of eyelashes. He smiled revealing a chipped front tooth.

"You two are raising trouble wherever you go. It was not hard to find you."

She smiled back, though it seemed to take a ridiculous amount of effort.

"Where are you taking us?"

"There is a place nearby where we can hide until dark. You can rest there and before sunup you will go to Otto's. He'll get you back home."

*Home.* The word left her thunderstruck. Where was home? Back in the States? Here in Guatemala where she'd served as the missionary nurse since she was old enough to remember?

She shot a look at Shaw, pulse thrumming. Would he stay here until he'd murdered Escorpion and probably been killed himself?

Rainwater dripped from his strong profile and his sweet song sang once again in her memory. She knew in that moment that part of her would always be connected to Shaw Wilder. The tenderness he'd shown in the cave had twined itself around her heart and she didn't think it would ever dislodge. Nor did she think she wanted it to. He was hard, angry, vengeful, bitter . . . but God had allowed her to see into his soul, and what she'd seen there had been unforgettable.

*What is going on? Why do you feel something for a man like that?*

Nina had been so sure of herself, of her mission, of her heart. Now she felt certain of nothing except that she grieved for Shaw and she yearned to think of something, anything, to ease his pain.

They passed a fat crocodile settled into the mud on the bank and several dugout canoes filled with youngsters trailing fishing lines. The children stared at her with frank curiosity. Here and there, a modest dwelling peeped through the foliage in small clearings along the shoreline, the owners forever engaged in a battle to fight back the encroaching jungle. She knew the *indigenas* here probably sustained their families growing maize, rice, cane, and sapodilla. In a way, she envied them. They had suffered so much, they had so little, but they accepted blessings as they came; and hardship along with them.

Tito nodded to a group of young men fishing from a rock that protruded from shore. They nodded back.

"Will they tell Escorpion's men?" she asked, feeling the tingle of fear start up again.

Tito shifted slightly. "They are grateful to Otto for giving them jobs and throwing fiestas for them."

Nina noticed he had not exactly answered the question. "What if Escorpion's men offer to pay them?" *Or hurt their families?* She couldn't bring herself to say it aloud.

Tito shrugged. "They know you are a missionary and many know of your father, so we shall see which weighs more."

She thought back to Arturo who had no difficulty making such a decision, and Nina shivered.

# CHAPTER 20

The dense vegetation thinned until they slowed near a ranch, a handful of cattle eyeing them from the banks. Tito pulled the boat to shore and tied it to a mahogany tree before helping Nina from the boat and waiting respectfully for Shaw to climb out.

They followed him up the rise of a hill where they found an ugly rectangular structure built of concrete blocks under a gray sheet metal roof.

Tito didn't go inside. Instead, he pushed the door open for them. "I will come and get you tonight, or sooner if necessary. Rest for a while. Dulce will make you some food."

Nina gazed at the impeccably tidy living room with no furniture except for a wooden table and three chairs. She caught a glimpse of the kitchen beyond a small doorway, outfitted with a humble wood-burning stove and a refrigerator. The smell of frying tortillas made her mouth water.

"Do you have a phone?" she asked, but Tito had already disappeared out the door.

A woman, no more than a young girl actually, poked her head out and signaled Nina to sit at the table.

"Hello," Nina said in Spanish. "My name is Nina."

"Dulce," she returned. "Please sit. I will bring you food."

"I need to wash. Is there a bathroom?" Nina asked, hopefully.

Dulce nodded and pointed to a small door.

With a surge of joy, Nina hurried into the bathroom, relieved herself, and washed her face and hands. The sheer luxury of cool, clean water playing over her fingers inspired her to leave the tap running much longer than necessary. Grateful for the small blessing of no mirror, Nina pulled her hair into the best braid she could manage and tried to straighten her sodden clothes. A small tap on the door startled her.

She opened it to find Dulce, her gaze riveted to the floor as she handed Nina a bundle of clothing. Nina accepted the offering gratefully and struggled out of her wet jeans and shirt. She rolled them into a ball and stuffed them into her pack.

Dulce had provided a long wrap skirt embroidered with a series of meticulous designs, a belt, and a soft smock blouse with short sleeves. She wrapped the skirt and secured it tightly with the belt, tucking in the blouse to contain some of the extra fabric intended for a larger woman. Though she would have preferred a good pair of jeans, she was thrilled at the blessing of dry, clean clothing to wear. Guatemalans, no matter how poor, valued neatness of appearance and so she would do her best.

When she entered the kitchen, Dulce bustled about.

"I want to thank you for helping us," Nina said.

Dulce continued patting the tortillas into neat circles.

"You don't need to do this. I know it is a risk for you, to assist me," Nina continued. "I have enemies."

Dulce continued to pat. "I am not afraid."

"I am," Nina said. "People around me are getting hurt." She looked longingly at the soft circles of dough. "If you want to leave, I understand. I don't want you to get hurt."

Dulce finally looked into Nina's eyes. "My father was a good man. He fell from the tree, he broke his hip and could not farm. My brother began to work for Escorpion as a runner." She pinched and prodded the dough. "They paid him in cocaine and he became an addict until the drugs gave him a heart attack at only sixteen."

Nina groaned. "Oh, Dulce."

She shrugged. "Now my father has a broken hip *and* a broken heart. I will not help the man who killed my brother with his drugs." She wiped her hands on an apron and gave a curt nod. "You eat now."

Two tin plates offered a couple of fried fish, some boiled squash, and the customary stack of soft tortillas, and Dulce set them next to a bottle of hot sauce. Nina thought there could be no finer cuisine in the world than the simple country food that Dulce had prepared in the tiny kitchen.

Dulce's face appeared troubled. "The señor?"

Nina knew a single Guatemalan woman would never approach a strange man, let alone speak to one. Nina patted her arm. "I'll go talk to him and see if he will come and eat this delicious meal."

Dulce smiled in relief and disappeared back into the kitchen.

Nina took a deep breath and headed outside to face Shaw.

* * *

The rain had stopped, but Shaw didn't notice it for a while. He sat on the stump of a ceiba tree and watched the water ripple along. He tried to guess at the time—somewhere past two o'clock, he supposed—but he found he didn't care. Axel was dead. Not a person, not like Beth, but he felt as if his heart had been cut through by a sharp blade. Pain, sorrow, shock . . . and then anger followed, sinking poisonous fangs deep into whatever tender part might have been left.

He burned, rage tearing at his innards. He leapt up from the stump and grabbed several rocks, pulling them from their muddy mortar and throwing them as hard as he could into the river. One, then two. The sweat poured from his forehead, and the sharp stones cut into his flesh. He didn't care; he just hurled them far at the water as fast as he could manage.

"Shaw," Nina said.

He hadn't heard her approach and he didn't want her there. He didn't want anyone near, ever. He kept his back to her.

"I'm sorry," she said.

He threw the rock in his hand and turned on her, surprised to find her dressed like any other Guatemalan woman. "And why would you be sorry? This is God's will, isn't it? Isn't that what you're going to say? God wanted Axel to die for some important reason because He's in control, right?"

She looked at him with eyes full of pity. It only stoked his rage.

"Isn't that what you people say when something horrendous happens, Nina? God is in control. Accept it. Well, you know what? I don't accept it." He knew he was shouting and he couldn't stop. "That's something weak people do who can't manage their lives. I'm not going to hand over my life to God because . . . He's my enemy. Do you understand that? He's my *enemy*."

She raised her hands as if she would touch him, face anguished. "He's not your enemy. He loves you."

"*Loves me?*" The words hardly passed his lips. "This God that killed my sister and ruined my mother? That's love?"

Nina exhaled. "Shaw, things happen in this world. Accidents, illness, pain."

"He causes those things."

"Sometimes things just happen because we have free will and this is a broken world. Things happen, horrible things, terrible things."

"And He allows it."

"And sometimes He intervenes the way we want Him to."

"And sometimes He takes everything away." Shaw's voice broke. "Everything. That dog was all I had left and the stupid beast loved me, Nina. He loved me and he trusted me and he drowned in that river for me."

"I know it feels like that . . ."

He cut her off. "So why should I worship that God? Why should I lie down and pretend that He loves me?"

"Because that's faith." Her voice trembled, soft and strong at the same time. He had to force himself to keep looking at the earnestness in her face.

"Believing that He has greater things in store for you, believing that your strength comes through Him, not through you, that's faith and it's strongest when we're the weakest."

She went to him then and circled him in her arms. He remained rigid, determined not to yield to that tender caress, no matter how gentle, how sweet, how full of emotion and sorrow. He kept his arms at his sides while she whispered in his ear.

"I'm so sorry, Shaw. I'm so sorry."

When she let him go, he saw that tears stained her face.

"Don't cry for me," he choked. "I'm not worth it."

She cocked her head slightly, the braid falling over her shoulder. "That's where you're wrong."

After a moment that stretched into eternity, she wiped her face and went back into the little house.

He stayed outside, pacing along the muddy bank, walking up and down the steep hillside as he watched evening approach with its darkening sky, from blue to gray. Nina tried again to get him to eat, but he refused. The smell of the food which should have bathed him in pleasure didn't even register. He wondered if anything would give him pleasure again. He heard Dulce beating the dust from the hammock and helping Nina into the canvas cocoon, securing the mosquito netting firmly into place. He hoped she could sleep, rest.

If her God was willing, they would get her to Otto's and he would see her safely home. And Shaw would be free to complete his mission against Escorpion. A boiling desire for revenge replaced the numbing grief. He felt invincible then, unfettered by any restraints that might take him off his dark course, buoyed by hatred, strengthened by wrath.

Nina's words came back to him.

Faith is strongest when we're the weakest.

He would not be weak. He would not let his enemies win. He would not let God take away the only thing he had left, the acrid burning drive for vengeance.

The thought spurred him into action. He entered the house. The heat inside felt stifling and Nina slept in silence inside her cocoon of mosquito netting. He pawed through the kitchen, putting anything he thought might be useful into his pack. Apples, water, a packet of tortillas, matches. Then he made his way back outside and examined the phone he'd taken from the cop.

Maddened to find it locked and secured with a password, Shaw surged with rage again and he hurled the phone far out into the water. It seemed to take the anger along with it, leaving him spent.

He found a spot on the porch in the sun. Putting his jacket over his head to discourage the hungry mosquitos, he slumped against the wall. He suspected Tito had climbed up to a vantage point on the hill behind them, keeping an eye peeled for Escorpion's men. The roads would be difficult for the Jeep to navigate in this remote area of the Petén; but eventually, they would get through. They would search every village, talk to every local, bribing and threatening until they figured out where Shaw and Nina had gone. It was just a matter of time.

A pang of anguish swept over him as he remembered that he no longer had Axel's exceptional ears to alert him of the enemy's approach. Had the dog suffered? Shaw hoped fervently that the end had come quickly and no fear had stricken his friend in those final moments, no sense of abandonment by his human companion.

He blinked back the tears that stung his eyes as they rose.

No room for weakness.

Only for revenge.

*"Don't cry for me. I'm not worth it."*

*"That's where you're wrong."*

His heart squeezed. "No, Nina," he whispered to the night. "That's one thing I'm right about."

He trained his tired eyes on the river, watching and waiting for the enemy.

* * *

Swaddled in layers of mosquito netting and enveloped in the lazy heat of the quiet house, Nina slept. She awoke with a start at the sound of movement outside. The dim room told her that sunset had passed. Eyes gritty and head pounding, she forced her mind to awaken. Her heart beat fast as she tried to recall where she was and how she'd gotten there.

The current of grief surged as she remembered in vivid bursts. The boat, shots in the water, Shaw's terrible mourning. She wanted to flop back down on the hammock and drift back into sleep that would take the memories away, but there was no escaping it. Axel was gone and Shaw had retreated to a place so dark and bitter she could not reach him there.

She couldn't, but God could.

She said a fervent prayer as she fought the netting. Just as her feet touched the floor, the door opened and Tito stuck his head inside. "Señorita Truman, it is time."

"Thank you, Tito. I'll be there in a moment."

When the door closed again, she hurried into the bathroom, savoring the comforts of indoor plumbing one last time. She carefully stowed the skirt Dulce had given her and slithered into her jeans which were mostly dry. She hoped it wouldn't offend Dulce, but the jeans were better for running; and it seemed she was doing more than her share of that lately. But perhaps this last leg of the journey would go without complication. With Escorpion close? And the cop working for Fuentes no doubt freed by now and searching as well?

She indulged in one more luxurious hand washing before she pulled on her still-soggy shoes, and grabbed her pack, and hurried out of the bathroom.

Dulce emerged from the kitchen with a paper bag, warm to the touch. The smell of fresh tortillas and the tangy banana fragrance of fried plantains tickled her nose.

"Thank you, Dulce. You have been so kind."

"*Que le vaya bien.*"

Go with God.

Nina could not think of a better sentiment for that moment.

# CHAPTER 21

Nina emerged into the semi-cool evening. It took her eyes a moment to adjust to the darkness before she noticed three horses standing patiently with Tito holding the reins.

She blinked again. "Horses? I thought we were going by boat."

Tito shook his head. "They will expect us to stick to the river. This way will take longer, but it improves our chances to get to Otto's alive. We'll meet the boat farther upriver."

*Alive.* She swallowed. "Tito, can I use your phone?"

Tito shrugged and handed it to her. She dialed her father's number first. It rang ten times before she gave up and dialed the embassy and got their recorded message. She wanted to try the emergency number, but Tito was already in the saddle and Shaw stood next to her. She couldn't figure out why until he offered his cupped hands to help her mount. She handed the phone back to Tito and allowed Shaw to hoist her up.

The saddle felt stiff and unnatural. Both Shaw and Tito appeared perfectly relaxed, the reins slack in their hands, legs fitted expertly in the stirrups. "How long?"

"We should be there before sunrise." Tito guided his horse to the trail that stretched away behind the cement house.

"Will Dulce be all right?" Nina called.

"She's already gone, and no one will ever know she was here," Tito called back.

*No one will ever know.* Something about the phrase made her stomach tighten. Perhaps it was the darkness of the jungle that seemed to swallow them up as they filed along the narrow trail.

*The jungle could swallow a person altogether,* she thought, recalling the stories of people who had disappeared into that green maw.

*Stop it,* she told herself sternly.

The wind rattled the trees and sent drops of water slithering down her back. Jungle creatures moved and undulated around her, croaking frogs, disgruntled birds disturbed at their passing, the constant thrum of the insect armies busy at work. She pulled her jacket up around her neck to ward off the stinging bugs, but it was of little help. Lumps stood out on her hands and temples where the bloodsuckers had found their prey. Mosquitos had their purpose in God's kingdom, she knew, but in her book they had no redeeming qualities.

She thought she saw movement in the tree to her left. Shaw must have seen it too because he pulled to the side and waited for her horse to pass before he filed in after her.

"What is it?" she whispered.

"Probably nothing."

She scanned the tree line, noting the scratches furrowed into the bark. Shaw's "nothing" might turn out to be a puma, one of Guatemala's most beautiful and determined hunters. Sleek and silent, they did their stalking at night. She knew from talk she'd heard at the clinic that the puma could take down a large animal by breaking its neck with one mighty bite. She swallowed.

Better pumas than pythons.

Tito had a rifle slung across his back, but she found more comfort in Shaw's vigilant lookout. He looked more alive now, and it encouraged her somehow; but she knew the anger and despair would still be there when the sun rose to reveal it in the depths of his eyes.

Time passed slowly as they crept through the forest. In the beginning, she heard the river coursing along somewhere to their left, but as the hours ticked by, the slope steepened and led them away from the water. Though the few hours of rest had sustained her somewhat, her body felt heavy with fatigue and her dry throat scratched.

She thought suddenly of Anna, the strange woman who had given her the note.

*Run or die.*

What had happened to her? Had Escorpion caught her at the airstrip and killed her?

Nina didn't think she could bear knowing that another living being had come to harm trying to help her. The list had grown long enough. Josef, Roque, Axel . . . and she looked at Shaw.

They traveled another hour in silence until Nina noticed the trail widen, showing signs of heavy use.

"Village?" Shaw called to Tito.

"A few houses and a *tienda*, if you can call that a village," Tito answered. "Ahead is a narrow pass leading up to Otto's. There is only one route. We will stop here to see if the way is clear ahead."

"Or if Escorpion's men are waiting to ambush us," Shaw muttered.

The thatch-roofed houses of the dark village silvered in the moonlight. A man stood on the porch of the smallest house holding a lantern. Tito excused himself to speak to the man, calling to Nina before he did so. "Go inside the *tienda*. There is water there."

The notion of a cool drink enticed her and she slid off the horse, handing the reins to Shaw.

"Do you want some water?" she asked.

He didn't look at her. "No. You go. I want to hear what Tito's discussing."

She nodded and went inside.

The tiny shack was dark, with no source of electricity that Nina could find. It smelled of fried beans. Most of the meager merchandise sat piled in cardboard boxes that would probably be displayed in a more seemly fashion during business hours.

She found a bottle of water in one of the boxes and fished around in her backpack for some quetzals to leave as payment. The back door opened and someone entered holding a light.

Nina blinked and held up a hand to screen her eyes. "Hello. Thank you for allowing me inside your shop. Tito told me I could buy a bottle of water here." She held up the money.

The figure moved to the counter. The woman, silhouetted in the lantern light, had long hair, braided into thick plaits wound around the crown of her head. Something about the posture, the narrow face, the long fingers that enfolded hers, seemed familiar.

Nina's breath caught in surprise. "Anna?"

She nodded and held a finger to her lips.

"How did you get here?" Nina whispered.

Anna shook her head. "I knew you would come this way. I came to warn you."

"Warn me of what? Are Escorpion's men waiting?"

Anna squeezed Nina's fingers painfully.

"Listen to me. You are heading to Otto, but he is not your friend."

"What are you talking about?"

Anna chewed her lip. "He wants to kill you because of who you are."

Nina leaned forward. "I'm a missionary nurse. Why would he want to kill me?"

"That's who you were raised to be. Otto knows about your real parents." Horses huffed softly outside and Anna's head jerked toward the noise. "We have to go before they find out I'm here."

Nina came closer, still holding on to the trembling hand. "You need to tell me the truth right now."

Anna shook her head. "No. We have to go."

Nina held fast. "I don't know who to trust anymore. People have been trying to capture me. I'm not going with you unless you give me a good reason."

"Very well." Anna sighed and extracted her hands from Nina's grasp. She turned away for a moment, and Nina heard her suck in a deep breath as if she dreaded what came next.

She faced Nina again and gently stroked her upper arm. "My mother worked at an orphanage in the highlands for many years."

Nina's nerves tingled as Anna moved closer. She was going to hear, to finally know, the truth about who she was. "She knew me when I was a baby there?"

Anna nodded, tears filling her eyes. "I am sorry, so sorry, that my mother did not tell me sooner. I . . . she disowned me many years ago. I was involved with a boy and we were not married. I only returned to her just before she died. We both found ourselves with nothing and no one except each other." She sighed. "So many deaths now, so many." The tears spilled down her cheeks.

Nina embraced her, and she remained stiff in the circle of Nina's arms.

"You could not understand," she whispered. "You have a father to care for you, a career to call your own, school if you wish it. The United States to return to when your mission work is done. You have everything."

Nina pulled away slightly at the anger she heard. Anna's profile did not betray the hurt and bitterness in her words.

"It's okay. Tell me the truth, Anna," she whispered into the woman's ear. "Please tell me."

"This is not easy," Anna whispered.

Nina felt a sudden prick, a pinch of pain. She yanked away. There on her lower arm was a tiny bead of blood.

Anna watched her, eyes round, the hypodermic needle still in her hand.

"Why?" Nina gasped, her mind whirling.

"You must not go to Otto," Anna said, but her words sounded tinny, odd.

*Get to Shaw*. Nina turned to the door, but the room swam in her view. *Which way?* She only needed to make it a few steps to help, to Shaw. She tried to walk, but her knees wobbled and she had to grip the edge of the counter to keep from falling. Her legs refused to take her to safety.

*Call out to him.* Fear prickling her body, she opened her mouth to scream, but Anna appeared beside Nina in a flash, her palm pressed hard over her mouth. Nina tried to move, to roll away, but she didn't have the strength.

She slipped to the floor, only vaguely aware of Anna throwing a blanket over her and the feeling of being dragged by her ankles over the dirt.

* * *

Shaw listened to Tito carefully, but he couldn't follow the conversation taking place in one of the Mayan dialects.

When Tito concluded his business, he returned to Shaw.

"There is no sign of Escorpion or his men. No police either. I have phoned ahead and Otto will send his people to be sure we can pass safely."

Shaw heaved a sigh of relief. It was almost over. He would deliver Nina to Otto and that would be that. An uncomfortable feeling swept over him at the thought. They would both be better off when their worlds were disentangled. An angry man with murder on his brain and a naïve missionary who still wanted to serve this country full of people trying to kill her did not have any business together.

But his mind pulled up the images of her in the cave: The comfort he both gave her and drew for himself; the look of joy on her face as she devoured the crawfish; the strange realization that he wanted to keep that joy safe no matter what.

*Hasn't she cost you enough? Beth came here to be with her friend and died. Axel is gone now, too.*

Shaw's own safety in Guatemala had been forfeited as well. There would be no going back to the trailer, no more hiding from what he had to do. A tremor rippled through his innards. He forced himself to tune back in to Tito's update.

"We will be there in less than an hour," Tito said.

*Less than an hour.* Shaw started to call for Axel and stopped as the grief washed over him anew. He cleared his throat and headed for the horses.

Shadows shifted along the ground in the moonlight, his own twisted and strange. One shadow near the back wall of the *tienda* froze as he neared. Interest piqued, he moved closer, hand on the knife at his belt. The shadow detached itself from the darkness and moved hastily away. Too large for an animal and . . . Shaw's breath froze in his chest . . . dragging something along behind from the sound of it, something heavy.

He yelled for Tito and took off after whoever it was. A man? Too small, but maybe a teen or a . . . woman. He sprinted faster to catch her before she got to the trees. Close enough now to see the braided hair and thick folds of skirt.

"Anna," he shouted.

She straightened, letting go of her burden, and ran full out for the cover of the jungle.

Tito rounded the corner then and Shaw stabbed a finger at the direction she'd taken. Tito and the man with the lantern set off in pursuit.

Shaw wheeled around and charged back to the bundle lying on the ground. Heart jackhammering against his ribs, he knelt next to it. He knew it was Nina even before he pulled away the corner of the blanket that covered her face. She was completely still, the kind of lifeless stillness that he had seen too many times in too many places. Holding his cheek to her mouth he concentrated over the thundering of his own pulse. A tiny puff of air. She was breathing.

*She's alive.*

Joy leapt to life inside him.

He had to see if she'd been stabbed or cut, if a flow of blood needed stopping before her life ebbed away, but the moonlight was not strong enough. It only succeeded in painting her delicate face in silver, shadowing the lush fringe of eyelashes, the peaceful curve of her mouth.

Frantically, he patted his pockets for a flashlight, realizing he'd left it in the saddlebags. He forced himself to leave her there, sprinting to the horses and retrieving the flashlight Tito had given him. In seconds, he knelt at her side again, gently unfolding the blanket, pouring the light over her clothing, looking for blood. Finding no wounds, he turned her as gently as he could manage onto her belly and scanned again with the light. No cuts or wounds.

But still no sign of life.

He returned her to her back and felt her head gingerly, tenderly, checking for a bump or gash.

Tito ran up, puffing. His eyes rounded. "Rodrigo is tracking, but she had a vehicle hidden so she has already gone." He squatted next to Shaw. "Alive?"

He nodded. "I can't find any wounds yet."

Tito added his own light to Shaw's. "There," he said. "On the arm."

Shaw squinted until he saw it too, the dark pinprick, the small drop of dried blood. His mind reeled. "Drugged?"

Tito's face turned grave. "Or poisoned."

# CHAPTER 22

Poison could not cause more hurt than the emotions coursing through Shaw's veins at that moment. She could not die, this sunny woman with the heart that beat steadily for a God he used to know. God would not allow that, surely.

*You won't take her. You can't take her.*

He stood so abruptly he almost knocked Tito over. "Call Otto. Tell him what's happened. We'll get to him as fast as we can."

They'd run out of choices. They had no vehicle, and the nearest clinic had to be hours away. As long as she kept on breathing, he could keep the black despair away. He gathered up the folds of the blanket. With Tito's help, he mounted the horse, her limp body cradled in his arms.

"Let's go," he barked at Tito who scrambled onto his own horse. They left the shelter of the village behind, once again swallowed up by the darkness.

Shaw let the horse lead the way, grateful that the beast kept close to his companion. He rested his head on her soft hair, every now and then pressing his cheek close to her face to ensure she was still breathing. She felt so small that she didn't seem to add much weight. He pulled the blanket up more snugly around her shoulders to fend off the mosquitos that buzzed around.

"Better than snakes," she would probably say.

He smiled into the darkness, throat thick, wondering again why God had brought him to this point, racing through the jungle with Nina Truman in his arms. Why did he care so much? Why did the terror bite so strongly at the thought that Nina might die there, in the circle of his embrace? Not long ago, he'd considered her responsible for his sister's death, a reminder of how callous and harsh God could be that she would live when his sister did not. Now he found himself unsure. Where blame had been, another feeling crept in. Acceptance? Forgiveness? Shaw squirmed in the saddle.

Love?

He slapped at a wet branch that brushed his face. Not love. He would not love anyone again. Especially a woman who served the God who punished him at every turn. He was too filled with hatred, scarred by anger, too unworthy of love.

*"That's where you're wrong."*

He disentangled a leaf that had fallen and become entwined in her hair. Why couldn't he do something? Rouse her with his words? Get her to a doctor? Why hadn't he seen Anna enter the tienda? Why?

He felt exhausted and weak. So many *whys*; and never, it seemed, never a *because*. Pressing Nina closer to his chest, he sang softly, a private song that he hoped she could hear deep down in the part of her that remained with him.

*I can't see why a boy should sigh when by his side . . . Is the girl he loves so true . . .*

Another eternity of traveling led them to the top of a heavily wooded hill. Otto's men were good, or perhaps Shaw was too distracted by Nina to notice them until they emerged from behind the oak trees at the top of the trail. As Shaw dismounted, one of the men drove a small SUV into view and Shaw transferred Nina as gently as he could manage to the backseat before climbing in next to her. Tito remained under the dripping canopy of trees, the horse's reins held in his hand.

Shaw rolled down the window and called to him. "Coming?"

Tito shook his head, a faint smile on his lips. "I will go back and return the horses. From here, it is your business."

Shaw stuck out a hand and Tito hesitated only a moment before he stepped forward and shook it. "Thank you," Shaw said. "I owe you my life and hers."

Tito's face clouded for a moment. "*Adios,* señor."

"*Hasta luego,*" Shaw said, hoping he really would see Tito later.

"*Que dios lo quiera,*" Tito answered, turning away and guiding the horses along the dark road.

May God want it so.

* * *

Nina's throat burned. She craved nothing more than to gulp down deep swallows of something, anything to quell the heat. The thirst eclipsed all the other messages her senses screamed at her; the darkness, the all-over cramping in her muscles, the mumblings she couldn't decipher, and the residue of fear.

She opened her eyes and flashes of light blinded her. Gradually, the light subsided into one soft glow from a bedside lamp. The blurriness retreated until she could make out walls painted a soft eggshell color. Underneath her was a mattress, not the hard leather of a saddle.

"She's awake." The voice shot through with excitement, and it took her several moments to identify the speaker as Shaw. Her body fought to bring her fully into the present. Blinking to clear her vision, she saw him leaning over her, a rare smile on his mouth. The maelstrom of sensations funneled into one: Joy.

Shaw was there with her. She reached out a hand, clumsy and shaking as he clasped it, and he kissed the tender skin on the underside of her wrist.

"I . . ." Her voice came out weak as a kitten's.

"It's okay. You don't have to talk."

He kissed her again on each fingertip with such tenderness she thought she must be hallucinating.

"Where . . . ?" She tried to sit up.

He pushed her gently back down onto the bed and pulled the covers up and tucked them under her chin. "You're safe. You're at Otto's."

Through the sweet rush of emotion, something else nagged at her, clawed at the edges of her happiness. She tried to make sense of it. The last thing she remembered . . . the prick of a needle, a smothering blanket, the long-haired woman. She bolted upright so fast it made her head swim.

"She drugged me. She said Otto wants to kill me."

A low rumbling laugh sounded from the doorway. A short man with a head of black hair and a thick mustache leaned against the jamb. "This is amusing to me," he said. "If I wish to kill you, it seems I will have to wait in line behind the others who are doing their best to make this happen."

"You're . . ."

"Otto Solis," he said with a bow. "My people brought you here after this woman who is holding you in such regard injected you with a drug."

Her eyes searched his round face, the amused curve of his lips under his mustache. Why would he have gone to the trouble to bring her here if he wanted her dead? But there were so many things she did not understand, so many people trying to get their hands on her.

"Do you know who my parents are?"

Otto cocked his head. "I hold many pieces of information, interesting bits that I am filing away to be used in due time, but I have no knowledge of your family history. As far as I am knowing, your father is *El Monte*, the great white mountain, is he not?"

Nina nodded, the ache in her head settling like a weight behind her eyes. Slowly, she slid back onto the bed. "I thought I was born in Mexico, but I recently found out that the orphanage was lying. I was born here in Guatemala. Anna said her mother worked at the orphanage and she knew the truth."

Otto frowned. "Hard to say what is the truth from this woman, no? But I will check into it." He paused. "With your permission, of course."

Nina stole a look at Shaw whose gaze hadn't left her face for even a moment. He had ultimate confidence in Otto; and Nina, though she couldn't explain it, had ultimate confidence in Shaw.

"I would be grateful, Señor Solis."

He flapped a hand at her. "Ah, you must call me Otto. Señor Solis is the name of an old man and I do not wish to be this for some time."

She tried for a smile and coughed. Shaw handed her a glass of water which she gulped greedily in spite of Shaw's urgings to sip it slowly. She took in the neat room with its painted shutters and swept tile floor. They'd made it to the oil palm plantation. "Are we safe here? From Escorpion's men?"

Otto laughed again and gestured broadly around the room. "I am a great man in these parts, as great as the tenacious scorpion who chases you. If he is coming, I am knowing this in advance and he will meet with stiff resistance." Otto walked to the door, eyes twinkling. "Besides, I have extra protection from a new man. He is quite good when he is not eating my hats." Otto whistled.

Nina heard the rapid staccato of nails on the hallway floor just before Axel burst into the room and threw himself on Shaw.

Nina cried out at the sight of the exuberant dog wrestling with an incredulous Shaw.

Shaw rolled around, enduring a lavish licking before sitting up, clasping the animal in a bear hug. His expression morphed into pure wonder and happy disbelief.

"Axel?"

"In the furry flesh, so to speak," Otto said.

Shaw battled against tears, his voice hoarse with emotion.

"Where did you find him?" he rasped.

Otto brushed a bit of fuzz from his neat white shirt. "I send teams of my men in search of you. Tito, he finds you first in the boat while the others watch from the bank. There is gunfire and so my men take cover. Sensible. Tito continues on with you because he is extremely brave, but not so sensible. After the shooting stops, my men emerge to find a dog lying on the bank, half in the water, blood coming from the wound on his head. Since they are looking for a crazy *gringo* and his dog, they decide this beast must be taken back here."

Shaw peered at the wound on Axel's head. "The bullet must have grazed him, and he blacked out after he got to shore."

Otto sighed. "It is an interesting journey for my men when this dog awakens and tries to tear them limb from limb until they wrap him in a burlap sack and bring him here. Axel is most ungrateful. I offer him sanctuary and the choicest of meat and all the dog does is whine and pace the hallway. He does not eat, he does not drink, only he paces and paces and chews my hats while awaiting his master's return."

Shaw laughed, the strong, jubilant sound thrilling Nina to the core. The dog trotted to the bed and gave Nina a friendly nose poke to the thigh. She stroked his fur. "Oh, Axel. I'm so glad you're alive."

Axel's brown eyes met hers and she thanked God for bringing Shaw's best friend back to him. He scampered back to Shaw again, as if to collect the affection he'd missed in their time apart.

"Otto, how . . . ?" Shaw began, choking on the words.

"How can such a troublesome *gringo* repay the kindnesses which I have showered on him and his ungrateful canine?" Otto finished. "Perhaps you will be buying me some new hats."

Axel added his two cents with a loud bark that mingled with their laughter.

Otto bowed again. "I will leave you to freshen up and then we will have a snack while I tell you about my ingenious plan to get Señorita Truman out of the country."

He bowed again and the door closed behind him.

Shaw sat on the floor, rubbing Axel's flanks while the dog laid his head on Shaw's leg and stared at him in adoration. He murmured quiet words to Axel, tender and raw, which Nina tried not to overhear.

She sat up inch by inch, allowing her dizziness to subside. She wanted to ask again if Otto was a man to be trusted, but the question seemed irrelevant. If Shaw had had any doubts to start with, they would have been answered when Otto returned Axel to him.

His gaze shifted to her and his cheeks colored slightly. "I thought he was gone."

"I know."

"And . . ." He cleared his throat. "For a few minutes, when I saw you lying on the ground . . ." He let out a gusty sigh. "I thought you were, too."

The emotion in his face made her breath catch. "I guess God isn't finished with me yet."

He chuckled. "I guess you're right. We're going to get you out of here and you can go back to your work." He looked away. "That's what you want, isn't it?"

Nina shifted on the bed. "Yes, but I'm not sure what that will look like."

He arched an eyebrow.

"I've been thinking about what you said, about hiding from things. I've spent my whole life trying to please my earthly father, and no matter what the birth certificate says, he really is my father." She twisted a corner of the tufted blanket. "It's time to forge my own relationship with God. *My relationship*, not my father's or my mother's or the teachings that I've studied since I was a child. It's time to come to God on my own and listen to what He's telling me to do, even if it scares me." She sighed. "I guess maybe thrashing around this jungle has brought that home."

Shaw stood up, and Axel did the same. The lamplight accentuated the fatigue on his face, the scratches and bruises. "What is that, do you think?"

She sucked in a breath. "I think maybe it's time to go to medical school, if they'll have me." She couldn't quite believe she'd said the words aloud, the tickling desire that she'd felt since her youth, blossomed into a fully-formed truth. Giving voice to the words made them real and she felt suddenly assured of what God wanted for her life.

She didn't know what reaction she expected from Shaw, but he broke into a dazzling smile. "Good for you, Nina Truman."

He lingered there, his eyes searching her face as if trying to convince himself she really was safe and well in spite of all they'd been through. "So, I guess our adventure is almost over." His smile faded away and he stepped back. "You're going home. Happy ending."

She reached for his hand and tugged at his fingers. "But what about you?"

He took her hand in his and closed his eyes, grazing his lips over her knuckles, sending tender emotion shivering through her insides.

"I'm staying here."

"Shaw, you don't have to go through with it. Killing Escorpion is wrong and you'll throw your life away."

"I don't have a life," he whispered.

"Yes, you do. You have Axel . . . and you have me."

He raised his head slowly and gazed at her with exquisite pain etched across his face. "You still think I'm worth something, don't you?"

She moved closer and pressed a kiss to his temple. "Yes, so much more than you can see."

He shook his head and something hard crept into his eyes. "I can't let him get away with murdering Beth and trying to murder you. I can't do it."

"He will be punished, Shaw. Here or in the next life."

"I wish I could believe that."

"I wish I could help you believe it."

The sound of an engine startled them. Axel growled low in his throat and Shaw went to the window, peering out through a crack in the shutters while fear roiled through her.

"It's not Escorpion," Shaw said, the softness in his voice stripped away now. "Probably more reinforcements, but I'm going to check it out."

"I'll go with you," Nina said, swinging her legs over the side of the bed.

He headed for the door. "Stay here. You need to rest."

She stood, ignoring the soreness in her back and legs. "I thought we'd established that I don't always do what you command."

"I'm still hopeful you'll see reason one day."

"A perpetual optimist." She giggled.

His laughter sounded like the sweetest song she'd heard in a very long time.

# CHAPTER 23

Nina emerged shortly from the tiny bathroom with a clean face and damp hair which she had pulled into some sort of knot on the back of her head. She wore a plain full skirt and blouse, her feet bare.

"Otto is some host." She fluffed the folds of her skirt. "He's left me some clothes."

Shaw chuckled. "Otto is quite the ladies' man, so I imagine he's got plenty for you to choose from. He's always got a new girl to entertain."

Nina scanned the room again. "This is a very nice place by Petén standards. Does the oil palm plantation bring in that much money?"

"The agrofuel business went crazy here. I've cleared land mines from a couple of properties for him. Biodiesel is the new thing, but Otto's been in the oil palm business for a while on the food end. He's got some deal with a manufacturer who buys his oil to make margarine. This amuses Otto as he thinks margarine is not fit to grease wheels."

"Ironic," she said.

"Good business, Otto would say."

Shaw remained silent as they traversed the terra cotta tiles, but he could hardly restrain his joy. Nina was alive. Axel was alive. He hadn't had so much to celebrate since he made it through police boot camp. Axel seemed more vigorous than he remembered, stopping to sniff at the ceramic pots bursting with tall hibiscus. When he got too far ahead, he stopped and sat, waiting patiently for the two humans to catch up.

Nina moved slowly and he kept within arm's reach of her in case she fell. At least that was what he told himself. More likely, his proximity was due to the fact that he couldn't bear to have her out of his sight again and he didn't think he could ever erase the picture of her lying on the ground from his memory.

*She'll be gone in a matter of hours, and then what will you do?* Having no answer, he settled on pushing the future from his mind and concentrating on the present. A hum of voices wafted in from the small room ahead, and the lightening of the sky outside the windows turned the walls from gray to golden as the scent of coffee made his mouth water.

Nina tugged at his sleeve. "Watch out."

"Why?" he said, wondering if he had missed something.

"You're smiling. You're going to lose that angry bear look you always cultivate."

He laughed.

"What time is it, anyway?" Nina said.

"Almost six a.m." He pushed open the door to the dining room, ushering her in first.

Otto sat at the table, peering at a map. A young woman with long black braids laid out plates on a sideboard next to a pot of coffee before disappearing into a back room.

Otto glanced up. "There you are. Fix yourself a plate and sit. There is planning to discuss."

Shaw made note that Otto's ever-present smile had disappeared, and his brows furrowed together. He bypassed the food and poured himself a cup of coffee, taking an experimental sip.

"Good," he said.

Otto shrugged. "My country, she produces the best coffee in the world and all of it is shipped away to the *gringos*. I must take pains to secure even the smallest amount for myself. This is crazy, don't you think?"

Shaw sipped the ink-black stuff. Otto had managed just fine. The rich, pungent brew was delicious.

Shaw sat at the table and watched Nina pile some sliced red bananas, black beans and tortillas on her plate. She snuck some to Axel, who wagged his tail happily, before she joined them.

"Here," Otto said, pointing to a spot on the map. "There is a place upstream. Tonight, my people will take you across the river and help you to the border and across into Mexico."

"I have no papers," Nina said.

Otto's lips quirked. "This is of small consequence to certain friends I have. You will be whisked into Mexico in no time and my people, they will be escorting you to the consulate there. This, I am thinking, will be sufficient." He sat back and smiled in satisfaction.

Nina toyed with a slice of banana. "We should contact the embassy here again. Tell them what we're planning."

Otto snorted. "The embassy here has been proving to be no help to you, señorita. It would not surprise me if Escorpion does not have an ear or two at the embassy. He has managed to track you every step of the way, has he not?"

She looked away, pinching her lower lip between her teeth. "Yes."

Shaw stroked Axel's head and took another mouthful of the excellent coffee. "What's bothering you, Otto?"

He tapped the table. "There is a small complication."

Shaw put his cup down. "What kind of complication?"

"Someone has arrived to offer assistance, even though I am through constructing an excellent plan." His brows drew together.

"Tell him to get lost. The less people involved, the better."

Otto rolled his eyes. "Spoken like a typical American. This is Guatemala, my friend. There is a pecking order here."

Shaw cocked his head. "What's going on then? Who's butting into the situation?"

The door of the dining room opened and a tall, thin man with crew-cut hair strode in. He wore a military jacket and neat khaki pants, and his black eyes took in every detail of the room before settling on Nina.

He took off his hat, tucked it under his arm, and reached for her hand.

She dropped her fork in surprise as he put his lips to her knuckles.

"Hello, Señorita Truman. It has been too long."

Shaw shot to his feet. "What are you doing here?"

Colonel Fuentes, his former brother-in-law, let go of Nina's hand and turned to face Shaw.

* * *

Nina struggled to her feet, moving around an alert Axel to embrace Colonel Fuentes. She remembered the last time she'd seen him, at Beth's funeral. He'd been grief-stricken, tears coursing down his creased face.

He clasped her hands between his own and squeezed. "I have been trying very hard to keep you alive."

Shaw moved next to her, Axel right there too, growling low. "You've been paying a cop to try and abduct her."

Colonel Fuentes stared calmly at Shaw. "You are mistaken. I will explain."

"Go right ahead," Shaw spat. "This should be good."

Fuentes let go of Nina's hand and pulled out her chair for her before selecting one for himself. "May I?" He directed the question to Otto who waved a hand in acquiescence.

The colonel sat and cleared his throat. "It is so good to see you alive, Nina. I feel you are all I have left to connect me with my sweet Beth." He shot a sideways glance at Shaw as he added, "And you as well." Turning his attention back to Nina, he softened. "She loved you very much."

Shaw could hardly stand to hear his sister's name on Fuentes' lips. "You got her killed." He heard Otto shift on the chair. His words might ignite a powder keg, but he couldn't stop them. "You had your hands in some business with the Mexican cartels and Escorpion didn't like it. He had my sister driven off the road to send a message."

Fuentes' mouth drew into a grim line. "Mr. Wilder, I wonder how you have come by this information."

"Doesn't matter. I don't hear you denying it."

"My business is of a private nature."

Shaw slammed his palm on the table so hard both Nina and Axel flinched. "What happened to my sister is my business. Do you deny that you're letting the cartels transport shipments of drugs across your property?"

"I do not have to confirm or deny anything to you."

"Yes you do," Shaw snapped. "Nina and I both loved Beth long before you ever met her, and we have a right to know why she was murdered."

Fuentes stared at him for a moment. "This anger is directed at the wrong person. I loved your sister very much, too. I also believe Escorpion arranged for the accident that killed Beth and that is why I have become involved in Nina's situation, to keep her alive because that is what Beth would have wanted."

*What Beth would have wanted.*

The words took some of the fire out of his anger. Shaw had spent so much time bent on exacting revenge from Beth's killer. Was that what she would have wanted? He shook the thought away. "She was your wife. You should have kept her safe."

Fuentes looked at his hands for a moment, the fingers laced together on the table. He sighed. "Yes, this is true. I told her not to go out by herself, to allow my driver to take her, and I should have forced the issue." A ghost of a smile crossed his face. "Yet I found Beth to be resistant to any kind of order." He looked at Shaw and flinched. "That is part of the reason I loved her."

Shaw met Fuentes' brown-eyed gaze and searched it. Was it sincere regret he saw there? Truth be told, it was one of the things he loved about his sister too, that bold approach she took to life, even after everything that transpired with their mother. She walked through the world completely unafraid and without bitterness. It knifed at him to realize that Fuentes adored the same things about Beth that he did. Fuentes had no right, this law-breaking peacock who strutted around like royalty. He got up from the table and strode to the window, trying to clear his head.

"I know Beth loved you very much, Colonel Fuentes," Nina said. "She told me so."

"Ah." Fuentes sighed again. "There will never be another woman like her. Though I kept her out of my business arrangements, she nonetheless concluded that I was partnering with the cartels." He laughed. "Oh, the tongue-lashing she gave me then, threats to leave me. Like a volcano erupting, so I promised to end the partnership."

"But you didn't," Shaw said bitterly.

"I found that I could not." He cleared his throat. "The people I was dealing with, they did not hesitate to send me a message by murdering a dozen of my workers at my ranch in the most grisly and inhumane manner imaginable."

"Yes." Nina gasped. "My father and I wanted to help, but the soldiers turned us away."

"There were none to help," Fuentes finished, his voice flat. "No survivors, not even the youngsters or the women. There were no kind deaths either, their injuries were meant to inflict the greatest pain possible."

"You finally figured out who your business partners really were," Shaw said. He expected a sharp retort from Fuentes, but instead there was only a resigned shrug.

"I had made a deal with the devil, so to speak, and there was no undoing it. At first, when Beth died, I assumed it was the cartel's work. It took some time to figure out it was Escorpion."

"Poor Beth," Nina whispered. "I miss her so much."

"She thought of you like a sister and when I spoke to her of trouble, possible threats due to my business activities, she extracted a promise from me that I would protect you from harm if it became necessary."

Shaw turned back to the table. "So you paid the cop to come and snatch her?"

Fuentes waved a hand. "There are many people on my payroll."

"Let me refresh your memory. The cop, the one I left handcuffed near the river. He's been tracking us."

Otto chuckled. "He is now, what is the word? *A laughingstock?* He showed up a filthy mess at the house of a *chiclero* who called the police to come and fetch him. Amusing to everyone but him."

Fuentes didn't smile. "Yes, he is one. The other two I sent are dead, I fear."

Nina stiffened, and Shaw put a hand on her shoulder. Something was about to explode, he could feel it. "What other two?"

Fuentes looked at Nina. "Josef and Roque."

She gasped. "But they helped me after the accident."

"You had your men shoot up that bus?" Shaw felt his hands ball into fists.

Fuentes shook his head, a frown on his face. "No. Their orders were different. The bus accident was entirely unexpected."

"Escorpion's work?" Otto suggested.

"I do not believe so," Fuentes said thoughtfully. "For two reasons. First, Escorpion is a *cobarde*, a coward, but he is concerned only with business. He has others commit murders when it suits his purposes, but he does not do so indiscriminately to his own people unless there is some profit in it for him."

"A real prince," Shaw muttered.

Otto set down his coffee cup. "And the other reason?"

Fuentes sat forward in the chair. "I enlisted Roque and Josef when I heard through my sources that Escorpion wanted Nina alive at all costs. Shooting up the bus would mean she could have been killed. That would not suit his plans."

Again, evidence that seemed to indicate there was a third party involved somewhere. Not Escorpion, not the police.

"But why does Escorpion want me?" Nina said, voice trembling. "Why is he after me? To pressure you to cooperate?"

"I do not think so." Fuentes eyed her closely. "That is a mystery which I have not unraveled."

"What about Anna?" Nina said. "A woman has been following us too, tracking us, and she drugged me to keep me from coming here." She sucked in a breath and continued. "She said she knows the secret of my birth parents and that someone wants me dead rather than let that get out." She raised her chin. "I wondered if that person is you, Colonel Fuentes?"

Shaw marveled at her courage. *Good for you, Nina. Let him have it.* He watched closely, but the expression on the man's face gave nothing away, except for a puzzled lift to the eyebrow.

"I know nothing about your parentage."

"I'm from this country, Guatemala. My parents adopted me here."

Fuentes stared at her. "This Anna. Can you describe her?" Nina did, and Fuentes looked to Otto. "Do you know of such a woman?"

Otto laughed. "I make it my business to know of every woman, but this one does not stand out in my memory. I am making inquiries. If she has not fled the Petén, I will find her soon and we will put all these questions to her personally."

Fuentes nodded. "In the meantime, I know only that Escorpion wants you and that it is in your best interest that he not find you."

"And yours," Shaw said. "It's in your best interest that Escorpion not get what he wants. The cartel is bankrolling you, and Escorpion is their opposition."

"True, but Escorpion has injured me by taking away my wife. I will do what I can, when I can, to make sure he does not get what he wishes." He looked at Nina. "I assumed you would have left with your father, but when you remained . . ." He shrugged. "You put yourself in danger."

Nina rubbed her hands across her eyes. "This is crazy."

Shaw gave her a squeeze on her shoulder, but he kept his gaze locked on Fuentes. "What were you planning to do with Nina when your cop snatched her? Get her out of the country? I guess you didn't foresee someone hiding a kilo of cocaine at the clinic."

Fuentes blinked. "You misunderstand."

"How so?"

"I sent Roque and Josef to plant the drugs in the shack at the clinic when I learned of your day excursion. They were not meant to snatch her. They were meant to arrest her."

# CHAPTER 24

He spoke so matter-of-factly, Nina was not sure she heard correctly. The room grew quiet and she listened to the ticking of the antique clock on the sideboard. "You had them plant the cocaine? You wanted them to take me to jail?"

He nodded. "Yes, they were to be there when you returned from Tikal, but they were delayed as they had to transport the injured to the hospital. By the time they arrived to arrest you, Mr. Wilder was there to disrupt my plans."

Shaw's eyes rounded. "Jail was your plan?"

Fuentes nodded. "She would be safe from Escorpion and the cartel. Alive and well."

Nina finally found her voice. "In prison?" she squeaked.

"Only temporarily. Soon the evidence would have disappeared and certain wheels would be greased to allow the charges to be dropped. The government would insist on revoking your visa. You would be speedily returned to the States, none the worse for wear."

Shaw let out a bitter laugh. "And there would be no reason for Escorpion, nor the cartel, to think you'd had your hands in it. If you snatched her outright, Escorpion would retaliate."

He shrugged. "I am a practical man."

Nina felt Shaw's anger rising up like floodwaters. "You are a coward," he said and spat.

Fuentes sat up straighter. "Perhaps I did not decide to become the action hero and sweep her away into the jungle, but what have you accomplished by this, Mr. Wilder?" His eyes bored into Shaw's. "You have nearly gotten her killed and attracted so much attention in your flight around the jungle that it was an easy matter for Escorpion to find you and murder two of my men, which now brings the police into this mad chase."

"I kept her from being arrested on fabricated drug charges."

"Ah yes. She is not in jail. An excellent effort. Now she must sneak across the border while both *la policia* and Escorpion's men are no doubt going to be on alert for such an action. Bravo, Mr. Wilder. I'm sure Ms. Truman is appreciative that she is not safely in jail."

"I am," Nina said, her voice loud enough to cut over Shaw's grunt of anger. "He helped me at great risk to himself. How was he to know what you'd planned?" Her eyes blazed. "You should have come to me and warned me of the danger and let me make my own decisions about how to handle it."

Fuentes huffed.

"He didn't want to risk Escorpion finding out," Shaw said. "This way he could keep his hands clean."

Fuentes looked suddenly contrite. "My hands will never be clean of Beth's blood. She is the failure I will take to my grave. The only way I could honor her was to keep you safe, and I would have done that if it were not for his interference."

Shaw stepped toward Fuentes and Nina put her hands to his chest to stop him. At the same time, Otto approached quickly, but stopped at Axel's ferocious bark.

"This is not accomplishing our task," Otto said. "Wherever the fault does or does not lie, we must get the señorita over the border tonight. Shall we be discussing the plan in more detail and leave the fighting for later? This, I think, is wise."

Nina continued to press her palms to Shaw's chest, feeling the beating of his heart against his ribs. Fuentes did not back away from Shaw's anger nor the growling dog, standing his ground until Otto took him by the arm.

"See here, on the map. I have constructed a plan which is no doubt brilliant," Otto said, leading him to the other side of the table. "We shall look at the route, no?"

Shaw followed them to the map, his body stiff with anger. Nina watched them trace out the plan. There was to be a boat crossing at two o'clock, well before sunup. She would be passed off from Otto's people who would escort her across the border into Mexico, and from there, home to her father.

Worry still roiled through her stomach when she thought about the fruitless phone calls she'd made to his cell. A niggling deep down in her stomach prodded at her. Something wasn't right. Someone was not telling her the truth.

She gazed at the men with their heads bent over the table. Fuentes. Otto. Shaw. She didn't trust any of them but Shaw.

And why should she trust him? He was going to kill Escorpion; he accused her of hiding from real life by staying in the jungle and leading Beth into the country where she was murdered. What logical reason did she have to trust him?

He looked up and their eyes met. Worry and anger still played over his face, but his eyes softened when they met hers. He stood. "We'll be ready," he said to the others, following Nina from the room.

Thoughts flew through her mind, stinging her with worries and fears like the voracious clouds of Petén mosquitos. What would happen on the final leg of the journey once Shaw was not there to stand by her side?

And how could she say goodbye to him?

The last thought was unexpected. Less than a week ago, he was only a memory from her past, the handsome older brother to Beth, a man she admired in a schoolgirl fashion from afar. Their days in the jungle had revealed who he really was, both the noble and brutal sides, and she found she did not want him to disappear from her life. Something about him called to her, stirred something deep inside her heart.

*What's wrong with you, Nina?* The trauma had addled her mind.

Shaw walked her to the door and stepped inside, closing it behind him.

"I don't trust Fuentes. He tried to have you jailed and now he's shown up here without invitation." Shaw began to pace, Axel eyeing him with his head resting on his paws. "Maybe he's spilled everything to his cartel buddies and they're on their way."

"I don't think he would do that."

Shaw rounded on her. "And how can you know?"

"Beth loved him. Your sister would not have fallen in love with someone evil."

"He's a drug runner, an opportunist . . ." Shaw struggled for more descriptors. "He's in the cartel, or he might as well be."

"Now, but not when she met him. I think he got in too deeply and now he can't get out."

"He tried to have you arrested."

She sighed. "It wasn't a great plan, but he thought it would work."

Shaw scrubbed his hands over his face. "You cannot be defending him. You cannot be that naïve."

"I know he's probably lying about some things, but he loved your sister and she loved him, too. You hate that, but it's the truth."

He looked like he wanted to break something. She moved closer and, on impulse, reached up to stroke his face. He imprisoned her palm against his cheek, eyes closed as he spoke so low she almost didn't hear him.

"I don't want to hand you over to people I don't trust."

"Why?" she said with a smile. "I'm the irritating missionary girl who's dragged you right into the middle of a mess. I should think you'd be glad to be rid of me."

He circled his arms around her waist and before she knew it, his face was inches from hers. "I don't know why . . . but I'm not."

"You're afraid I'll get hurt?"

He remained silent.

"It's okay to be afraid. I certainly am."

He sighed and grazed his mouth over her forehead, sending a warm current throughout her body. "Is that part of that *Faith is strongest when we're weakest* business?"

She wanted to stay wrapped up in that warmth. "Yes," she whispered. She hesitated before she added, "You could come with me. Into Mexico."

He pushed her chin up, forcing her to look into his eyes. "I have to stay."

"No, you don't." She gripped the material of his shirt. "You don't have to kill Escorpion. You can walk away from that hatred and leave it behind you."

"I can't walk away from what he did to Beth."

"She wouldn't want this for you. God doesn't want this for you."

His eyes roved her face and, for a moment, she thought he would bend down and kiss her. Instead, he moved away and strode to the door. "Try to get some sleep," he said. "It's not over yet."

The door closed softly behind him.

*No, it's not over yet,* she agreed. *God, help him to turn away from his hatred. Please, before it's too late.*

* * *

Shaw tried to sleep on a hammock slung on a screened porch that looked out on the neatly planted rows of palm trees shading the ground. Monkeys added their own noises from the nearby canopy of forest. The oil palms looked well maintained, and he watched a worker sever a massive bunch of fruits from the branches, adding to the pile of nobby, rust-colored clusters he had already collected. Business as usual, until dark.

A flurry of unusual activity would occur tonight . . . and then tomorrow, back to business, back to life in the jungle.

Back to tracking Escorpion and the mission that had been interrupted by one strange day. His mind wandered back over the bus accident and his first encounter with Nina freeing the little boy's father from the burning bus. She'd been crazy to risk her own safety for someone she didn't even know, of course. Crazy and wonderful.

Would he ever see her again?

He knew the answer to that. Even if his mission to kill Escorpion resulted in success, only a slim chance remained that he would survive, let alone get out of the country and back to the United States. And her life would be filled with possibilities of medical school and the lives she would change with her new degree. Pain squeezed at his insides.

He thought about the dichotomy; faith is strongest when we're the weakest. It might have been the only explanation for how a tiny, delicate woman could face her life and loss so courageously. An image of his father filled his mind then, patiently tending to his mother, bringing her flowers and helping dress and feed her, telling her stories he believed she could hear, deep down.

*And praying.*

Praying, for his ruined wife. For his dead daughter.

Shaw swallowed.

For his lost son.

*Who's the coward now, Shaw?*

The man who faced his grief every day and found the courage to offer it up to God? Or the man lost in the jungle, living on the fumes of revenge and hatred?

Maybe another way could be found to emerge from the darkness; maybe Nina was right. Axel, sensing his restlessness, looked up.

His gut told him the answer. *Too late.* He'd moved too far away from God, Nina, his father, his mother, and everyone else. All he had left was hatred.

He turned over and forced his eyes closed.

* * *

He slept in spite of everything, and ate the dinner meal with Otto. There had been no sign of Fuentes. Nina did not come either and he wanted to go and find her, but Otto stopped him.

"She is enjoying the bath my lady has prepared for her. Women need these rituals, do they not? The little pamperings and primpings. It brings the smile back to their faces."

Shaw sat back and toyed with the fish on his plate.

Otto eyed him, a sly smile playing across his face. "So this Nina Truman, she is quite lovely, yes?"

"Yes."

He paused. "Tiny, and yet she has a fire about her." He pointed to his chest. "Here, inside."

Shaw speared a piece of fish and swallowed it, his cheeks growing warm.

"It is hard to resist a woman with such fire."

The fish stuck in Shaw's throat so he gulped down some coffee to help it along.

"I am thinking that you are sweet on this girl, no?"

"No," he almost shouted. In a quieter tone he added, "No, she's just my sister's friend and I'm trying to get her out of a jam."

Otto smoothed his mustache. "So you are risking the bullets and machetes and drug fiends because she is your sister's friend? This is all?"

Shaw glowered at Otto. "This is all." He tried to put just the right tone of finality in the last word.

"Very well," Otto said, laughing. "I am just looking out for you. Like a mother hen clucking about finding her young rooster a lady hen to love. Every rooster needs a hen, no?"

"You should know. You've had a coop full of them."

Otto laughed. "This is true. I grow tired of the birds too quickly because there is always one coming along with brighter feathers and that sparkle in the eye. It turns my head."

Shaw clenched his teeth. "Let's talk about something else, mother hen." He lowered his voice. "Has Fuentes gone?"

"Sadly, no," Otto answered. "He remains until Nina is delivered across the river, in spite of my encouragement of the good colonel to depart."

"Do you trust him?"

Otto leaned forward. "He is a weak man who joins up with the *Mexicans*." Otto spat out the word. "Soon, they are controlling him like a puppet on strings. Weak," he repeated, lip curled. "You cannot trust a weak man who gives away his power."

"I never trusted him in the first place."

Otto's eyes rolled in thought. "This will be a small operation tonight. Only two men and the boat captain. Very small, you see, to call little attention to our efforts." He took a cigar from his pocket and lit it, puffing solemnly. "Fuentes is well connected. He has many foot soldiers, which is why the Mexicans are seeking him out."

"So what do we do?"

"We watch to be sure he is not bringing any other guests to the party tonight."

Shaw nodded. "And if he does?"

Otto looked at him with all traces of humor gone. "Then, I am fearing, my little plan will become bloody very quickly."

Shaw's heart thudded. Nina *could not* get caught in the crossfire. He would make sure of it.

Otto walked to the desk and took out a gun, handing it to Shaw. "Our enemies are coming in many forms, my friend. We should be remembering it was a woman who got nearest your *amiga* last time, and stuck a needle into her arm. If it had been poison, you and I would not be having this conversation. Many enemies in our henhouse."

He didn't need Otto's reminder. That point had been hammered home since he'd pulled Nina from the burning bus. "Hard to tell the foxes from the hens."

"There can be no second chances now," Otto said.

Shaw weighed the gun in his palm, the cold metal chilling his skin.

Through the cloud of cigar smoke, Otto nodded as Shaw tucked the gun away and returned to his hammock to watch the minutes tick down.

# CHAPTER 25

Her mind consumed by what would transpire in the next few hours, Nina felt thoroughly satisfied to be completely clean for the first time since she'd boarded the bus.

Carmelita filled the old cast-iron tub with deliciously hot water and added some fragrant herbs which perfumed the tiny bathroom. Nina washed and scrubbed, rinsing her hair again and again, applying the small bar of soap to every possible square inch until the water grew cloudy. She would have loved to drain the water out and fill it again, but she didn't want to waste. When she finished, she dried and dressed in a skirt and blouse. Carmelita entered the room and held up a hairbrush.

"Oh, thanks very much," Nina said, holding out her hands.

Carmelita waved them away and herded her to a chair where she began to brush out the thick curtain of Nina's dark hair. Her fingers found the shorn section and she raised a questioning eyebrow.

"It's a long story," Nina said with a laugh.

Carmelita began to braid Nina's undamaged hair into a thick plait down her back. On impulse, Nina caught her eye in the mirror. "Do you know a woman named Anna?"

Carmelita started for a moment. "Anna? There are many Annas in this country."

Nina described Anna to Carmelita. The woman looked studiously away as her fingers flew through the strands.

"No, I do not know any woman like that."

"Her mother was a nurse at an orphanage here in Guatemala. Are you sure you don't know of her?"

Carmelita dropped the brush on the table. "No, señorita."

"How long have you worked here?"

"Only a few months."

Nina suspected from the long looks Otto had shot in her direction, that there may have been more between Otto and Carmelita than boss and employee. "Do you like working at the plantation?"

She nodded. "It is a blessing to have work and Señor Otto is good to me. I am able to care for my mother and put aside something for when I am no longer needed here."

"When will that be?"

Carmelita flashed a quick look. "Things change quickly." She finished the braid and tied it with a ribbon. "I must go now."

Nina wanted to keep her talking, but the woman scurried out the door. She had the unsettled feeling Carmelita had more to tell about Anna.

She brooded about it until the sun dropped below the trees. Part of her desired to go find Shaw, to sit with him and spend the last minutes of their time together in undisturbed quiet. The other part flooded with grief at their upcoming parting and the knowledge of what he meant to do after she found safety and solace in Mexico.

She spent the long hours praying, and packing and repacking her small bag which she tried her best to spot clean in the sink. Finally, the clock read one-thirty and there came a knock at the door.

She flung it open, hoping to see Shaw, but a man she didn't know summoned her.

She followed him outside into a dark night, lit only by a sliver of moon and the rays from two flashlights.

"*Buenas noches*, señorita," Otto called, waving her over to a horse. "We ride these beasts tonight."

She approached and found Shaw there suddenly, helping her

into the saddle. His hands lingered on her arm. He looked as if he wanted to say something, but Fuentes rode up, mounted expertly on the back of a black horse, and he nodded solemnly at her. Fuentes, Otto, Nina, and Shaw started down the trail that paralleled the river, Axel following along.

The water sparkled in undulating ribbons next to them, flecked by the moonlight. How lovely it would be to ride under other circumstances, but far too much worry weighed her down. She prayed silently as they went along.

Otto pulled his horse to a stop under the trailing vines and examined the ground carefully. "Tire tracks."

Shaw rode next to him in a flash. "Jeep?"

"Maybe," Otto said. "Rain has blurred it. It is hard to be telling when it has passed this way."

The skin on Nina's arms prickled. All around her, shadows danced in the darkness, reminding her how easy it would be for someone to track them as Escorpion had done before. Axel remained on high alert, but he didn't bark or sound an alarm. Yet.

Otto spoke in rapid Spanish, and Fuentes readied his rifle.

Nina swallowed, remembering the sound of Escorpion's bullets plunking into the water around them, the sight of Shaw's face when one of them found its mark in Axel. She forced herself to keep breathing regularly as they continued on, the trees thinning around them, leaving them exposed. Goose bumps danced over her arms.

Otto sped up the pace until the horses trotted, and Nina found it took all her concentration to stay seated on the jostling saddle. She wished she'd taken up Juan Carlton's offer to teach her to ride. It seemed a lifetime ago that she'd sat next to his broken body, ignoring Anna's command for her to run away. What would have happened if she had gone with Anna then? Would she know the truth about her parents, or would she be dead?

She certainly wouldn't have gotten to know Shaw, the man who got her out of the bus wreckage before it rolled down the ravine in a ball of fire. She shot a look at Shaw, and she found the determined set to his shoulders comforting.

Branches slapped at her, wet and clammy. Uneven ground pitched her forward and backward in the saddle. When she thought she couldn't stay mounted a moment longer, they reached a cluster of trees set back from the riverbank. Even the constant chorus of jungle insects fell still.

A small dock stacked with large wooden crates that had seen better days held an old coil of weathered rope. She saw no sign of a boat along the inky water, but Otto did not seem perturbed.

He cracked a smile, teeth white in the darkness. "We are early. Plenty of time to relax and enjoy our adventure before the boat arrives. It is a lovely Guatemalan night, no? The stuff sweet ballads are made of."

Fuentes dismounted, but he didn't loosen his grip on the rifle. Shaw helped Nina from the horse and down to her shaky legs. He kept a supporting hand under her elbow.

"Everything looks okay," he said. "It will be over soon."

She nodded, trying to sort out her cascade of feelings. He led her to a box and she sat, ridiculously grateful to have escaped the heaving saddle.

He stood next to her. "Call the embassy as soon as you can," he said.

"I will."

"And call me when you get back to the States. I don't know when I'll pick up a new phone, but I'll get one eventually." He hesitated. "I'll . . . it will make me feel better to know you're back on American soil."

She nodded. Silence stretched between them. "I'll miss you," she finally blurted out.

He caught up her fingers and squeezed them. "Don't miss me. Just go on with your life and be an amazing doctor."

"I will," she said, voice thick with emotion. "And then I'm coming back to Guatemala to run a clinic." She imagined what it would be like to find him here then, with Axel, untouched by any further violence. His eyes searched her face and she saw that he hadn't given up his plan to punish Escorpion. He would not be there when she finished medical school. This truly was their last moment together before hatred tore them apart.

Shaw drew close and whispered in her ear. "You really are going to be a great doctor. I'm proud of you, and Beth would have been, too."

Tears pricked her eyes and she pressed her head to his chest. "Shaw…"

He kissed her then, gentle and sweet, and it awakened a feeling of unbridled joy. The connection between them was fragile and tender. Something had changed inside him, somewhere in that frantic trek across the jungle. Though she couldn't tell exactly what or when it had occurred, she prayed it was enough to transform him, that a spark would turn to flame and burn away his smoldering need for vengeance.

* * *

The sound of a motor thrummed through the darkness and broke the spell. Tension roiled through Shaw, overflowing the exquisite emotion he'd felt a moment before when he'd kissed Nina. The boat still lingered a mile or so downriver, but if something was going to go bad, this was the time. Shaw paced, peering into the trees, checking the rocky hillside above them, using his binoculars to track the progress of the boat.

He saw no sign of anyone posted on the crag above, no indication of anything amiss. The vessel crept toward them, only a dim light illuminating the silhouette of the captain.

They came near enough for him to see the boat with a powerful outboard motor and a covered cabin. The captain's companion loosened a skiff and rowed over to collect Nina so that the larger boat could avoid the rocky shallow water near the dock.

Shaw held her hand and once again tried to put his feelings into words, but like the elusive lyrics to a forgotten song, he could only wrangle up the tune. He could only hope to pass the emotion to her through one last kiss. He pressed his mouth to hers, with all the tenderness he could manage.

When they parted, she looked up at him, eyes wide, and a gentle smile on her lips. She touched his face, her skin soft as the breeze against his cheek.

"Be careful," he whispered.

"You too." Reluctantly, with pain knifing through his stomach, Shaw handed her down into the rough wooden skiff and watched as she glided away across the water.

Shaw still felt wary, but he could make out no sign of trouble. Axel had grown bored with the proceedings and had gone off to sniff the wooden crates.

It didn't seem real that Nina was no longer with him. He saw her dark head, her hand raised to wave goodbye. His heart felt as though it had torn at that moment, and the cold river water flowed in to drown him.

Axel whined. Perhaps he felt it too, that loss Shaw could not explain.

Otto and Fuentes watched the boat churn away from the dock, still alert for ambush. The only sound that broke the silence came in the form of the chugging of the engine and the melancholy breeze rifling through the leaves.

The dog pawed at a heavy crate.

"You're going to get splinters," Shaw snapped. Axel continued to worry at the wood, shoving his nose against the side.

Shaw moved over and freed a small flashlight which he carefully shielded with his hands, directing the light downward. The crate showed nothing unusual. It was nailed shut. He trailed the light over the dock around the bottom. His whole body went cold when he saw the dark streak partially concealed by the crate. Heedless of any noise he might make, he yanked at the lid, heaving against the nails that fastened it down.

The wood top didn't budge. Searching frantically, he found a thin metal pry bar tucked behind one of the stacks. Shoving the bar under the lid, he forced down on it with all his weight. Boards protested with a shrill shriek that startled some small animal into flight through the bushes.

"What are you doing?" Fuentes demanded. "You are making too much noise."

Shaw had loosened the top enough to push his hand inside and wrench off the wood panel.

He shone the light inside, and all three men joined him to peer down at it.

A man lay at the bottom of the crate, bloodied and battered. He appeared to breathe, but that could have been Shaw's senses playing tricks on him.

Shaw looked to Otto in horror.

Otto's eyes were huge with shock. "This is my man, the one who is supposed to be piloting the boat."

All three faces turned toward the departing boat.

Shaw dropped the lid and raced to the edge of the dock. Nina had already boarded, and now two other silhouettes appeared from concealment, letting loose with sprays of automatic weapons that flashed through the night.

Shaw called out her name. "Nina!" But the sound of it was lost in bullets that pounded the dock, tearing into the wood and sending all of them taking cover behind the crates; including Axel, who hunkered down next to him, barking. Shaw risked a look to find that the boat sailed quickly away, the gunmen continuing to pepper the dock with bullets. He tried again to make for the water, but a shot grazed his shoulder and he went down, his cheek grating against the weathered wood of the dock. Crawling back behind the crate with Axel tugging him along, Shaw's mind fogged over with pain and rage.

Nina was gone. Escorpion had bested them in the final move, taking out the boat captain and substituting his own men. Now Nina was on her way to the custody of a madman, his sister's killer. And they'd been too stupid and slow to catch on.

He slammed his fist against the crate, ignoring the pain in his shoulder.

Otto and Fuentes approached when the gunfire died away.

Otto's grave expression intensified. "He has outplayed me. He knew. Somehow, he knew." His gaze shifted to Fuentes. "Who did you tell of this plan? Someone in your employ who has talked out of school?"

Fuentes stiffened. "You forget who you are speaking to. I told no one. Perhaps the leak came from one of yours."

"Nonsense," Otto spat.

Shaw got to his feet. "It doesn't matter now."

Otto noticed the blood soaking Shaw's sleeve. "You are wounded my friend. Sit down."

Shaw shook off his hand. "Where would Escorpion take her?"

Otto blinked in surprise. "Where?" His eyes rolled in thought. "A place where we cannot go."

"Where, Otto?" Shaw said through gritted teeth.

He hesitated. "The closest spot is his home up the mountain. He would not expect anyone to challenge him there."

"Why not?" Shaw said.

"Because," Fuentes said, slinging his rifle over his shoulder. "He is well protected there, in a compound of sorts. The villagers nearby will protect him."

"Like your people would do for you before you signed your life away to the Mexicans," Otto said.

Shaw's shoulder burned. They eased the beaten man from the box and bundled him as gently as they could onto one of the horses.

Fuentes walked stiffly to his horse and mounted in one graceful motion. "If you want my help in going to fetch Señorita Truman, I will accompany you myself. Otherwise, I am certain we will not see one another again."

Shaw would be happy never to share the same country with Fuentes for the rest of his life, but he knew he'd need all the help he could get if he was going to get Nina out alive.

Otto broke the tension with a laugh. "And I, too, will accompany you, though you will please not to count on me to be doing something foolish like walking in front of a bullet. I am too much in love with the nice things in my life to end it for an American girl who does not even know how to make a decent tortilla."

Shaw would have smiled if not for the fire of pain and anger blazing inside him. Instead, he just nodded.

"I suppose," Otto added with a sigh, "that we must go about saving this damsel at this very moment? I am not to be eating any fine beans and eggs this morning?"

No one answered.

"Very well," he said. "We will stop along the way for some supplies suitable for storming a compound and deliver this poor man to the village. Perhaps I will find breakfast there, but first I am thinking we should bandage that shoulder."

"No need," Shaw said, moving toward his horse.

"But there is," Otto said quietly, voice suddenly sober. "Escorpion, he is a wily one and perhaps he has paid off some people who are watching." He pointed to the ground. "A blood trail will be easy to follow, no? How foolish if Escorpion were to know we are coming. So much better if he believes he has killed us."

Shaw looked at the spatters of his own blood, black in the moonlight. He knew Escorpion wouldn't be too surprised at all to know that Shaw pursued him. He recalled the drug runner's quiet warning at the airstrip.

*"You are a stranger, and you have crossed a line from which you will not return."*

He sat patiently while Otto wrapped a length of cloth around his shoulder, steeling himself against the pain when he cinched it tight.

Escorpion was right. He had crossed a line and he might not return.

But then . . . neither would Escorpion.

# CHAPTER 26

The bizarre situation unfolded in violent spurts. Nina was handed aboard the boat and abruptly shoved to the bottom, a man's body holding her immobilized to the deck. An explosion of gunfire vibrated the wood underneath her and stabbed through her ears until she started screaming.

She thought at first that Escorpion's men fired from the bank as the maelstrom of sound confounded her senses. After several more moments, the gunshots diminished and the man released her to sit upright. Head spinning, she tried to get her bearings.

"Have they found us?" She crawled to the side and peered at the dock, now far in the distance. Had they killed Shaw? Fuentes and Otto? Were they all lying dead?

She turned to the captain. "What happened?"

He ignored her.

The man who had pinned her to the bottom of the boat smiled, an unpleasant grin. "Escorpion will be happy to see you," he said with a laugh.

She looked at him in horror, her stare shifting from the captain to the laughing man, and over to the other gunman in the stern of the boat. These were not Otto's men. They had not been firing to scare away Escorpion's people, but to kill her protectors.

Her head snapped toward the dock again. *Shaw*, her heart cried out. Had he died there? Was he bleeding to death next to the others because of whatever twisted game Escorpion played? Because of her?

The captain laughed along with the other two, and Nina made a decision in the span of a heartbeat. With their laughter ringing in her ears, she leapt over the side of the boat.

The water enveloped her, cold and heavy, but she kicked immediately to the surface. She didn't think they would shoot at her after taking such pains to take her alive. The current tugged and tossed her as she set out for the bank, grasping at her heavy clothing and threatening to suck her to the bottom.

She *would not* be drowned by this river. She *would not* be taken by these men. And above all, she *would* make it back to Shaw. If he'd survived it all, he would need her.

Water blinded her and she stopped for a moment to get her bearings until she heard a splash and the shouts of the men on the boat. They'd pulled the vessel into a tight arc to circle back to her location, but the current fought them too.

She swiped at the hair plastering her face and made out the blurry outline of the trees. With all the strength she possessed, she stroked through the water. As the bank grew closer, she made out the rocks piled in irregular mounds.

*Head for the rocks,* she thought. The men outnumbered her, but she was small. She could find a place to hide and make her way toward the dock when she could. Her arms felt leaden, muscles complaining from the accumulation of fatigue over the past few days. She kicked harder, willing herself on, pushing her body against the tug of the current.

Once she began to sense the water becoming shallow, the choppy movement of the waves thrust her toward the shore. Five more hard strokes and she got her feet under her, gasping, standing, the water up to her waist, rocks and gravel shifting under her feet. She struggled to wipe her eyes as a hand from out of nowhere grabbed her hair.

Nina pulled and kicked at her captor, but he held fast, oblivious to her assault. He yanked her backward and slipped something around her wrist. In a matter of moments, she felt the sting of her hands tied behind her back, held fast by plastic restraints. He turned her and she once again looked at the man from the boat. He no longer laughed, but a look of triumph beamed from his face. He didn't speak as he pushed her onto the shore.

Sodden and exhausted, Nina decided he wouldn't see her cry.

He forced her along the bank to a place where the water deepened, allowing the motorboat to come close. While they waited, he pressed so close to her that she could smell his sour breath as it landed on her face.

"I am going to take you out to the boat," he said. "We have orders not to kill you, but that is as far as it goes." His eyes wandered along the length of her torso. She suddenly became excruciatingly aware of the outline provided by her wet shirt, knowing that whatever this man decided to do, she was helpless to stop it. Fear surged through her.

"There are other things we can do without ending your life." He put a hand on the collar of her shirt, causing her to flinch as his fingers grazed her skin, flicking under the wet fabric.

"You might hurt me. Escorpion wouldn't like that." It was a shot in the dark, but the man hesitated for a moment.

He leaned in close. "I could make sure not to leave any marks," he whispered.

At that moment, she truly understood what it meant to be powerless at the hands of someone else. Breathing became a sheer act of will.

*God, please, please.*

A voice called from the boat. The man held her close for one more moment. "Remember, señorita." Her legs trembled violently as he dragged her into the water, marching her out until her feet no longer touched bottom. Fighting the panic caused by her bound hands, she had no choice but to let him put his arm around her neck and float her on her back toward the boat.

Once again, they lifted her aboard and seated her this time on a bench. She shivered with cold and exertion, her mind reeling.

The captain dialed his cell phone. "She will be there in two hours," he said.

Despair crept over her as she watched the boat journey deeper downriver, no more hope of escape.

The only thing she could think about was Shaw Wilder.

* * *

They decided to risk a fire. After hours of rough travel and a quick stop at a shack, Shaw coaxed a flame to life from underneath the dilapidated remains of what had once been a storage shed. Just enough of a rusted tin roof remained to deflect the drizzle and provide fairly dry tinder for their use.

Shaw didn't want to stop, but even he could see that they needed to rest. The bandage Otto had applied had almost seeped through with blood. Fuentes feared his horse had collected a pebble in his hoof which required attention. Axel looked exhausted too as he flopped down next to Shaw and promptly went to sleep. If only Shaw could do the same. Instead, he tried to keep from grinding his teeth as Otto patiently fed the flame which admittedly felt pretty good. Shaw accepted a cloth from Otto's pack and secured it around the old bandage, ignoring the pain. He didn't know whether the bullet had gone through or lodged somewhere in his shoulder. Best not to think about it since he couldn't do anything to treat it anyway.

Otto took something wrapped in leaves from his pack and unwrapped it. Attaching it to a stick, he held it over the fire, causing Axel to open one eye.

"Where'd you get the fish?" Shaw asked him.

"A gift, pressed upon me by the *chiclero* when we stopped to deliver the wounded man."

"Along with the pistol?"

Otto laughed. "I am not aware that you are noticing that."

"I try to notice everything. It keeps me alive."

Shaw's stomach growled as the flames began to crisp the skin of the fish. Fuentes stood several yards away, tending to his horse, and Shaw noticed Otto sneak a look at him.

"You still don't trust him?" Shaw muttered.

Otto kept his gaze on the fire, the flames reflecting in his dark eyes like some internal lightning. He answered in a near whisper. "He has made friends with our enemies."

The past few days had caused Shaw to rethink his definition of friends and enemies, justice and revenge. He thought about tender-hearted Nina then, a woman who believed even he—a man bent on murder—could be worthy of God's love.

A spark separated itself from the fire and floated away into the black velvet night. It occurred to him then in a sizzle of clarity, with the jungle humming and pulsing all around him, that his mission for revenge might not be for Beth after all. Was killing Escorpion a way to quench the fire inside him rather than the means to secure justice for Beth? Who would his revenge serve? Not his dead sister. She would not condone it, even if it would prevent Escorpion from spreading his network further. It was not for Beth, nor for the good of Guatemala. Despite all of these realizations, however, the hatred still ran swiftly through him.

*Escorpion does not deserve to live,* he thought savagely. *If I'm the only one strong enough to kill him, then so be it.*

Nina's earnest voice whispered through his memory. *Your strength comes through Him, not through you. That's faith, and it's strongest when we are the weakest.*

It was not the time for weakness. He left Otto to his cooking, got to his feet, and moved away from the smoke to suck in a few lungfuls of clean jungle air. He found himself drawing near to Fuentes, who now stood in the shelter of the trees, his horse nibbling the sprigs of tender grass. Fuentes looked away at the ridge of mountains silhouetted by the faint moonlight, so lost in his thoughts he didn't seem to hear Shaw's approach.

"Horse okay?"

Fuentes turned to him and nodded. "A small stone. I removed it."

Shaw glanced at the mountain ridge where Fuentes' gaze had returned, but he found he could not think of a thing to say to this man whom he wished his sister had never clapped eyes upon. Fuentes was from a different world, a strange and barbarous reality where loyalties were bought and sold and the current of drugs flowed just as swiftly as the Usamacinta River.

"I was born in the highlands," Fuentes said.

Shaw waited in silence.

"Beth said we should return there, leave my ranches behind and raise chickens." Shaw could hear the smile in Fuentes' voice even though his face turned away. "Can you imagine? To leave all my wealth, all my cattle and houses and land and return to the highlands to raise *chickens*?" He sighed, a low and soft gust, like the breeze trickling through the leaves. "It was ridiculous, impractical and obviously impossible. The incredible thing is that she made me almost believe I could. *Almost*."

The quiet stream of emotion in that last word stunned Shaw; regret and pain reverberated through those two syllables. *Almost.* Beth's love had almost been enough to change the corrupt colonel. Fuentes had been almost ready to leave his life with the cartel behind, nearly convinced by Beth's love that his soul was worth more than his status, his acquisitions, his self-importance.

Almost.

But Fuentes had been so rooted by those things that he couldn't cut them loose. He could not humble himself, weaken himself, for anyone, even Beth.

*When I am weak, then I am strong.*

He found Fuentes looking at him.

"I notice you have your sister's eyes."

Shaw's throat thickened. Fuentes had loved Beth; like Nina, like Shaw. None of them, he reasoned, shouldered the responsibility for her death. No one except Escorpion. If he ever got the chance, he vowed to apologize to Nina for blaming her.

"You loved her." Shaw pushed the words out, grating over his throat and out into the humid air. "I understand now that you never meant to hurt her."

They watched each other in silence, the crackle of the fire playing counterpoint to the murmur of life tucked invisibly all around them.

"I did not save Beth," Fuentes said quietly. "But I will help you save her friend."

They stood there, the rain thickening around them, until they turned without a further word and joined Otto in the paltry shelter.

* * *

Nina strained at the plastic bands around her wrists, but the effort proved futile. Gradually, as the boat took her farther and farther away from Shaw, she grew still, her eyes resting on the water. There was little talk from the men until they docked the boat some two hours later, moving her to a waiting vehicle. The man who had captured her earlier pushed her roughly onto the backseat so that she pitched facedown with a small cry.

The boat captain spoke harshly to him in a language she did not understand. The meaning was clear anyway; as he well knew, she was not to be harmed.

*Yet.*

She decided to press her advantage. "My wrists are bleeding. Please take off the restraints."

The captain and the other man exchanged a look. She thought they would ignore her request as the captain slid into the driver's seat, but the other man removed a small knife from his belt and cut the restraints from her wrists.

Maybe an opportunity of escape would arise when they slowed or stopped. The small hope evaporated when the man with the knife climbed in the backseat next to her, pulling her nearer and belting her into the middle seat, out of reach of the door handles. She tried to make herself as small as possible, but his body touched hers anyway, sending a ripple of disgust through her.

She tried several times to ask why Escorpion wanted her, why she'd been taken. Though she knew they would never answer, it gave her some sense of control to try. The road became steeper, the vegetation changing from jungle to the towering conifers typical of the highlands. They finally turned onto a neatly tended road, set back amongst the trees so that it became nearly invisible. The driver punched a code into the elegant gate and they drove through. She saw a fenced paddock with a dozen beautiful horses silhouetted in the moonlight.

Her pulse hammered hard in her throat, and she prayed prayer after prayer as they moved deeper into the trees. The outline of something—more of a castle than a house—loomed in the darkness. The moonlight caught on the pale stone cupolas and the dark wooded doors. Cleverly tucked amidst the trees, she could hardly pick out the dimensions of the structure. The car pulled up a graveled horseshoe drive and stopped in front of the massive black beamed doors.

Stomach tight, she climbed out, sneaking peeks out of her peripheral vision, hoping for the chance to bolt. She wasn't even sure it would help since she had no idea in which direction to flee. They pulled her into a foyer with a high ceiling, the interior cool and dark, and her eyes struggled to adjust to the wall sconces emitting a buttery light that softened the stark interior.

Her knees shook as the captain and the man suddenly withdrew, closing the doors behind them.

"Wait," she called to the closed door, panic suddenly overwhelming her good sense. She pounded a fist on the wood, yanking on the handle, and finding she couldn't open it.

A woman's voice called from the spiraling stairs in the corner.

"That won't do you any good." Nina shivered as Anna stepped into the poor light from the wall sconces, dressed in a neat skirt and blouse, hair coiled into a fat braid pinned to her head.

"I am glad you have finally arrived," she said, a note of disapproval in her voice.

Nina could not figure out how to start. *Who? Why?* The questions tumbled around in her brain as Anna moved closer, and Nina stepped back.

"You drugged me," she managed.

"You are a stubborn girl. You would insist on going back to the American and his friend." There was a tone of derision in the last word. "I tried to explain it to you, but there was no time."

"Explain what?"

Anna gave her an appraising look. "We need to get you into dry clothes before you catch a chill. I am told you dove into the river."

"I'm not going anywhere with you," Nina whispered through her chattering teeth.

Anna's expression of calm didn't change in the slightest. "There is a room upstairs, a very nice room. We will go there."

Nina shook her head, pressing farther against the wall behind her. Then she noticed a man who had slipped in from the side door behind the stairs, and he stood in the shadows with his arms folded.

"You will come with me or Juan will make you go." Anna shrugged. "Either way, there is no getting out of here."

*Oh yes there is, I just have to find it.*

When Juan moved closer, Nina started up the stairs after Anna. She led the way to a small bedroom with a cream tile floor and a bed covered in beautiful linens. A peaked window broke up the line of soft, muted prints on the walls.

Anna's nose wrinkled in disgust. "Bathe and dress. Everything you need is here. I will come back to take you to him in the morning."

"Escorpion?"

"Of course."

"Tell me why I'm here," Nina said, catching her arm and clinging tight. "Please, Anna."

Anna pried her fingers away, eyes blazing with sudden anger. "You are here because he desired it and because he is a man of his word." The words hissed out with such force that Nina let go and shuffled back.

Anna disappeared out the door and closed it hard. Nina waited a moment before she tried the handle. Locked. No surprise.

She went immediately to the window looking down over an oblong courtyard, and she felt dismayed to find a grillwork of iron bars crisscrossing the glass. Down below, a pool glinted in the darkness, and strategically placed lights hinted at well-tended plants around the periphery. She tested the bars anyway and found them shut tight.

A quick scan of the room netted her nothing of use; no scissors, heavy ornaments, not even so much as a nail file. She had been imprisoned; a well-appointed, comfortable one, but a prison nonetheless.

Her thoughts returned to Shaw. She desperately wished for the comfort of his embrace, the warmth of his eyes, the rare thrill of his laughter.

*Is he alive?* she wondered for the hundredth time. Or had the bullets ended his life, and Otto and the Colonel's, too?

# CHAPTER 27

As they finally found the paved road the next morning, Shaw's neck itched from the mass of mosquito bites, and his shoulder throbbed an incessant painful rhythm. They might have missed it entirely if Otto hadn't pried the information from a fisherman they'd encountered sometime in the wee hours of the morning. He'd had to ease the information out of the man with friendly banter and sweeten the conversation with a handful of quetzals.

"Has he got cameras other than the one at the gate?" Shaw demanded.

Otto shook his head. "The man would not say, but I am finding that quite likely."

They stayed back from the road and shared Otto's binoculars to check for any signs of movement. Except for a car parked in the gravel driveway, the place seemed like a still photograph. When the car engine started abruptly, the three men retreated into the shadows, horses well out of the line of sight.

"That's the boat captain," Fuentes whispered as the car passed through the gate.

Shaw ground his teeth. It went against every instinct he had to let the man go who had snatched Nina away. He forced himself to stay motionless as the car vanished into the jungle. The less men at the compound, the better.

He again trained the binoculars at the castle façade. "Doesn't look like he's got sentries."

Fuentes remained pensive.

"Looks can deceive. We must watch for a while before we go in," Fuentes said.

Shaw knew he was right, though the idea of waiting another minute rankled him. Hunched in the trees, water dripping from the branches, the inactivity burned inside like acid.

Was Escorpion hurting Nina? Defiling her? A vein throbbed in his temple. He figured he understood now how Axel felt when he forbade him to go after the bad guys. Seconds ticked into minutes; ten, fifteen. Their patience paid off though when two men with rifles slung over their shoulders made their way in a slow circle around the main house, the glowing tip of one of their cigarettes marking their way. It soon became evident that they performed this check at regular intervals, radioing in their progress.

Shaw wanted to climb the gate himself the next time the men vanished around the back, but Fuentes stopped him. "Listen."

The sound of an engine reverberated through the trees. The captain and his cohort returning? It might be their only chance to secure the gate code. He told Axel to stay and crept forward, keeping to the trees.

Otto held out a hand to stop him. "This is folly, my friend."

Shaw shook him off. "Keep the dog quiet," he said as he moved away.

He stayed to the bushes, shoving his way through, head low until he got near enough to spot an SUV winding up the road. Shaw didn't recognize the driver, nor could he get a good look at the person in the backseat. Didn't matter anyway; he had only one mission now.

The gate code.

He forced his way along, scrambling to keep up with the vehicle, pushing through the foliage when the driver stopped and reached out a hand to punch in a code on the security gate. Shaw had his binoculars up in an instant. He heightened the focusing power and committed the numbers to memory; or at least he hoped he'd gotten the numbers correct. It had taken only an instant for the driver to finish before the gate opened and closed again behind the vehicle. Shaw remained still until he spotted the camera mounted on a pole and shrouded by a pine, in perfect position to record anything that passed through the gate; and no doubt passed it along to a monitor in the main house. He eased back and returned to Otto and Fuentes to report his findings.

"I'll open the gate after we take out the camera. Hopefully, they'll think it's a mechanical failure and come to investigate. We won't have much time before they figure it out."

"And if you have gotten the code wrong?" Otto said.

Shaw shook his head, not wanting to allow for that possibility. "I didn't."

Otto sighed. "Ah, such confidence. It makes me wish I was a young man again."

Fuentes spoke quietly, his eyes still on the gate. "How will we disable the camera?"

"There's a wire running down the pole. One of us will cut it while I put in the code."

"That will be me, I am thinking," Otto said. "And then I will depart quickly and continue my efforts to speak to someone at the embassy on your behalf."

Shaw felt disappointed, but not surprised. Otto had done much already that risked his standing and position. He wasn't about to risk his life, and he'd flat out said as much. "Fair enough."

He thought about asking Otto to take Axel with him, but he knew Axel wouldn't go. He felt the comforting weight of the dog leaning against his leg. A friend in good times and bad; truly, the best kind.

"And how to get into the main house?" Fuentes said thoughtfully. "It looks well-fortified, and there are, of course, the guards."

Shaw looked toward the horses, their coats luminous in the moonlight. "I think we'll just have to make a little diversion."

Fuentes nodded, a small smile on his face.

Otto clasped Shaw in a bear hug that pushed the breath out of him. "I am wishing things would have turned out differently, but there is no good in wishing. There is only the storming of the castle, and I leave that to you who are young and foolish." He leaned close. "Remember there are foxes in our henhouse," he whispered into Shaw's ear. "If he shows his teeth, kill him."

Shaw wondered if Otto referred to Fuentes or Escorpion. Fuentes stepped closer and Otto broke off.

Fuentes took Shaw's hand and shook it solemnly. "For Beth."

Shaw's heart chimed in silently. *For Nina.* As they readied themselves to enact their plan, Shaw looked up at the Guatemalan sky. He should have been terrified, but he wasn't. Maybe being so close to Nina had caused some of her dauntless courage to rub off on him. He clung suddenly to her belief that things would turn out as they were meant to.

He brushed away a drop of cold water that slid down his temple.

*I know You and I don't agree on much, but if You're there . . . God, use me to get her out alive.*

His prayer astonished him, but his calm resolve surprised him even more. He couldn't deny the almost detached sensation that he had stepped into line with some sort of divine plan that would unfold and sweep him along with it.

Otto made little noise as he moved toward the pole, his knife at the ready. Shaw had no time to pinpoint Fuentes' location as Otto whistled long and low and cut the cord.

Shaw punched in the code. For a long moment, nothing happened. His mind whirled as Axel pressed hard against his leg. He'd gotten it wrong. Guards would come, find the damaged camera and the whole place would swarm with security. The sudden and quiet hum of the gate made his skin prickle in relief as it slid open on oiled runners.

He and Axel, followed quickly by Fuentes, were through the gate in an instant. He allowed himself one more look backward, but he couldn't see any sign of Otto. Fuentes already ran toward the corral as the gate slid back into place. Shaw caught up quickly and helped him undo the latches. Fuentes slapped one of the horses firmly on the rear. In a rush of sudden movement, the horses began funneling out the gate as Fuentes continued to urge them forward. He flashed Shaw an enthusiastic smile.

"The most fun I have had in long months," he said.

They ducked low and edged close to the house, slinking behind some flowering plants just as the side door flung open and the two guards came out. They came to a dead stop, as they spotted the horses milling in confusion in the front garden and wandering around the side.

Shaw held Axel by the scruff of the neck, catching the shouts as the men took off in pursuit. The door they had just exited hadn't closed all the way.

*Bingo*. Shaw and Axel headed inside, with Fuentes right behind them.

* * *

The morning found Nina huddled on the floor, still wearing her muddy clothes. She had not been able to find any way out of the locked room. She pinned her flailing hopes on her father. Perhaps he had discovered part of what had happened and contacted the embassy and they had become aware that something had happened to her. The thoughts didn't calm her enough and she began to prowl again, searching the bathroom for anything that might help in an escape. Nothing. She looked at her muddy hands and sodden clothes, eyeing the clean garments hanging on the peg. When she did find a way to flee into the jungle, she'd last longer wearing dry clothes.

With no way to lock the door, Nina wedged her shoe in the gap underneath. At least it would slow someone down. She filled the corner tub with hot water, wondering how Escorpion had managed to create such a luxurious castle in the middle of a rugged mountain terrain. It was disgusting, really, the way he lined his pockets with blood money and indulged in such extravagances at the price of the people he used.

Quickly stripping off her clothes, she hopped into the near-scalding water and washed at record speed, soaping and rinsing as efficiently as she could. She examined the clothes; another skirt and a gauzy top. Nina retrieved her old shirt and found that it had nearly dried, and a small tear separated the sleeve from the shoulder. She saw a brush and yanked out the tangles before pulling her mass of hair back into as severe a ponytail as she could manage. It would help when she broke free not to have her hair catching on every branch and twig.

Nina could only guess how she looked since the bathroom hadn't been equipped with a mirror. She hoped her appearance came off as severe and composed instead of terrified and alone, which seemed to better fit the bill as soon as she reentered the bedroom. A shout from outside brought her to the window, but she couldn't see a thing except the maddening courtyard.

She remembered an old movie she'd once seen. Maybe she could hide under the bed and, when Anna set to work looking for her, she could make her escape. Probably ridiculous, but at least it was something. She just lifted the comforter and peered into the gap when the door opened suddenly.

"He's ready for you now," Anna said from the doorway.

Nina jerked to her feet.

Anna surveyed her from her head to the hem of her skirt. "The other blouse, it is better. Put it on."

Nina's chin lifted. "I'm here against my will and I don't have to please my abductor. If you want that other blouse on me, you're going to have to make me wear it."

Nina thought that Shaw would have been proud of her answer, and it gave her a tiny measure of comfort.

Anna's eyes narrowed and she sighed. "We must not keep him waiting," she said, turning on her heel and leading the way out the door.

If nothing else, she would at least be able to put her questions to Escorpion himself, at last. Nina felt a deep shiver of dread as she followed. Was she ready for the answers?

* * *

Shaw slid the lock home on the door. It might only buy them a few minutes, but he'd take anything he could get right about now. The entrance emptied into a narrow tiled corridor with no windows. Axel hadn't gone berserk, so he knew there must not be anyone else in close proximity. Fuentes moved ahead of him and found a small room crammed with computers and monitors, all very new and expensive. On one of the screens, two dark horses devoured the carefully tended flowering plants in the terra cotta pots that flanked the driveway. Escorpion would not be pleased, he thought with a grin.

Axel tensed and Shaw looked to the rear door. Fuentes took up a position behind, partially screened by a tower of equipment. Rapid footsteps echoed outside and Shaw warned Axel with the flick of one stiff finger.

"Wait."

The door flung open and a skinny man—more of a boy, really, with a wisp of a mustache and pimpled skin—plowed in, fumbling for a gun holstered on his belt. His eyes shifted in terror between the growling Axel and Shaw. Fuentes stepped behind him and clamped a hand over his mouth.

"No noise, boy," Fuentes whispered in Spanish.

The boy raised his hands, his fingers trembling. His brown eyes grew huge as Axel bounded up and gave him a thorough sniffing.

Fuentes tentatively removed his grip and faced the prisoner, hands on his rifle. "Tell us how many men Escorpion has here."

The boy tried twice before the words came out. "Th–three guards plus me. I only manage the computer systems."

"Who else?" Shaw growled.

The boy's terrified gaze shifted from Axel to Shaw. "A housekeeper and a driver. That's all I know."

It was probably true and Shaw didn't want to frighten the boy any further, so he gave Fuentes a slight nod.

Fuentes took off the boy's belt and used it to tie his hands behind his back. Securing a roll of tape from the desk, he applied it to the boy's mouth and pushed him toward a storage closet.

"It will be over soon," Fuentes whispered. "Do not cause any trouble."

Shaw's heart pounded as he surveyed the cluttered office. As they'd suspected, the whole place had been monitored carefully, so their own entrance into the building had no doubt been observed by anyone paying close enough attention. He scanned the tiny screens. Hallway, kitchen, outdoor patio area, pool. Upper floors showed one small room that housed a bed with a figure seemingly asleep under the covers.

*Nina?* He peered closer, but another screen caught his eye. Two women, one leading the other along a poorly lit corridor.

*Anna.* The woman turned up at the strangest times. And the other?

Nina.

His breath caught. He would know that determined profile anywhere. She didn't appear to be injured, nor were her hands bound. The monitors didn't cover the back area where Anna led her. Almost as if she felt him watching, Nina stopped and raised her face so the lamplight caught her expression. Fearful, expectant, but still with that same poised sense of calm that he now knew came from somewhere higher up. He couldn't take his gaze off her, mesmerized by those dark eyes.

Fuentes looked over his shoulder. "Where is the woman taking her?"

Shaw knew. "To Escorpion," he hissed. "Let's go."

They headed down the hallway and up a circular set of stairs. Below, they heard a door open and the men who had been chasing the horses burst into the foyer.

There was a flash of light as the guards began to fire at them. Shaw and Fuentes bent low and continued onward, Axel right behind them. Bullets zinged off the iron railings, and Shaw felt the heat of one flick past his temple. They hit the top of the stairs, but the long corridor ahead offered no cover from the shooters above them. With one nod to Fuentes, he and Shaw slammed through the nearest door, their combined weight snapping through the bolt.

Shaw saw him first—a tall man dressed in western clothes, holding a lamp above his head, ready to smash it down on Fuentes, or maybe Axel.

Shaw shouted to Axel, but it took all his concentration and strength to try to close the door against the two men who had thrown themselves at it. Fuentes joined him and they heaved at the thick door until they managed to get it shut. Fuentes dragged a heavy mahogany wardrobe in front of it, and they worked together to set it into place.

Shaw whirled around, panting. The man still held the lamp over his head as Axel barked at a deafening volume. Shaw called him off and Axel backed up a step, hair still raised on the scruff of his neck.

Fuentes ran to the window. "Barred. I will see if I can kick them away."

"I've been trying for days now," the man said, lowering the lamp. "Who are you?"

Shaw looked around for some other piece of furniture he could use to barricade the door against the pounding, but saw nothing except the bed. The heavy wrought iron frame might prove worthy, and he set to work dragging it to the door. It wouldn't hold for long.

He joined Fuentes at the window, and they took turns kicking at the heavy bars. The man asked again. "Who are you?"

Shaw shot him a look. Something about the tall frame, the shock of hair. He stopped mid-kick, almost losing his balance as he put the pieces together.

"Dr. Truman?"

He nodded. "Yes. And you are?"

Shaw tried to overcome his shock. "I'm Shaw Wilder, the guy who's been trying to keep your daughter alive."

# CHAPTER 28

Even Fuentes stopped kicking for a moment. "*El doctor?* Nina's father?"

Dr. Truman nodded, his face stricken. "Where is Nina? Is she hurt?"

Shaw shook his head. "She's here. That's who we were going after when the shooting started."

The doctor looked as if all the life had suddenly drained out of him, and it left his face paper white. He slumped against the wall with a groan.

"I hoped he was lying. I prayed that she'd gotten out of the country before he got his hands on her."

"How did you get here?" Shaw asked, his mind spinning. "Nina thought you were with your brother. She tried to call—"

"They got me on my way to the airport. When Nina phoned, I managed to answer it, to try to warn her before they took it away and locked me up here, like an animal."

"But what was the reason for that?" Fuentes demanded.

"Insurance," the doctor said grimly. "If Escorpion couldn't get his hands on Nina any other way, he'd use me as leverage to get her to come here willingly."

"And you know the truth, don't you?" Shaw said. "You know why he's after her."

His mouth quirked. "I only have guesses."

"Something to do with why you lied to her about her adoption?"

The doctor looked at Shaw for a long moment. "When we adopted her, we were told she was born in Mexico and we had no reason to disbelieve what the birth certificate said. Recently, an old lady from one of the villages we tend told me Nina's certificate was altered, that she was the daughter of a very dangerous family who wished her dead. I didn't believe it, until Escorpion began to make inquiries. I wanted to tell Nina the truth, but it became clear that doing so here would put her in danger and I would not allow that. I arranged for us to go home where it was safe." He looked at Shaw defiantly. "She's my daughter and I did what I felt was best to protect her. I intended to talk her out of coming back."

Shaw almost smiled. "That might be like trying to tell a fire not to burn."

He nodded. "I see you've met my Nina."

A shout from the hallway snapped them back into action and Shaw began to alternate kicks with Fuentes until one of the bars gave way. One more began to loosen as the shouts grew in volume and the pile of furniture against the door trembled.

Shaw kicked until his muscles ached, and the bar slowly bent away. Fuentes slipped easily through the gap, followed by Shaw, Axel, and the doctor who struggled to get his long legs clear. The window opened onto a flat roof running the length of the building, a sort of upper story patio with clusters of elegant chairs and more potted plants. Glass windows set into the plaster looked down on a plush sitting room fifteen feet below with inlaid tile floors and a wood-burning fireplace.

A door set in the corner of the roof would lead them down, but they might run squarely into the third guard or more reinforcements called in from the village. Still, it looked like their best option. Behind them, one of their pursuers squeezed his head and shoulders through the bars. Shaw led them to the stairwell door and pushed Fuentes into the gap, handing Dr. Truman the gun Otto had supplied back at the plantation, relieved to see him handle it with confidence.

"You might need this. Get him out of here, take Axel. I'll draw them off and meet you."

Fuentes gripped his arm. "That is foolish."

"Sorry, best I can come up with," he said.

Dr. Truman shook his head. "I'm going after Nina."

Shaw shoved them and a reluctant Axel into the stairwell and pulled the door shut behind them. "I need you to go for help," he said, before the door clicked shut.

*Besides, I'm not leaving here without Nina.*

* * *

Anna paused before an ornately decorated door to straighten her hair and smooth her skirt. She looked fearful about what might come next.

Nina's pulse quickened. "Why would you work for Escorpion? His business is drugs."

Her nostrils flared. "I came to him for protection and he gave it to me. He has not betrayed me."

Anna's eyes indicated that someone else had, someone who had once been dear to her. Nina flashed back on the moment in the bus when Anna had looked at the shooter with the oddest expression of tenderness.

"The soldier who shot up our bus. Who was he?"

She started, lips tightening. "This is not important. Escorpion provided safety for me, security."

"In exchange for what?"

Anna smoothed her skirt again.

"In exchange for what?" Nina repeated more forcefully. "Anna, what was the price for these favors?"

"Information."

"About me?"

"As I tried to tell you, my mother worked in an orphanage. She remembered a tiny baby, a girl brought in secrecy by her nurse."

"Me?"

Anna nodded.

Not a Mexican orphanage like her father and mother had always told her. Guatemalan. And her father had recently learned the truth, but chosen to conceal it from her. His lie lanced through her again like the sharp fangs of the *barba amarilla* until she forced the feelings in check. He must have been trying to protect her from whatever truth lay beyond the closed door.

"No one could know who the baby was and my mother kept the secret until just before her death," Anna whispered. "As soon as it got out, your life was in peril. I tried to warn you. I tried."

"What is the secret?" Nina demanded, grasping her wrist as she reached for the knob.

The door swung open and Escorpion stood on the other side. He regarded her placidly. "Do come in please," he said. "And we will talk."

Nina's body grew cold and she swallowed hard. The feeling of dread rippled through her at what the next few minutes would hold. She suddenly didn't want to step through that door, to know the secret that would certainly change her life.

*Who am I?* She both longed for and feared the answer to that question.

She heard Shaw's deep voice rumbling through her memory. "*You're Nina Truman. You're the girl who can fix a flat tire and eat crawfish and craves milk legs.*" The thought pulled her mind back from the brink of panic, the edge of despair that threatened to suck her in.

*Nina Truman*, she reminded herself. The woman God made her to be, a divine identity she would never lose, no matter what Escorpion had to say.

It gave her the strength to move her legs forward. Escorpion held the door as she and Anna entered. He closed it behind them, sliding the bolt home. He walked to a chair and sat, gesturing for her to take a seat across from him. Anna was not offered a chair, nor did she make any effort to secure one.

Escorpion's gaze searched Nina's face, inch by inch as if he looked for some important clue there, an answer to a puzzle that had stymied him. His long hair was smooth, flowing around his face like a dark shadow.

"A missionary. Raised as an American," he said, his voice heavy with disgust. "I would not have guessed it if Anna hadn't told me."

Nina gripped the chair arms. "Guessed what?"

His eyes remained flat and expressionless when he answered. "That you are my sister."

The pronouncement left his lips and nothing but silence followed. The room fell so still that she could hear the soft ticking of an antique clock on the sideboard.

"I think you are mistaken."

Deep down though, she knew with calm certainty that he wasn't. Somehow, there was truth in that terrible pronouncement, a fact that could not be wished away no matter how much she wanted it. He seemed to regard her now like an insect caught on a pin.

"I am not mistaken," he said calmly. "I have seen your records, the recent ones as well as your altered birth certificate, blood type, date of birth, the mention of the birthmark. I have also taken the liberty of having your DNA tested using hair taken from your brush. We are a match in so many ways. There is no mistake. You are my sister."

"I was told I was born in Mexico."

"A lie. You were taken out of the country and delivered to a Mexican orphanage where the doctor and his wife adopted you." He sighed. "They did not know, I imagine, of your true identity, but recently your father began to put the pieces together as I sent my people out to find you. Perhaps this is why he made arrangements for you to leave the country?"

Nina circled back to the question that weighed most heavily on her. "Why was I given away?" It was the one sentence she could manage. At first, she thought he wouldn't answer.

"My father was a very powerful man and my mother . . ." He shrugged. "She did not wish to love my father or embrace the gifts he gave her, so she made plans to take her twin babies and run."

*More like she was terrified,* Nina thought. "Maybe she wanted a better life for them."

Escorpion's eye twitched. "He gave her everything and she threw it all away. She fled, like an ungrateful dog." Hatred sizzled through his words. "She attempted to take away his children, so he punished her. It was his right and duty."

"How?" Nina's stomach twisted into a knot. "How did he punish her?"

Escorpion looked straight into her eyes. "He had her killed. A car bomb."

The words landed in her mind like the deadly explosives he described, puncturing her heart, embedding themselves like pieces of shrapnel deep inside. *Car bomb.*

"Your . . . *our* father had our mother *murdered*?"

Escorpion did not answer, his black eyes stark in his pale face.

"What kind of a man does that?" Nina whispered, sickened.

"A man who will not tolerate betrayal." Escorpion crossed one elegant leg over the other. "He would not allow our mother to leave the property with me. You . . ." He lifted his shoulder again and shrugged. "You were another story."

"He let my mother take me knowing he was going to kill her?" The words fell like hard stones in the quiet room. "He wanted me dead, too." Her earthly father, one she had never had a chance to know, hated her so much he wished her dead. Pain almost overwhelmed her until she closed her eyes.

*God, You are my true Father.*

She clung to it as Escorpion continued. "He had his son, the one who would be loyal to him, who would carry on the family name."

"I guess that made up for murdering the rest of his family?" She almost laughed. "But somehow I didn't cooperate. Here I am. Alive."

"Yes. The nanny took you out for a walk just before the bomb went off. And here you are. Alive."

Alive, standing in front of a brother she had never known, after learning that her earthly father was a monster. *Why am I here, Lord? Why?* She looked at her brother, his expression filled with an intensity that she couldn't understand.

"There were whispers at the time of the bombing of course, that the girl baby had been spirited away to safety. My father heard of these rumors, but that is all they were, rumors. As time passed, it did not matter. My father died ten years ago and the issue died with him. I was . . ." He searched for the word. ". . . uninterested in your life until recently. Then I began actively searching for you and it came to my attention that Anna was in possession of information about your identity. She came to me just before the bus accident and I began to make plans to bring you here."

"Was that your thug who caused the bus to crash? Were you trying to pick up where he left off?" Her voice trembled. "There were innocent people on that bus, your people. Children and mothers."

Escorpion's lip curled. "I am not a terrorist, Ms. Truman. The bus shooting was not at my direction and it caused all manner of complication since you set off into the jungle with the American."

She didn't want to believe he was innocent, but she saw no hint of deception on his smooth countenance. "I had to run. Someone hid a shipment of drugs at our clinic." She left Fuentes' name out of it.

His eyes narrowed. "My enemies did not wish you to make it here to me, and they will be punished as soon as my business with you is finished."

Poor Fuentes. She had to find a way to warn him if she ever got out of Escorpion's castle alive. Nina felt like a bit of ash, tossed from the fire, whirled through a swirling current. She shot a glance at Anna whose gaze remained fastened to the floor, and then she glanced back to Escorpion.

"Why have you done these things?" she demanded. "You've killed police officers, had this woman try to kidnap me, shot at . . ." She fought for breath thinking about the bullets that raked through the air at Shaw. "You shot at my friends. Why did you bring me here?" She yelled now, unable to stop the flow of anger and frustration. "I have done nothing to you, nothing at all."

Escorpion shot to his feet. "You have something I require," he hissed.

"I have nothing. I'm a missionary with no house, no money, nothing."

*I am weak*, her heart whispered. *I've lost the man I love*.

The rush of emotion choked off her words.

The rear door opened and a man rushed in carrying a rifle. He whispered into Escorpion's ear.

"We must go to another location now," he said.

Nina heard the distant sounds of shouting. Something had gone wrong, something which caused Escorpion to breathe heavily, his face suffused in fury.

She stood as tall as she could. "I am not going with you."

He slapped her with such force that she fell backward onto the tile floor.

* * *

Shaw made sure the guards who finally shoved their way through the bars got a good look at him before he took off in the opposite direction from the stairwell. He had to buy Fuentes and the doctor some time. Between guns and Axel, they had a good chance of getting out and going for whatever help they could find. One guard squeezed off a shot which plowed into the plaster by Shaw's head.

He dove for cover behind a pillar and considered his options. There weren't many. The wall of windows behind him looked down into yet another one of Escorpion's luxury suites. Ahead of him, the two gunmen would separate if they were worth anything, and probably run him down. He glanced down through the glass into the room below. His own breath fogged the surface so he wiped it away, in spite of the pain in his wounded shoulder.

His body jerked as if he'd touched a live wire.

Down below, he spotted Nina, staring up at Escorpion, her face blank with shock. Anna stood nearby, and the missing third guard held a rifle at the ready. He watched in disbelief as Escorpion raised his arm and dealt Nina a backhanded slap that knocked her to the floor.

A formless cloud of rage swept through him with such force that it momentarily paralyzed him. From somewhere behind him, he processed more gunshots, the noise muted by his own roaring pulse. With nothing in his mind except Nina, he stepped back, took a running start, heedless of the hollered commands of the gunmen tucked away behind the plaster pillars. He hurtled toward the overlook and smashed through the windows, falling in a shower of glittering shards into Escorpion's den.

# CHAPTER 29

Shaw hit the floor feetfirst. The impact hurtled him into an upholstered setee. Rolling to his feet, he launched himself at Escorpion who grabbed an iron poker from the hearth and slashed it at Shaw. Still slightly off balance from the fall, Shaw deflected most of the blow, but it caught him in the ribs. He grunted in pain, but did not slow. They circled each other, Escorpion's eyes glittering, ready to strike with the poker. He had to finish it quickly, before the noise attracted any other attention. No time for fancy moves.

Shaw squared his shoulders and employed an old-fashioned running back tackle. Headfirst, he plowed into Escorpion's stomach with the fury of a charging bull, relishing the sound of the air being forced out of Escorpion's lungs on impact. The poker went spiraling away into the air, clattering against the tile as the drug runner fell backward. Even after the tackle, Escorpion still struggled to free himself.

Shaw jammed his forearm under Escorpion's chin. He pressed into the soft area under his throat. "Well, well," he panted. "Looks like you're on the bottom of this dog pile."

Escorpion's eyes flashed. "I will not lose to you, *gringo*. I will have what I want and you will not hamper my efforts."

"Brave talk."

"It's more than talk. It is a promise."

"You'll never touch her again," Shaw hissed.

Escorpion's face flushed an unhealthy purplish color. "You have a strong survival instinct, I will allow. I thought you were left on the dock to die, American."

"You thought wrong. You're going to let her go." He pushed harder on Escorpion's windpipe, fighting against the bitter hatred roaring inside him.

Escorpion flicked a glance sideways and smiled. "That is where you are mistaken."

Shaw heard it then, a small cry. Arm still at Escorpion's throat, he risked a glance to the side only to find the guard with his pistol held to Nina's temple. Her lips were pressed together, nostrils flared.

Escorpion's voice came as a sibilant hiss. "Mr. Wilder, you have mistaken your position here. You will release me," Escorpion purred, "or she will die right here before your eyes."

His breath caught. "You won't kill her. There's some reason you need her to stay alive. You're bluffing."

Escorpion's mouth curved into a cruel half smile. "How little you know me, American. I don't need to bluff. There are many means to an end."

Shaw's gaze shifted to Nina again and her eyes locked on his and flashed with fear. Her chin remained high though, that familiar spark of courage lingering on her face. He still suspected that Escorpion could be bluffing, but could he risk the consequences on a suspicion?

If he let Escorpion go, he would likely kill Nina anyway and emerge triumphant and unpunished, like he had after he murdered Beth. He found it hard to suck oxygen into his lungs against the intolerable anger.

He pressed farther into Escorpion's windpipe. "Then you'll die with no one to save you, just like my sister."

Escorpion's eyes flickered, then widened as he squirmed under Shaw's grip. "Ah. So that is our connection. It is surprising that I did not see the resemblance before. Your sister died to send

Fuentes a message, because he is a stubborn fool who would not listen."

White-hot ire sparked in his vision. "You had her murdered."

He stilled under Shaw's hands. "Then you know I will not hesitate to have Nina shot. Yes, I wanted her alive, but I will formulate a new plan that will serve just as well. I am not encumbered by feelings of guilt or loyalty. Purely a practical decision." Escorpion managed a smile. "It is a difficult choice for you. Do you kill me and have your revenge? Or give it all up, including your life, to spare the girl? It could be one of your ridiculous Western movies."

Drops of sweat slid down Shaw's face. The desire to squeeze until he crushed the windpipe in his fist loomed so strong he could taste it. Escorpion had killed Beth, and he needed to die as retribution. Shaw had planned for this one moment for so long, for what felt like an eternity. He'd hidden away in a hostile jungle, turned his back on his father and mother, all for this moment, the moment for which he had pined . . .

Shaw yearned for Escorpion to pay by dying quietly here on his expensive tile floor. But as he readied himself to murder the man whose life he held between his fingers, he heard Nina's sweet voice in the back of his mind, and felt the strange comfort of her words.

*Faith is strongest when we're the weakest.*

Killing Escorpion might make him strong for a moment. For that one beat of time, Shaw would hold the scoundrel's life in the palm of his hand, and then destroy it, the ultimate power intoxicating to contemplate. Strength for a moment . . .

He hesitated as a thought wormed into his mind, as he wondered which might be the stronger choice: To go ahead and fulfill his longtime plan and squeeze the life out of his sister's murderer . . . or to separate himself from the burning need for vengeance? Nina's gentle touch and steady faith trickled through the winding avenues of his mind as the balance in his soul teetered back and forth between hatred and love.

*I am weak . . .*

He clenched his teeth and ground them against one another. He couldn't choose weakness and let Escorpion live, branding himself the loser. He would have his revenge. Fingers clenched, he started choking the life out of him.

Escorpion's mouth opened as he gasped for air, his fingers curled reflexively around Shaw's. Shaw leaned in, throttling him, watching the cruel eyes grow panicked and the thrashing more frantic. He tried to push harder, to take the life owed to him, to Beth.

And then something shifted deep within his soul and he faltered. His fingers lost their will to squeeze and he found he couldn't finish.

Against all reason, something inside him stood up, something stronger than the hatred, mightier than the desire to punish. He turned and stared at Nina's beautiful eyes, a crystal tear painting a trail down her face. He suddenly remembered more of the verse, from those long-ago days when his mother read to him on sultry afternoons.

My grace is all you need. My power works best in weakness.

He wondered if Nina saw the strange transformation in him that happened in the space of a moment as he let go of Escorpion's throat and rose heavily to his feet. The guard removed his pistol from Nina's temple and swiveled it to Shaw.

He tried to tell Nina with his eyes. *Run, run for the door. Do anything you can to survive.*

The guard took aim.

"No," Nina shouted, running for Shaw, but Anna caught her and pinned her arms behind her.

"Don't kill him." Tears ran down Nina's face now. "We've called the embassy. They'll come and find out you murdered him."

Escorpion got awkwardly to his feet, his cheeks oddly flushed. "They will find nothing," he spat at her. "No sign that either of you were ever here." He spoke to the guard in Spanish before turning back to Nina.

"I will kill him later, after we move to another location." He flicked a look at the guard. "But he does not need to be conscious."

Giving Shaw no time to block the blow, the guard's gun connected with his skull. Nina struggled to reach him as the world dissolved into blackness.

* * *

Nina couldn't stop the tears as Anna led her to a small room that adjoined the suite. It looked as if it had been designed for some sort of storage with no windows or doors and only a small overhead bulb for lighting.

"You'll stay here while they ready the car," she said. "It will be over soon."

The guard dragged an unconscious Shaw into the room and dumped him on the floor.

Nina knelt next to him. "He needs medical attention. Please."

Anna shook her head sadly. "It hardly matters. He is going to be dead soon anyway."

"Why?" Nina shouted, rushing at Anna, who took a step back behind the guard. "Why is this happening? Why are you helping him?"

"He will care for me, reward me," Anna said, her voice soft. "I have no other way to survive."

"You can't trust him. He's a criminal."

Anna's eyes were flat, empty of everything but a profound sadness. "I don't trust any man, but he is the only choice I have. I am sorry." She hurried from the room and the guard slammed the door shut. Nina pounded on the door, screaming at Anna, Escorpion, the guard.

"You have no right to do this!" she yelled. "No right." There was no answer from outside. She hammered until her fists stung and then she dropped to the floor next to Shaw, gently turning him over. Tearing a section from the bottom of her blouse, she wadded it up and pressed it to his head to stop the flow of blood. His eyes remained closed, his breathing shallow.

Shaw didn't deserve to die for her. She took his hand and held it to her cheek. "I'm so sorry," she whispered, kissing his palm as she wondered about the look she had seen in his face when he let Escorpion go. His entire purpose had been to avenge Beth, and he gave that all up back there on the floor of Escorpion's suite. Something changed in him then, and she knew he'd sacrificed himself for her. Her own tears drenched his face as she prayed for him, her mind and heart tumbling over each other.

She still couldn't understand why her God-given call, the mission that sent her to this beloved country, would result in her murder and Shaw's. How could that serve Him, furthering the kingdom as she'd believed? No answer came, no explanation. The only thing left was prayer and she put herself to it earnestly, rocking slowly back and forth on her knees, pouring out her soul to God. They weren't the prayers taught to her by her own father, but the flow of feelings, a soul-wrenching plea for grace, for mercy, for the compassion of a loving heavenly Father.

Shaw stirred and his eyes blinked open. Nina bent close. "I'm here." He tried to sit up, but she held him down. "Stay still. You've got a head injury."

He struggled to get up anyway, but groaned and sank back down. Only Nina's hands kept his head from hitting the hard floor.

"Where . . . ?"

"Locked in a storage room. They're going to take us somewhere. I don't know where or why."

He squeezed his eyes shut and then opened them again. "Are you hurt?"

"No." She traced a finger along his cheek and resettled the makeshift bandage. "Shaw, you had him at your mercy. You chose me over your revenge," she said, voice trembling.

He sighed. "I let him go."

"Yes, you did."

"And now we're locked in a closet."

Nina tried to lift the heaviness she heard in his voice. "At least there are no mosquitos."

He groaned again. "If it's true that God works best in weakness, I'm about as weak as you can get."

She fought to breathe. "You did the right thing. Even if we both die here, you did the right thing."

"Do you think so?"

Her words seemed small and inadequate to communicate the enormity of what she felt. "I am absolutely certain of it."

He caught her fingers and pressed them to his lips. "You made me believe I was worth something to you . . . and to God."

She began to cry again. "Shaw, I'm so sorry that I involved you in all of this."

"I think God had a hand in it too," he said. "Your father's here. Escorpion took him as insurance in case he couldn't get his hands on you."

She felt smothered. Her father would die also. "No. Not him, too. If only he'd told me the truth sooner."

"I don't think he realized the risk of keeping it from you. He was trying to protect you, to get you out of the country."

Her gasp morphed into a cry of pain. "He'll be killed. For some bizarre reason which I can't figure out, we're all caught in Escorpion's trap."

"There's a chance." Shaw filled her in on the events that led up to her father fleeing with Fuentes and Axel. "We've got to hope that they made it out. Got help somehow."

She nodded, lips pressed together, while tears ran down her face.

They stayed there for a while, Shaw squeezing her hand as she wept. He tried again to sit up, and this time she couldn't dissuade him. In the stark light, she saw his face turn a sickly shade and he sucked in deep breaths to steady himself.

"Got to get you out of here before that psycho comes back. Look for something, anything we can use as a weapon."

Nina didn't let go as he got painfully to his knees and then stood, leaning against her. She wrapped her arms around him and pressed him close. He returned the embrace, gently stroking her back.

"I'm not giving up yet," he said against her neck. "I'll leave Escorpion to the justice system, but I'm not going to quit until you're safe or there's no more life in me."

She smiled through her tears. "The odds are against us."

He shifted. "God doesn't play the odds. Isn't that what a missionary would say?"

"Absolutely," she whispered.

"Now about that weapon . . ." he started just as a hand rattled the doorknob.

Nina's stomach plummeted as the door opened to the guard, pistol ready, Anna and Escorpion behind him.

The guard tossed a rope to Anna. "Tie his hands behind his back."

She moved behind Shaw, looping the coil around his wrists and pulling tight, the guard supervising her efforts. Anna's expression resembled an apology, but Nina could not stand to see it and she glanced away to Escorpion. His blotchy, swollen face twitched, and he seemed out of breath as he spoke into a tiny cell phone.

"See that the surgeon is ready," he said, disconnecting.

*Surgeon*. A nameless feeling of dread pinched her spine and lifted the hair on the back of her neck. "Who is in need of surgery?"

Escorpion looked at her, brown eyes so like her own except flat and parched, like river stones left stranded in the sun by the retreating water. "I am."

For the first time, she looked at him with a nurse's view. The swelling of the face, shortness of breath, poor color. "Your heart?"

He nodded. "Ironic that the son, the favored child, is the one with a defective heart."

A defective heart, which appeared to have worsened to life-threatening status.

Nina's blood seemed to freeze in her veins. He searched for her using science to prove their familial connection beyond a shadow.

DNA. Blood type. Perhaps tissue samples.

*We are a match in so many ways.*

She grabbed the door frame for support, causing Shaw's head to jerk in her direction.

*A match . . .*

"That's why you brought me here, why you gave orders that I wasn't to be harmed." Her voice came out at barely above a whisper. "You are going to use me to save your own life."

He shrugged. "You are a missionary; certain of your God and your everlasting life, are you not? I will send you into that blissful future ahead of schedule. You should thank me."

It took a moment before Nina found her voice. "Shaw spared your life."

"Yes. Ironic that he has enabled me to take yours. I did warn him I was not the sentimental type."

She sank against the door frame, holding herself up on shaky knees. "You are my brother."

He huffed. "That is an accident of birth, nothing more. I told you earlier that you have something I require."

Shaw shuffled closer until the guard stopped him with a jab of the gun. "What is he talking about? What does he want from you, Nina?"

She tried to stop the whirling in her head, the dizziness that overtook her.

"He wants . . . my heart."

# CHAPTER 30

He'd known Escorpion as a murderer, a drug runner with no regard for anyone or anything that didn't serve his purposes, but Shaw found himself reeling from this newest revelation. That a human being, even one so vile, would hatch a plan to kill someone and take their heart . . .

Beyond the realm of possibility.

Escorpion would murder his sister to save his own life. Shaw fought against the rising sense of panic as the group made their way through the back corridors toward the graveled driveway. The whole horrendous plot had been set into motion months before, and he felt certain Escorpion had a medical team standing by at some well-supplied facility ready to harvest Nina's heart. His skin prickled in waves of horror.

He strained to hear any indication that Axel, Fuentes, and Dr. Truman had made it to safety and summoned help. A million-to-one shot, even if they had managed to escape the compound, but who would they find to help them? Otto had no doubt put miles between them by now, and the nearest village was several hours away. He guessed they could be waiting somewhere to ambush, but that hope seemed unlikely with the whole place under surveillance.

*No*, he thought grimly, *we're on our own.*

His head thundered with pain. *Think, think*. Above everything else, he had to keep Nina from being put in that car. If that happened . . .

He resisted a shudder. The one bright spot might be found in the ropes around his wrists. He'd flexed them when Anna had bound them, and it might have been his imagination, but he thought she hadn't pulled as hard as she could have to secure the bonds. Was there the slightest chance that she would help him get Nina out of the mess? He couldn't be sure what to believe from the woman who had betrayed them at every turn. Nonetheless, he continued working at the ropes every moment that the guard looked away as well as the times when they stopped to allow Escorpion to catch his breath.

The heavy front door swung open, flooding them with fresh and fragrant mountain air. The afternoon sky shimmered a brilliant blue where it appeared in the gaps between the trees. A sedan and a truck sat parked out front, and the guard gestured Nina toward the sedan. Shaw started to follow, but the guard stopped him and pointed to the truck.

He understood. Nina and Escorpion headed for the sedan, and Shaw realized his fate awaited out in the wooded nowhere beyond the castle where the guard no doubt intended to kill him. No trace, no mess, no one around to ask questions. His father would surely try to find him after a while, but what could he do really, especially with a sick spouse who needed him? Shaw's death would pile another measure of pain on the man who had lost his daughter and the future he'd had with his wife, lost everything but the profound rest he found in the Lord.

Shaw felt a deep craving to talk to his father and unpack the strange feelings of comfort he'd received in this jungle amidst the fear and pain. Somehow, he knew his father would understand.

He pulled at the ropes and felt them ease another small bit.

Escorpion waited for his driver to open the door for him, and he cast a triumphant look at Shaw. "You see, American?" He spread his hands. "I told you back at the airstrip that you are a stranger who has crossed a line from which you will not return. I always keep my promises. Consider that, while you are dying."

He slid into the backseat.

Shaw felt the rope slipping away. He tried to prioritize. Go for the guard. Take him out before the driver forced Nina into the car. While he considered his options, another man sprinted into the open space with a rifle in his hands, running for all he was worth.

Shaw heard a faint and familiar sound that sent his spirit soaring. He wrenched away the rope and dove for the guard just as Axel rounded the corner, targeting the running man.

"Get down, Nina!" Shaw yelled.

The distraction lent him the precious moment he needed to yank away the ropes and dive for the gun-wielding guard. Fortunately, he had no time to aim and just shot wildly, the bullet shattering the side mirror of Escorpion's car.

One punch sent him to the ground.

The driver exited the vehicle, his hand pulling a gun from his waistband as Fuentes snatched him from the car. With Dr. Truman's help, he pushed him to the ground, facedown.

Escorpion opened the side door and bolted back toward the house.

"I don't think so."

Shaw ignored the pounding in his head and took off after him. Escorpion moved quickly in spite of his bad heart. He nearly made it to the door, but Shaw caught him and spun him around against the stone façade.

Shaw fought off a wave of dizziness as he looked down at Escorpion.

"I will never be prosecuted," he panted. "No one will testify against me."

He was right, of course. Escorpion could very well avoid prosecution through a combination of bribery and threats. An idea landed in Shaw's mind like a thunderbolt, illuminating the path before him. Catching Escorpion had not signaled the end but the beginning.

"Maybe not, but you've just helped me find my new mission," Shaw said. "I'm going to spend the rest of my life working against you. I'm going to be here, helping the regular people thrive so they don't need drug runners like you. However I can help, whatever I can do." He smiled. "So even if you do escape prosecution, you'll become . . ." He leaned closer, delivering the finish like a knockout punch. " . . . *irrelevant.*"

Escorpion flinched at the words. "I will never be irrelevant. You are weak. You should have killed me when you had the chance."

Shaw put out a finger and tapped it on Escorpion's heaving chest. "I'll leave that departure date up to God, but thanks very much for helping me figure out my future." A shriek of metal rang through the air.

A vehicle with embassy markings crashed through the gates and beelined to the front, two soldiers piling out, guns at the ready.

"American Marines," Shaw said with a smile. "I'll let you tell your side of the story to them, but I'll warn you. They aren't as friendly as I am."

He stepped back as a Marine leveled his gun at Escorpion. "Mr. Wilder, step away, please."

"With pleasure," Shaw said, easing back and finding himself wrapped in Nina's embrace. Dr. Truman stood just behind her, his face suffused with joy.

"Did you mean that?" Nina whispered. "What you said about your new mission?"

"I sure did. Not sure how yet, but I'm going to make a difference here. First, I'll make a trip back to the States and have a long talk with my father and maybe sing some songs for my mother. She'd like that." He brushed the hair from her face. "I figure we'll both need to go back to the States. You've got medical school waiting, don't you?"

Nina turned to her father, her face shining. "Daddy, I'm going to be a doctor. I've been hearing that call for a long time, but I ignored it because I didn't want to leave you. Or maybe I was afraid to fail. I'm not sure." She looked at the ground.

Dr. Truman took her hands. "I'm a stubborn man, Nina. Your

mother always told me so. When she died . . ." He blinked hard. "I knew I'd failed her. She didn't tell me about her illness because she knew I was determined to see my mission through." He looked down at their joined hands. "My desire to minister blinded me to your mother's needs."

Nina kissed his hands. "I know she didn't see it that way."

He sighed. "I didn't want to lose you so I kept you close. It was the easy, selfish choice so I could have my mission *and* my daughter, but somewhere along the way, I forgot to acknowledge that your call might be different from mine. I guess I didn't want to entertain that thought."

"It's okay, Daddy." Nina wrapped her arms around him. "I haven't regretted one moment of our time here. Well, except for the running-for-my-life part."

He blinked back tears and breathed out heavily. "Nina, I'm so sorry I kept the truth from you. I was scared that Escorpion would come after you and I would fail you like I failed your mother. I underestimated your strength." He looked at her closely, a smile playing across his lips. "Maybe I've always underestimated you."

She squeezed his hands. "I understand why you did that and it's all forgiven." Dr. Truman embraced Nina, and Shaw stepped back to give them some privacy.

Axel joined Shaw and gave him a thorough sniff. Shaw knelt gingerly next to him. "Good work, boy."

"He is a good tracker," Fuentes said. "We encountered two new guards that required subduing and Axel was most helpful."

Shaw laughed. "Yep, he's the best soldier I've ever worked with." He got to his feet and extended a hand to Fuentes. "I owe you an apology. I think I understand now what Beth saw in you."

Fuentes' throat worked as he struggled for words. "And that is all I could ask for," he said, returning the handshake.

"What will you do now?"

He looked off into the mountains. "I believe I will disappear into the trees and find myself a nice little house somewhere. With chickens."

Shaw didn't want to say it. Fuentes must have read the thought in his mind.

"The cartel will look for me, and maybe they will find me, or maybe they will take my land and not think me worth the pursuit. In any case, I will start my little flock of chickens and watch them grow for as long as I can."

Shaw smiled. "I wish you success, friend."

Fuentes returned the smile. "And I, the same for you."

They both started as a woman's scream cut the air followed by a single shot.

Shaw's heart leapt until he saw Nina still safe in her father's embrace. Both Marines looked toward the sound but were occupied with securing the prisoners. Shaw didn't waste any more time as he sprinted into the woods, fighting through a wave of dizziness. He pushed aside leaves and branches until he nearly fell over a body.

Dr. Truman and Nina followed behind him, and they all stood there looking down at Anna, on her side with blood trickling from a bullet hole in her chest. Her lips moved laboriously. "I loved him." She gasped. "I trusted him."

Shaw dropped to his knees next to her. "We'll get you help."

With one trembling finger, she touched his chest. "Love her always," Anna said as her eyes closed.

Dr. Truman pushed him aside, intent on providing what help he could.

"Go tell the Marines we've got another shooter," Shaw commanded, and Fuentes disappeared back into the trees.

Axel went rigid as he caught movement in the bushes. Shaw crept closer, giving Axel the signal to wait. Circling around behind the thick cluster of vegetation, he gave the dog the okay.

Axel barked and charged, and a man emerged from the bushes. Shaw caught him neatly around the knees and brought him to the ground, kicking away the gun.

Otto sat up, waving off Axel. The dog shook his head in confusion.

Shaw blinked hard, wondering if he could blame his head injury for this new development. Otto could not have gunned Anna down in cold blood. "Otto? You shot her?"

Otto sighed. "It is something which I had to do."

"Why?" he managed.

"Because," Nina said, walking up to Shaw, eyes wide. "He's the one who shot up the bus, and Anna knew it."

* * *

Nina berated herself for not figuring it out earlier. The look Anna had given the shooter, the way she'd warned her from going to Otto. The fact that she knew the true story about Nina's birth.

Nina looked at the sweating figure sitting on the muddy ground, the charming rogue who had sheltered her; or so she'd thought. "She loved you. She told you about me and you tried to kill her. Why?"

Otto smoothed his mustache. "I am a fox in the henhouse. Women are my downfall. I must have them and love them, but then my eye wanders, you see, and the other one becomes more pretty than the one in my arms. I grew tired of Anna, she could not understand this. After she told me the secret of the señorita's birth, I am deciding to get rid of Anna because she will perhaps hamper my plans."

"What plans?"

"To restore order to this mess that is being made." He waved a hand irritably. "Fuentes did not know how to manage things. He gets in bed with the cartel, a disaster in the making. Paah." He spat on the ground. "I hear talk that Escorpion will not live long without a new heart. I am positioned well with my plantations and my holdings. Why should it not be me that takes over Escorpion's territory once he is dead? I will not be so weak as Fuentes and allow myself to be a puppet in my own country."

"So you shot up the bus, figuring Nina would die, and Anna

too," Shaw said. "And when I found you there you pretended it was somebody else."

"Two birds, one stone, so to speak. When Nina Truman dies, so does Escorpion. When Anna dies, I am free of that complication." He sighed. "So like a woman. Neither of them do as they should, and both survive."

Nina noticed Shaw's shock and the betrayal in his eyes, and she put a hand on his arm.

"I trusted you," Shaw said. "And all along, you were trying to make sure Nina never made it to safety."

Otto shrugged. "Things would be going smoothly if my men had taken her into Mexico."

"Where she would have been killed," Shaw said.

He sighed. "But this Fuentes, he has to go and arrange for her to be arrested, the idiot, which sends her into the jungle and this whole ridiculous race begins."

Shaw spoke slowly, as if he'd just awoken from the dream. "You cannot trust a weak man who gives away his power."

Otto raised an eyebrow.

"That's what you said about Fuentes. I should have realized you were working against him. I thought you were a man of honor."

"I am looking out for myself. This does not make me dishonorable."

"You sound like Escorpion," Nina said.

Otto bristled. "I am to be a much better leader than Escorpion."

"No," Shaw said, sadness in his words. "You are to be escorted to prison, right alongside him."

A Marine jogged over and Shaw filled him in on the details. Nina couldn't listen to it for one more moment, and she walked away to a small patch of sunlight that infiltrated the thick canopy. She breathed deeply to take in a lungful of the humid air.

She'd survived. The nightmare had reached an end at last.

Shaw was alive, and her father, and Fuentes, and even Axel

who had wandered off to chase after a bird. She knew it hadn't merely been her own struggles that had brought her through the ordeal, but God, her true Father, leading her to this place where she now found herself. In spite of the ugliness she'd seen, the death of Anna, the murder of her biological mother by a man who had left a legacy of hate for his son, Nina felt something odd. Her heart surged with . . . joy.

God had stripped away her fear. She realized with a spark of delight that during the flight for her life, she'd forged her own, deeply personal relationship with her Lord and Savior. She would leap into medical school knowing full well that's where He intended her to land. Her dream, and His.

And then she would return to Guatemala, to the jungle where she'd almost lost her life, where she'd found a new one. A bird flittered from branch to branch, light and delicate as a breeze. Shaw's arm slipped around her shoulder, and her heart began beating faster.

She looked up into his eyes and smiled. "I'm sorry about Otto."

"Me too. I thought he was the one person I could trust. How wrong could a guy be?" He rubbed a hand over his face, marred by myriad bruises and scrapes. "Maybe if I'd figured it out sooner, Anna wouldn't have had to die."

She took his hand and squeezed it. "Otto is a bad man, and he's also a top-notch liar. You couldn't have known."

His eyes traveled over her face as if he searched for something he'd lost. He smoothed her hair, fingering the shorn ends. "Sorry about your hair."

"It will grow back."

After a silent moment, he told her, "This will probably sound nutty, but I feel like my heart did, too. When I met you, my heart grew back."

She pressed her cheek against his chest, soothed by the steady beating until he pulled her to arm's length.

He cleared his throat. "I meant what I said about coming back here. An idea sort of grew inside me back there with Escorpion. I can hardly believe I'm saying this, but I'm going to make a difference to these people, help them find their way so the cartel or whoever takes over after Escorpion will find it harder to get recruits. I don't know how, but it's burning inside me and I can't stop thinking about it. God's finally gotten through to me. There's a way to make things better here, and Axel and I will find it."

She smiled, wrapped in the wonder of his transformation. "You aren't the man you were."

"Nope. I'm still a stubborn, hot-tempered gorilla and I let myself get lost in hatred," he said with a chuckle. "But now I know what I'm meant to do. I envied that in you, that you knew what you were here for."

"I thought I did. Now I know I'm meant to be a doctor." Her lips trembled. "I'll miss you while I'm in medical school."

"I'll be around." He looked suddenly nervous, a little boy asking to join in a big boy's game. "I'll be back and forth between here and the States. My mom and dad deserve better from me than I've given them." Another long pause. "When you're ready to go back to Guatemala . . ." He cleared his throat again and the last part came out in a rush. "Maybe we can come back together."

Her pulse seemed to hammer so hard she could feel it through her whole body. "Together?"

He remained silent for a moment. "Nina, I'm not good with words," he whispered, his voice thick with emotion. "I . . . I love you. That's it, the bare bones of it. I love you, I love your spirit, I love your faith, I love your soul, and I want you next to me for the rest of my life. I think God meant us to be together and I hope you feel that, too." Then he kissed her tenderly, awakening a swirl of sweet emotion that circled through her like a haunting melody.

She traced a finger along his cheek, this strong man who fought through the jungle and found the fire that lit his soul along the way. There could be no one else to walk alongside, no one better suited to share every moment of struggle and rejoicing. They were meant to be together.

"I love you, Mr. Wilder."

Tears glimmered in the corner of his eyes, matching the ones that crowded hers. His hands squeezed hers convulsively and he tried to speak, and then stopped. After a deep breath, he opened his mouth again and sang softly as he took her in his arms. He pressed his face to her temple, hands cradling her shoulders. *"I can't see why a boy should sigh when by his side is the girl he loves so true."*

Nina knew the next few lines, and the anticipation awakened in her a greater joy than she had ever known.

Shaw's words mingled together with the birdsong and the pulse of life all around her. She already knew what her answer would be, and her heart beat with its own happy music.

*"All he has to say is: 'Won't you be my bride . . . for I love you . . .' "*

# DISCUSSION QUESTIONS

1. In the opening of the novel, Shaw believes that missionary work is useless, like shoveling sand uphill. Why do you think he believes this?

2. Have you ever been so overwhelmed by shock or tragedy that you were unable to pray? What advice would you give others in that situation?

3. Axel plays an important part in the story. He's a dog that can never be persuaded to give up. Describe an animal that has been a blessing in your life. Does it share any qualities with Axel?

4. Shaw's mother paid a terrible price during her own mission trip. Both Shaw and his father react differently to the tragedy. Discuss the differences in their reactions and how each viewpoint affects their life choices.

5. Nina makes the decision to run with Shaw into the jungle. Did she make the right choice at that point? What choice would you have made?

6. Escorpion believes Americans are arrogant. Why do Americans sometimes have that reputation outside the U.S.?

7. Shaw says he's a realist while Nina has a more optimistic view of life. Which character trait describes you? What are the advantages and disadvantages of each trait?

8. Shaw's father believed it was in God's power to heal his injured wife, yet God did not do so. Discuss an experience you've had where God did not move in the way you wanted Him to. How did you react to it? How does Shaw react to his mother's situation?

9. Shaw wants God to explain himself about his mother's accident. Have you ever desired such a thing? What is some biblical advice about how to deal with situations where we cannot understand God's intentions?

10. Shaw is entranced by Nina's optimism, which he doesn't understand. Why is optimism an attractive quality in people? Who do you know who you would describe as optimistic, and where does their positive outlook come from?

11. What does the Bible say about vengeance? How are we to handle our vengeful feelings when we are wronged?

12. Nina struggles to identify which country is her home. What is your definition of home? Has it changed over the course of your life?

13. Shaw believes God cannot love him because He has allowed so much loss and heartache in Shaw's life. How would you respond to someone who voiced these feelings?

14. What does it mean that faith is strongest when we're weakest? What has it meant in your own life?

15. Nina and Shaw both have a new mission. How do you think their lives will turn out?

16. What is your own personal mission? What do you feel God put you on earth to do?